the Archie® DIGEST LIBRARY

Betty and Veronica®

– in –

The Rival

Spotlight

visit us at
www.abdopublishing.com

Exclusive Spotlight library bound edition published in 2007 by Spotlight, a division
of ABDO Publishing Group, Edina, Minnesota. Spotlight produces high quality
reinforced library bound editions for schools and libraries. Published by agreement
with Archie Comic Publications, Inc.

Library of Congress Cataloging-in-Publication Data

Betty and Veronica in The rival / edited by Nelson Ribeiro & Victor Gorelick. --
Library bound ed.
       p. cm. -- (The Archie digest library)
    Revision of issue 117 (Feb. 2001) of Betty and Veronica digest magazine.
    ISBN-13: 978-1-59961-267-6
    ISBN-10: 1-59961-267-4
      1. Graphic novels. I. Ribeiro, Nelson. II. Gorelick, Victor. III. Betty and Veronica
digest magazine. 117. IV. Title: Rival.

PN6728.A72 B493
741.5'973--dc22

                                                              2006050276

All Spotlight books are reinforced library binding
and manufactured in the United States of America.

Contents

Betty AND Veronica®

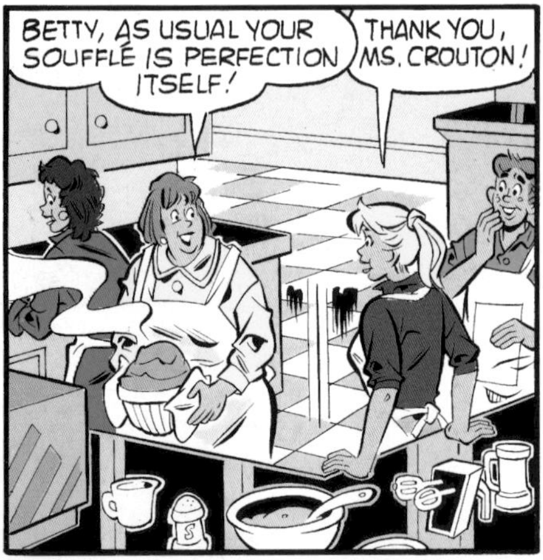
BETTY, AS USUAL YOUR SOUFFLÉ IS PERFECTION ITSELF!
THANK YOU, MS. CROUTON!

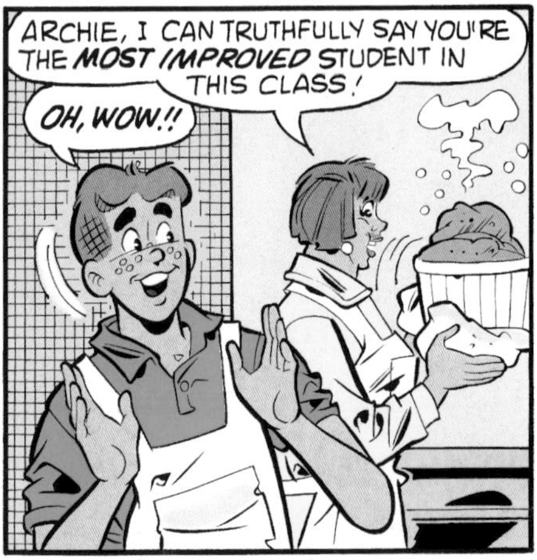
ARCHIE, I CAN TRUTHFULLY SAY YOU'RE THE *MOST IMPROVED* STUDENT IN THIS CLASS!
OH, WOW!!

SCRIPT: GEORGE GLADIR PENCILS: TIM KENNEDY INKS: KEN SELIG
COLORS: BARRY GROSSMAN LETTERS: BILL YOSHIDA
EDITORS: NELSON RIBEIRO & VICTOR GORELICK EDITOR-IN-CHIEF: RICHARD GOLDWATER

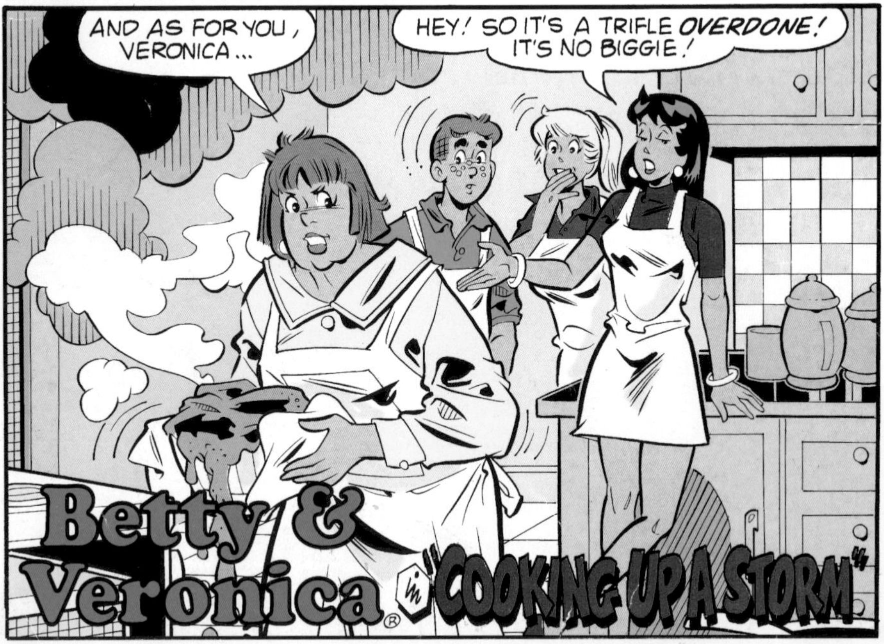
AND AS FOR YOU, VERONICA...
HEY! SO IT'S A TRIFLE *OVERDONE!* IT'S NO BIGGIE!
Betty & Veronica® in "COOKING UP A STORM"

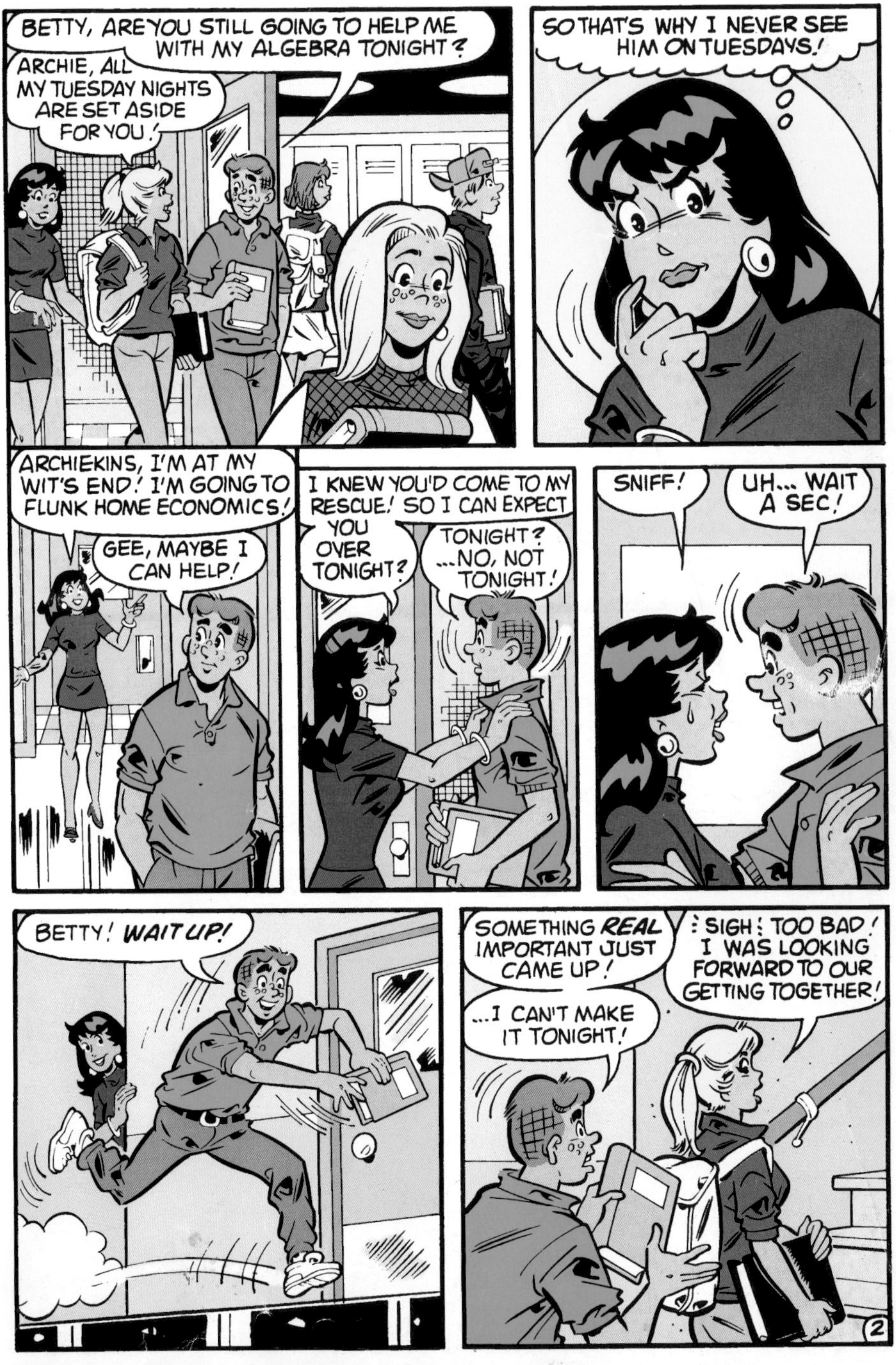
BETTY, ARE YOU STILL GOING TO HELP ME WITH MY ALGEBRA TONIGHT?
ARCHIE, ALL MY TUESDAY NIGHTS ARE SET ASIDE FOR YOU!
SO THAT'S WHY I NEVER SEE HIM ON TUESDAYS!
ARCHIEKINS, I'M AT MY WIT'S END! I'M GOING TO FLUNK HOME ECONOMICS!
GEE, MAYBE I CAN HELP!
I KNEW YOU'D COME TO MY RESCUE! SO I CAN EXPECT YOU OVER TONIGHT?
TONIGHT? ...NO, NOT TONIGHT!
SNIFF!
UH... WAIT A SEC!
BETTY! WAIT UP!
SOMETHING REAL IMPORTANT JUST CAME UP!
...I CAN'T MAKE IT TONIGHT!
: SIGH : TOO BAD! I WAS LOOKING FORWARD TO OUR GETTING TOGETHER!
2

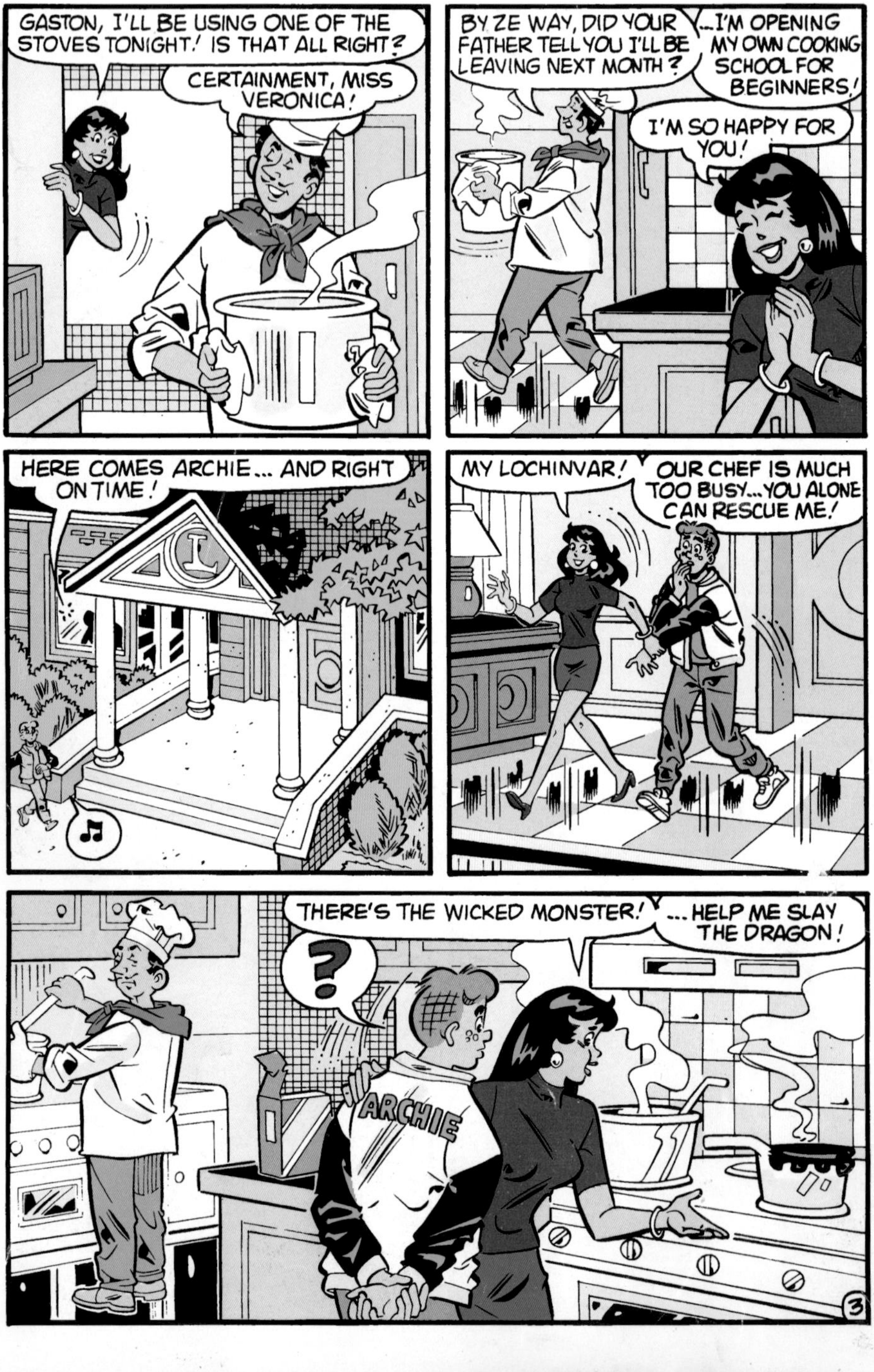
GASTON, I'LL BE USING ONE OF THE STOVES TONIGHT! IS THAT ALL RIGHT?
CERTAINMENT, MISS VERONICA!
BY ZE WAY, DID YOUR FATHER TELL YOU I'LL BE LEAVING NEXT MONTH?
...I'M OPENING MY OWN COOKING SCHOOL FOR BEGINNERS!
I'M SO HAPPY FOR YOU!
HERE COMES ARCHIE... AND RIGHT ON TIME!
MY LOCHINVAR!
OUR CHEF IS MUCH TOO BUSY...YOU ALONE CAN RESCUE ME!
THERE'S THE WICKED MONSTER!
... HELP ME SLAY THE DRAGON!
?
ARCHIE
3

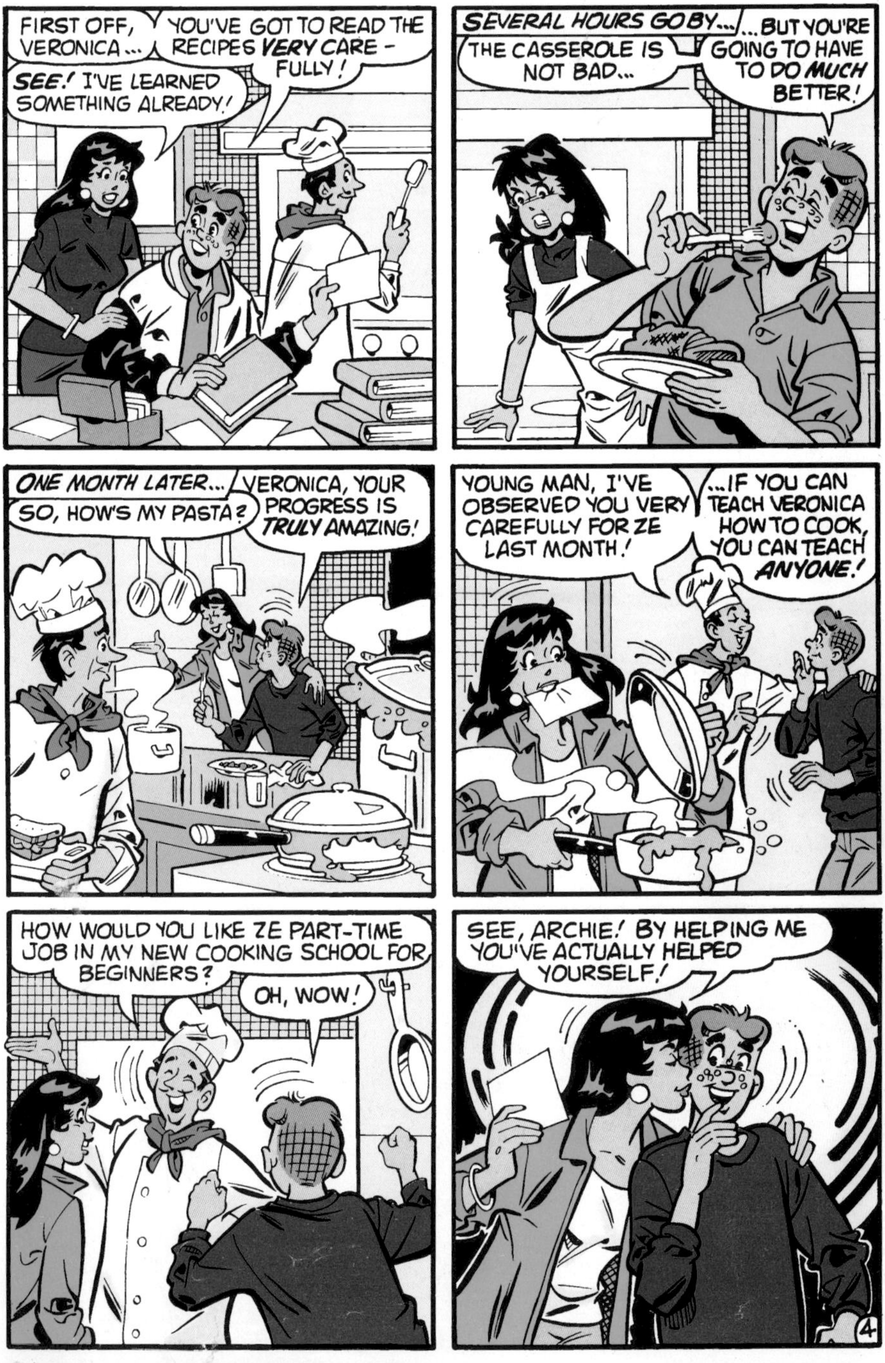
FIRST OFF, VERONICA ...
YOU'VE GOT TO READ THE RECIPES VERY CARE - FULLY!
SEE! I'VE LEARNED SOMETHING ALREADY!
SEVERAL HOURS GO BY...
THE CASSEROLE IS NOT BAD...
...BUT YOU'RE GOING TO HAVE TO DO MUCH BETTER!
ONE MONTH LATER...
SO, HOW'S MY PASTA?
VERONICA, YOUR PROGRESS IS TRULY AMAZING!
YOUNG MAN, I'VE OBSERVED YOU VERY CAREFULLY FOR ZE LAST MONTH!
...IF YOU CAN TEACH VERONICA HOW TO COOK, YOU CAN TEACH ANYONE!
HOW WOULD YOU LIKE ZE PART-TIME JOB IN MY NEW COOKING SCHOOL FOR BEGINNERS?
OH, WOW!
SEE, ARCHIE! BY HELPING ME YOU'VE ACTUALLY HELPED YOURSELF!
4

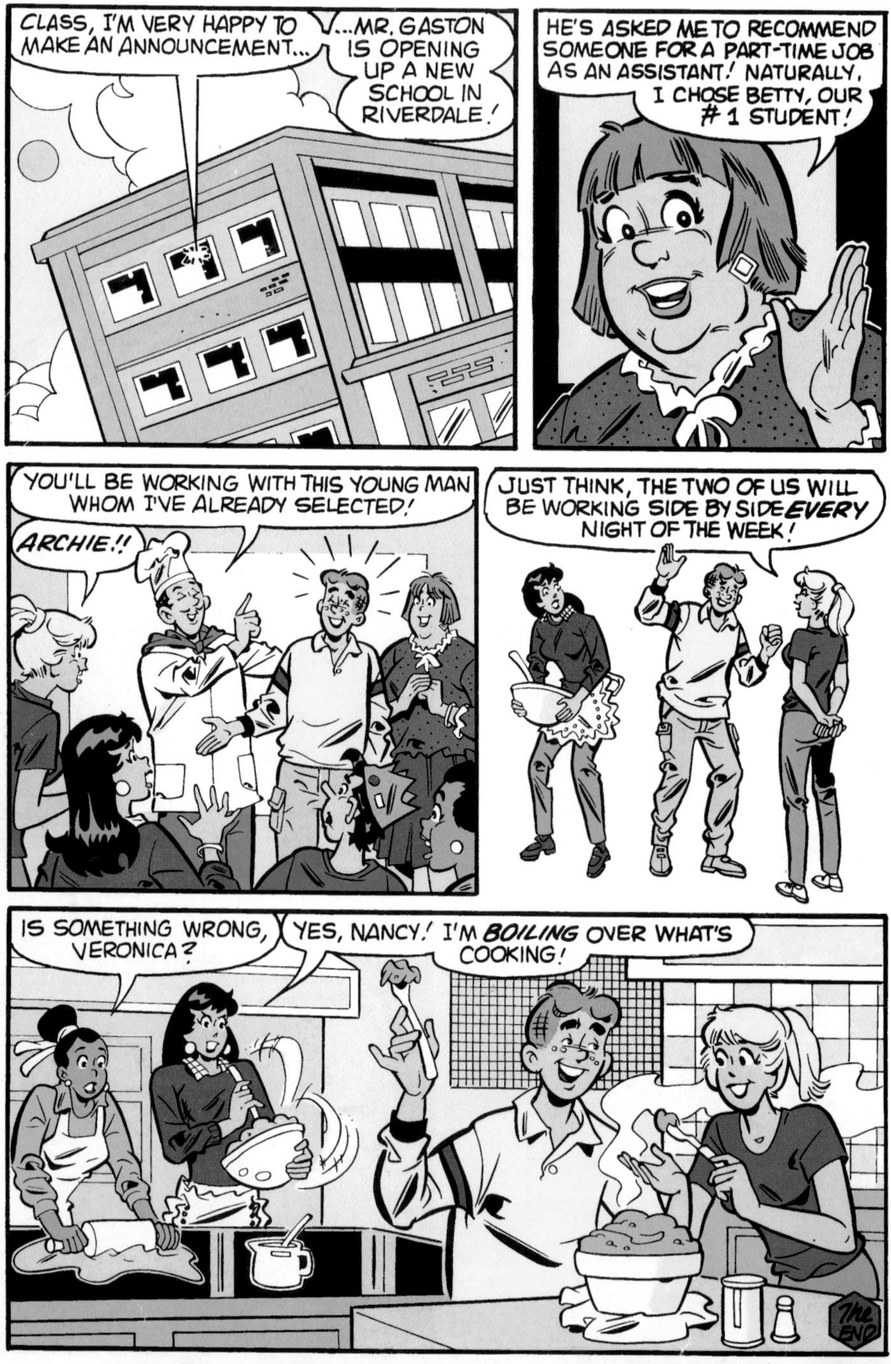
CLASS, I'M VERY HAPPY TO MAKE AN ANNOUNCEMENT...
...MR. GASTON IS OPENING UP A NEW SCHOOL IN RIVERDALE!
HE'S ASKED ME TO RECOMMEND SOMEONE FOR A PART-TIME JOB AS AN ASSISTANT! NATURALLY, I CHOSE BETTY, OUR #1 STUDENT!
YOU'LL BE WORKING WITH THIS YOUNG MAN WHOM I'VE ALREADY SELECTED!
ARCHIE!!
JUST THINK, THE TWO OF US WILL BE WORKING SIDE BY SIDE EVERY NIGHT OF THE WEEK!
IS SOMETHING WRONG, VERONICA?
YES, NANCY! I'M BOILING OVER WHAT'S COOKING!
THE END

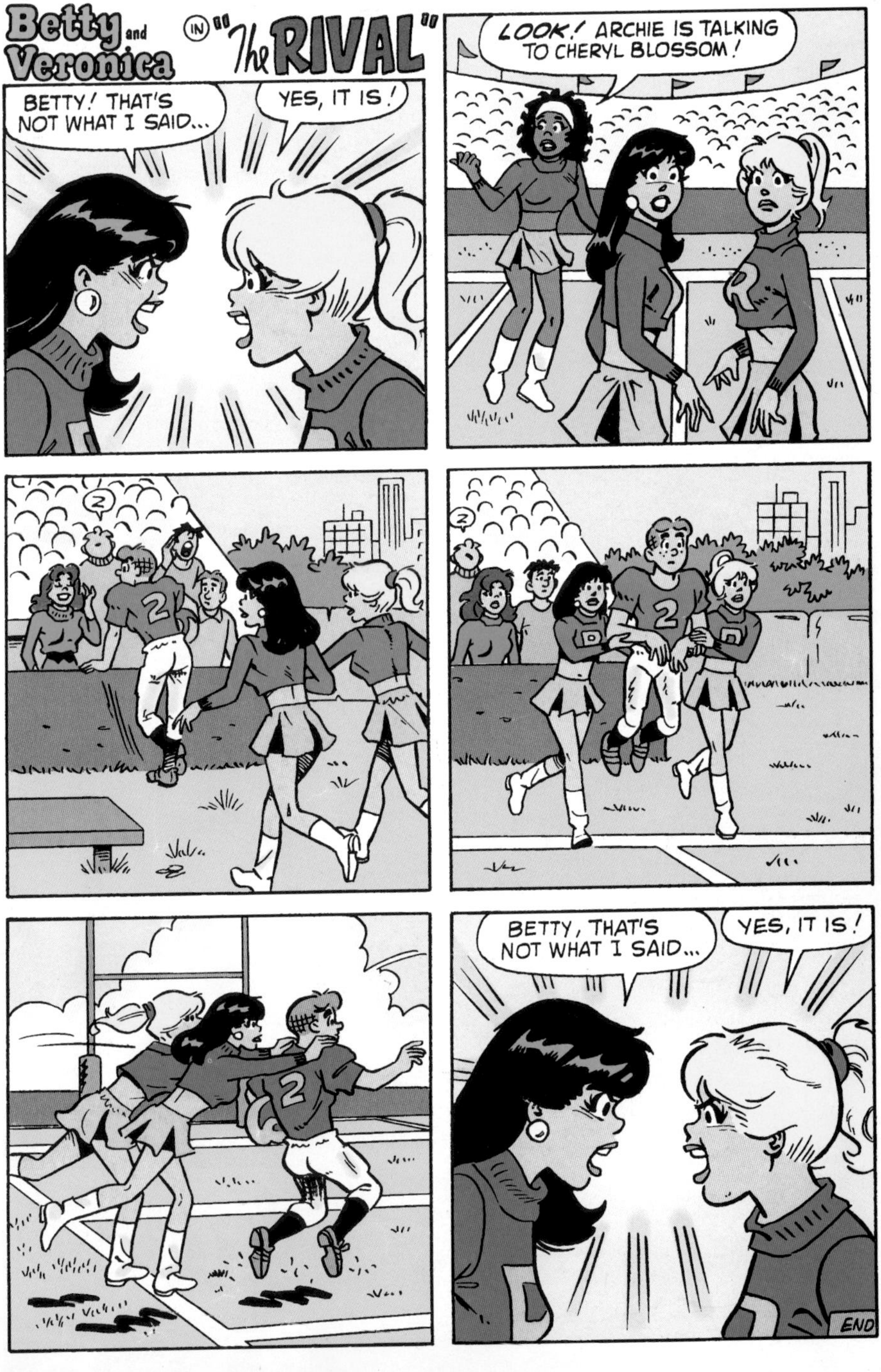
Betty and Veronica IN "The RIVAL"
BETTY! THAT'S NOT WHAT I SAID...
YES, IT IS!
LOOK! ARCHIE IS TALKING TO CHERYL BLOSSOM!
BETTY, THAT'S NOT WHAT I SAID...
YES, IT IS!
END

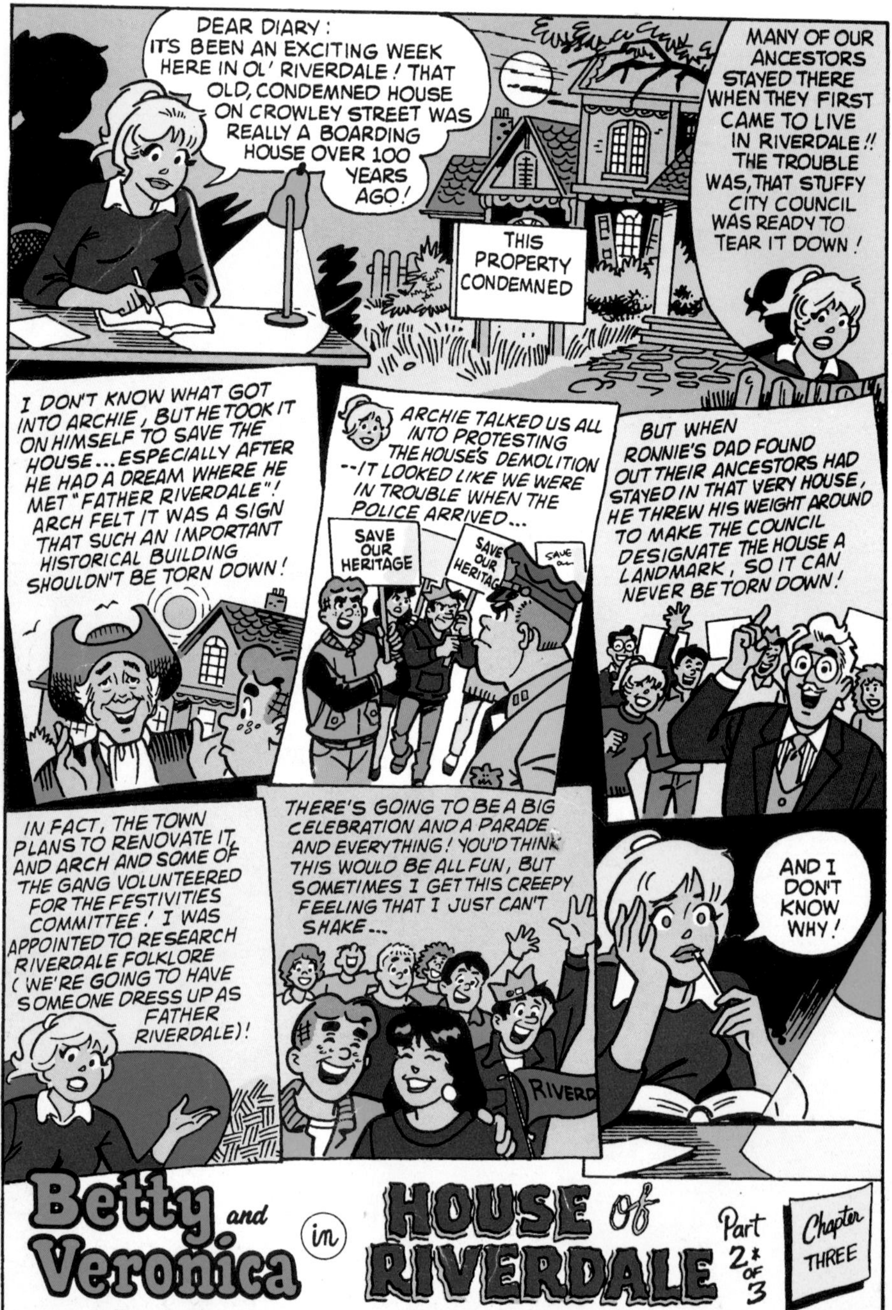
DEAR DIARY: IT'S BEEN AN EXCITING WEEK HERE IN OL' RIVERDALE! THAT OLD, CONDEMNED HOUSE ON CROWLEY STREET WAS REALLY A BOARDING HOUSE OVER 100 YEARS AGO!
THIS PROPERTY CONDEMNED
MANY OF OUR ANCESTORS STAYED THERE WHEN THEY FIRST CAME TO LIVE IN RIVERDALE!! THE TROUBLE WAS, THAT STUFFY CITY COUNCIL WAS READY TO TEAR IT DOWN!
I DON'T KNOW WHAT GOT INTO ARCHIE, BUT HE TOOK IT ON HIMSELF TO SAVE THE HOUSE... ESPECIALLY AFTER HE HAD A DREAM WHERE HE MET "FATHER RIVERDALE"! ARCH FELT IT WAS A SIGN THAT SUCH AN IMPORTANT HISTORICAL BUILDING SHOULDN'T BE TORN DOWN!
ARCHIE TALKED US ALL INTO PROTESTING THE HOUSE'S DEMOLITION --IT LOOKED LIKE WE WERE IN TROUBLE WHEN THE POLICE ARRIVED...
SAVE OUR HERITAGE
SAVE OUR HERITAGE
BUT WHEN RONNIE'S DAD FOUND OUT THEIR ANCESTORS HAD STAYED IN THAT VERY HOUSE, HE THREW HIS WEIGHT AROUND TO MAKE THE COUNCIL DESIGNATE THE HOUSE A LANDMARK, SO IT CAN NEVER BE TORN DOWN!
IN FACT, THE TOWN PLANS TO RENOVATE IT, AND ARCH AND SOME OF THE GANG VOLUNTEERED FOR THE FESTIVITIES COMMITTEE! I WAS APPOINTED TO RESEARCH RIVERDALE FOLKLORE (WE'RE GOING TO HAVE SOMEONE DRESS UP AS FATHER RIVERDALE)!
THERE'S GOING TO BE A BIG CELEBRATION AND A PARADE AND EVERYTHING! YOU'D THINK THIS WOULD BE ALL FUN, BUT SOMETIMES I GET THIS CREEPY FEELING THAT I JUST CAN'T SHAKE...
RIVERD
AND I DON'T KNOW WHY!
Betty and Veronica in HOUSE of RIVERDALE
Part 2* of 3
Chapter THREE
CATCH PART I OF "THE HOUSE OF RIVERDALE" IN JUGHEAD WITH ARCHIE DIGEST #162 ON SALE NOW!

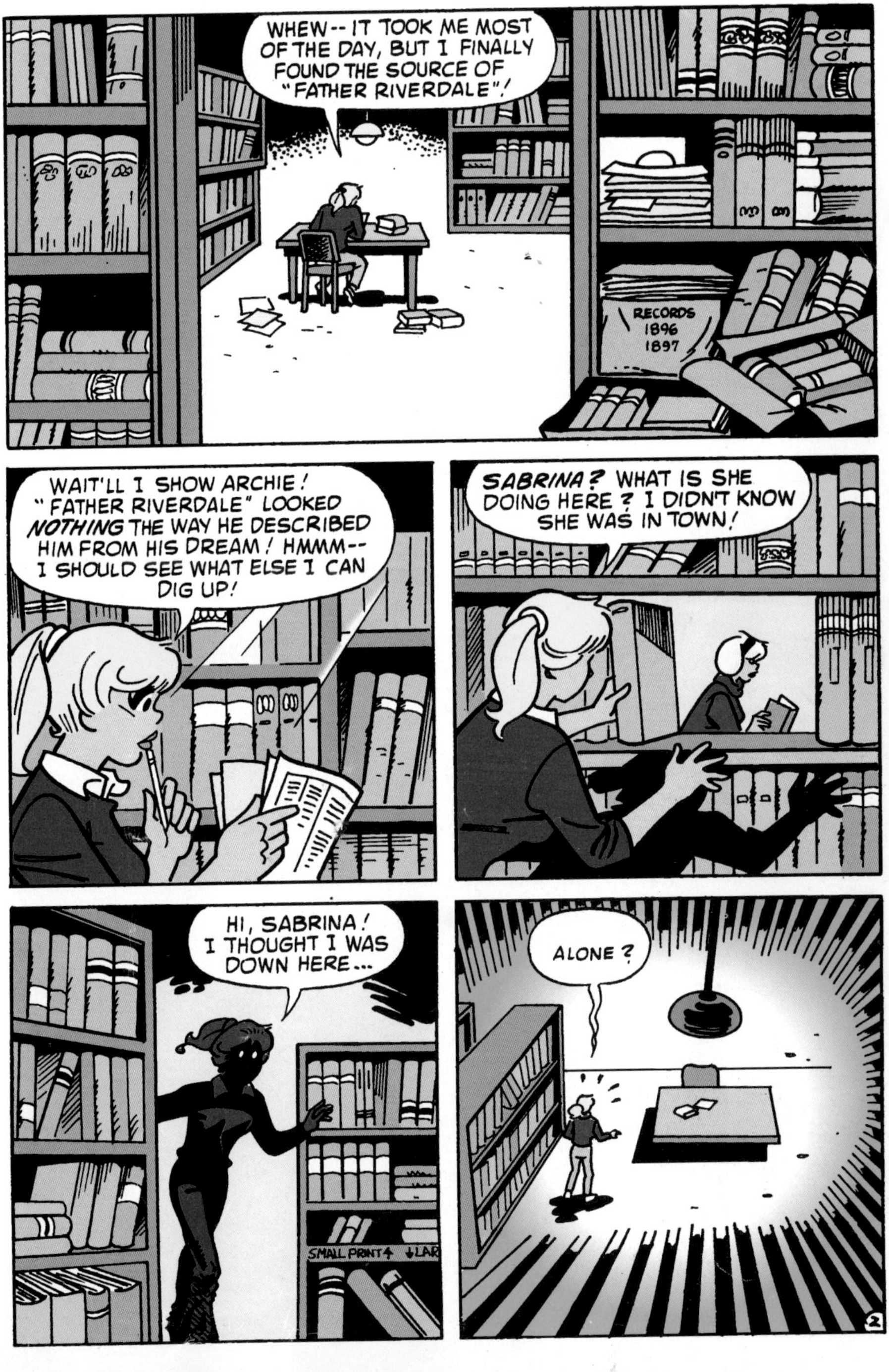
WHEW -- IT TOOK ME MOST OF THE DAY, BUT I FINALLY FOUND THE SOURCE OF "FATHER RIVERDALE"!
RECORDS 1896 1897
WAIT'LL I SHOW ARCHIE! "FATHER RIVERDALE" LOOKED NOTHING THE WAY HE DESCRIBED HIM FROM HIS DREAM! HMMM-- I SHOULD SEE WHAT ELSE I CAN DIG UP!
SABRINA? WHAT IS SHE DOING HERE? I DIDN'T KNOW SHE WAS IN TOWN!
HI, SABRINA! I THOUGHT I WAS DOWN HERE...
SMALL PRINT
ALONE?
2

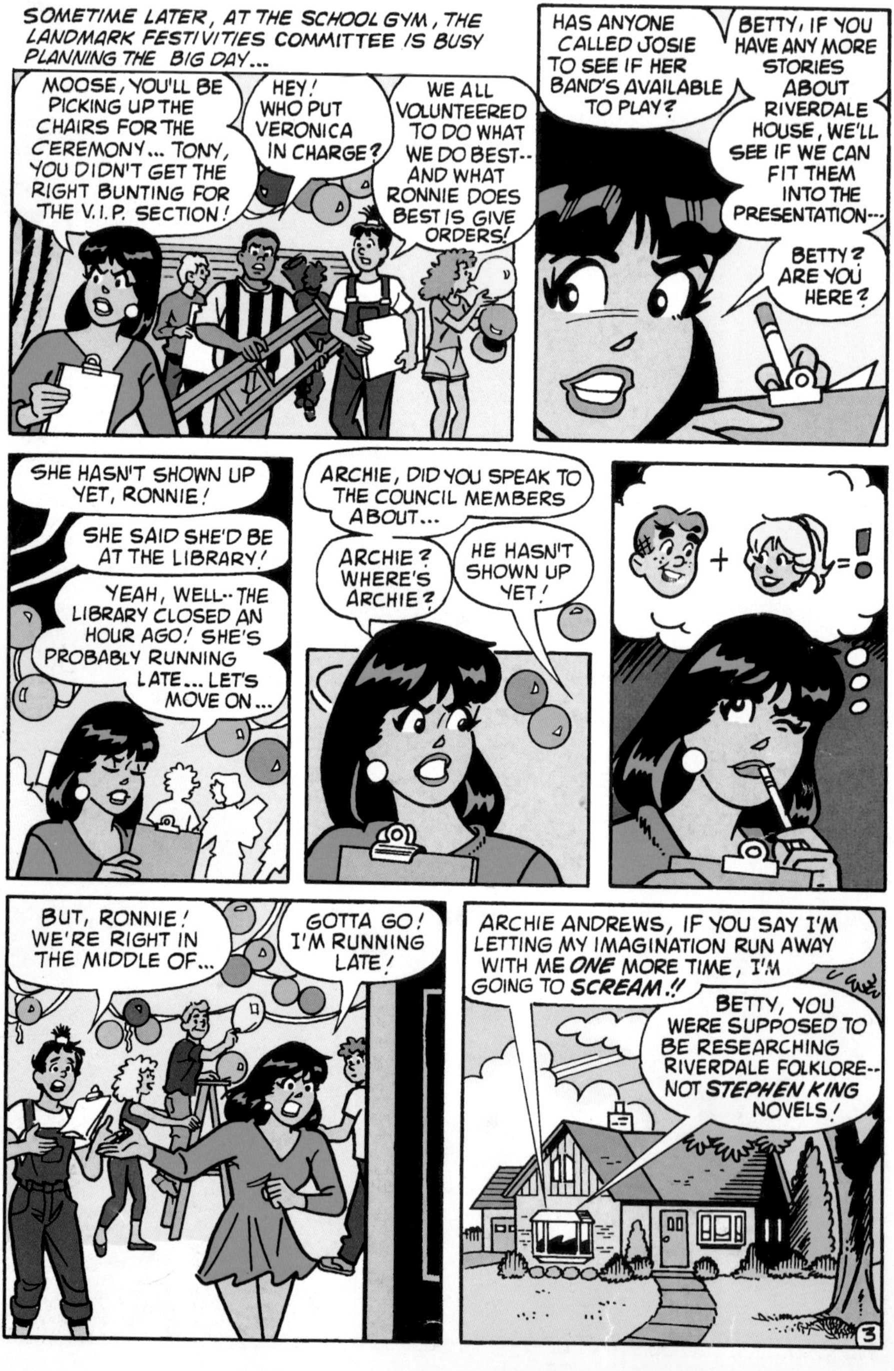
SOMETIME LATER, AT THE SCHOOL GYM, THE LANDMARK FESTIVITIES COMMITTEE IS BUSY PLANNING THE BIG DAY...
MOOSE, YOU'LL BE PICKING UP THE CHAIRS FOR THE CEREMONY... TONY, YOU DIDN'T GET THE RIGHT BUNTING FOR THE V.I.P. SECTION!
HEY! WHO PUT VERONICA IN CHARGE?
WE ALL VOLUNTEERED TO DO WHAT WE DO BEST-- AND WHAT RONNIE DOES BEST IS GIVE ORDERS!
HAS ANYONE CALLED JOSIE TO SEE IF HER BAND'S AVAILABLE TO PLAY?
BETTY, IF YOU HAVE ANY MORE STORIES ABOUT RIVERDALE HOUSE, WE'LL SEE IF WE CAN FIT THEM INTO THE PRESENTATION---
BETTY? ARE YOU HERE?
SHE HASN'T SHOWN UP YET, RONNIE!
SHE SAID SHE'D BE AT THE LIBRARY!
YEAH, WELL-- THE LIBRARY CLOSED AN HOUR AGO! SHE'S PROBABLY RUNNING LATE... LET'S MOVE ON...
ARCHIE, DID YOU SPEAK TO THE COUNCIL MEMBERS ABOUT...
ARCHIE? WHERE'S ARCHIE?
HE HASN'T SHOWN UP YET!
+ =!
BUT, RONNIE! WE'RE RIGHT IN THE MIDDLE OF...
GOTTA GO! I'M RUNNING LATE!
ARCHIE ANDREWS, IF YOU SAY I'M LETTING MY IMAGINATION RUN AWAY WITH ME ONE MORE TIME, I'M GOING TO SCREAM!!
BETTY, YOU WERE SUPPOSED TO BE RESEARCHING RIVERDALE FOLKLORE-- NOT STEPHEN KING NOVELS!
3

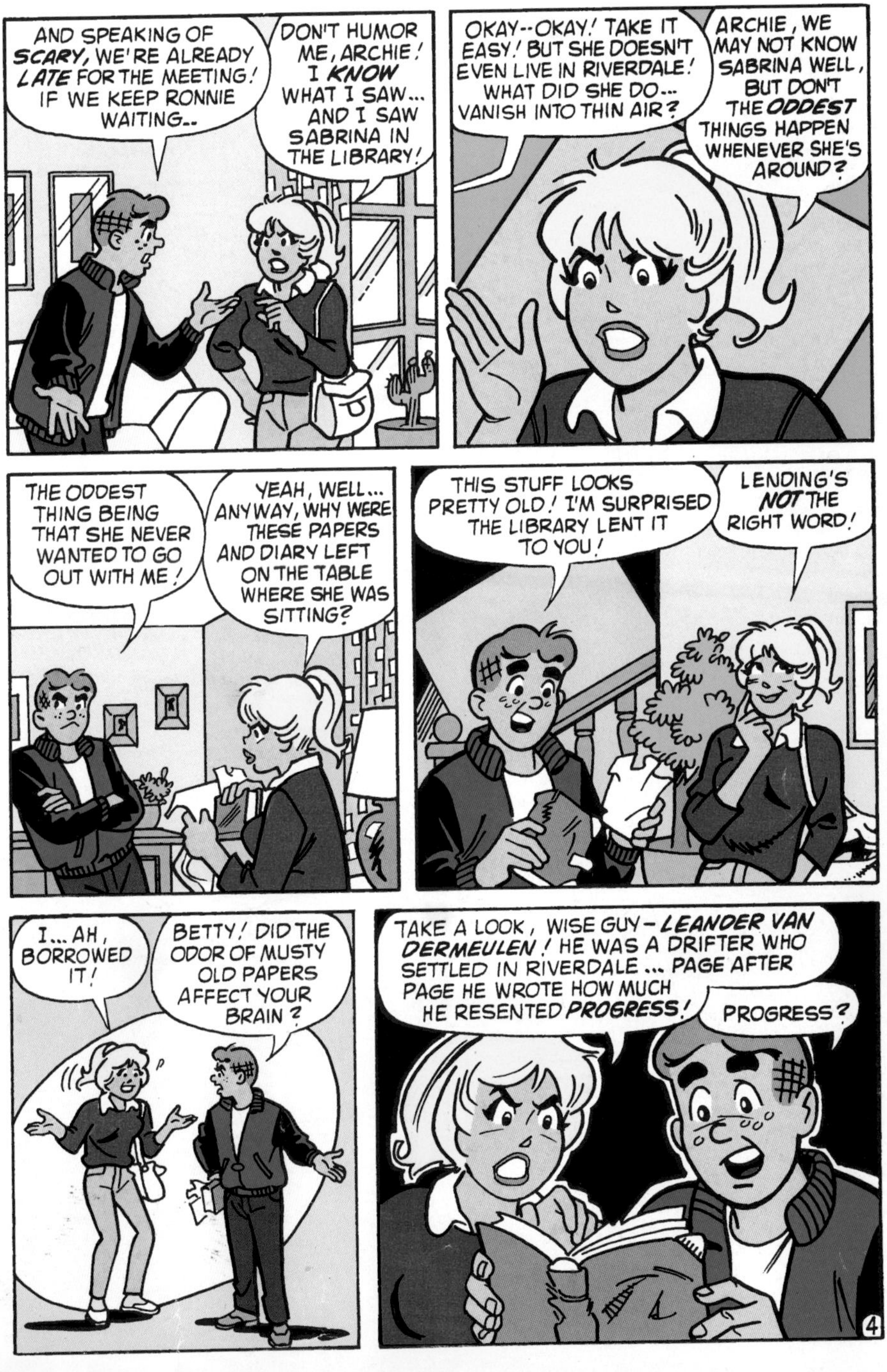
AND SPEAKING OF SCARY, WE'RE ALREADY LATE FOR THE MEETING! IF WE KEEP RONNIE WAITING..
DON'T HUMOR ME, ARCHIE! I KNOW WHAT I SAW... AND I SAW SABRINA IN THE LIBRARY!
OKAY--OKAY! TAKE IT EASY! BUT SHE DOESN'T EVEN LIVE IN RIVERDALE! WHAT DID SHE DO... VANISH INTO THIN AIR?
ARCHIE, WE MAY NOT KNOW SABRINA WELL, BUT DON'T THE ODDEST THINGS HAPPEN WHENEVER SHE'S AROUND?
THE ODDEST THING BEING THAT SHE NEVER WANTED TO GO OUT WITH ME!
YEAH, WELL... ANYWAY, WHY WERE THESE PAPERS AND DIARY LEFT ON THE TABLE WHERE SHE WAS SITTING?
THIS STUFF LOOKS PRETTY OLD! I'M SURPRISED THE LIBRARY LENT IT TO YOU!
LENDING'S NOT THE RIGHT WORD!
I... AH, BORROWED IT!
BETTY! DID THE ODOR OF MUSTY OLD PAPERS AFFECT YOUR BRAIN?
TAKE A LOOK, WISE GUY-LEANDER VAN DERMEULEN! HE WAS A DRIFTER WHO SETTLED IN RIVERDALE... PAGE AFTER PAGE HE WROTE HOW MUCH HE RESENTED PROGRESS!
PROGRESS?
4

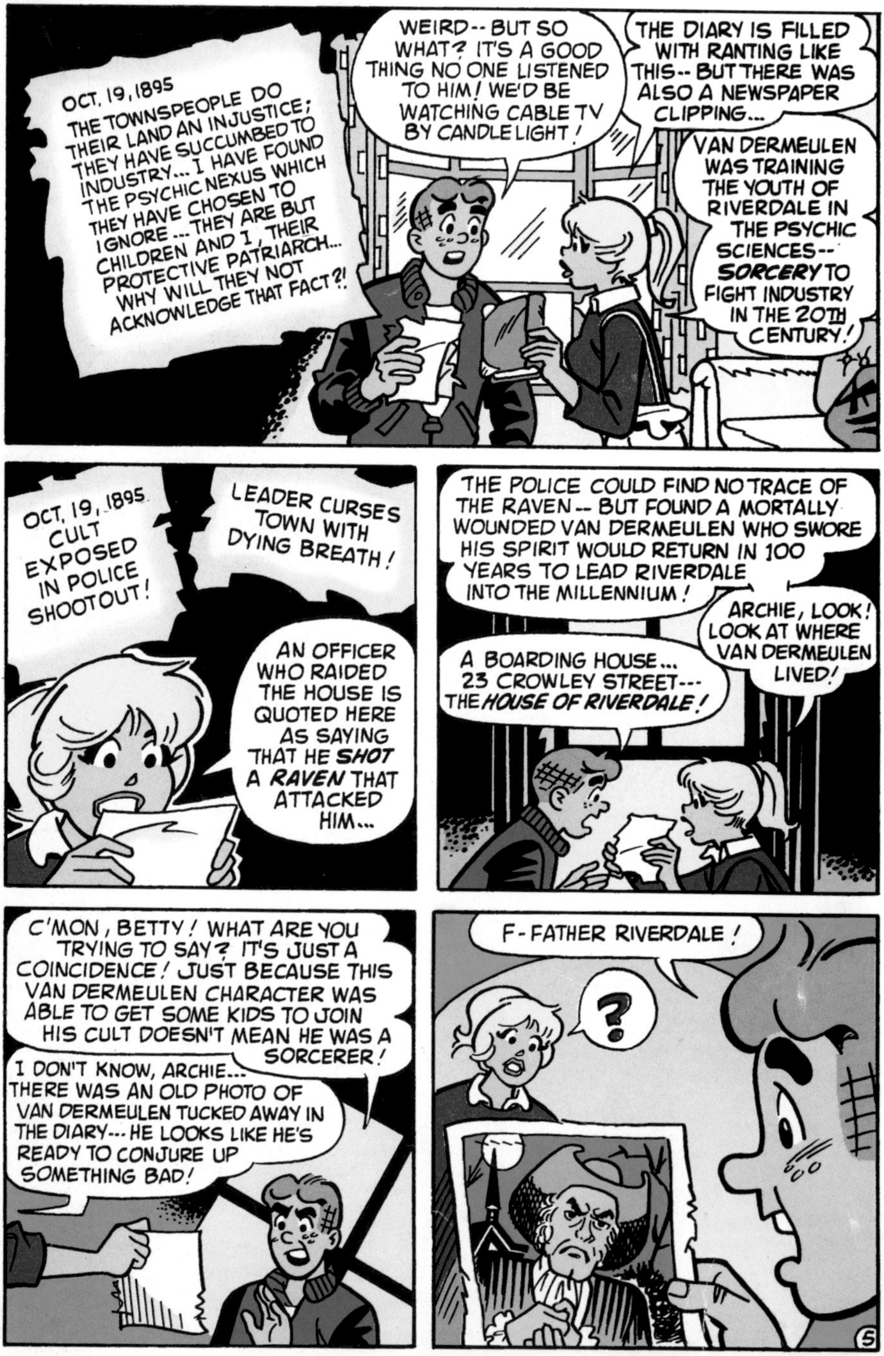
OCT. 19, 1895
THE TOWNSPEOPLE DO THEIR LAND AN INJUSTICE; THEY HAVE SUCCUMBED TO INDUSTRY... I HAVE FOUND THE PSYCHIC NEXUS WHICH THEY HAVE CHOSEN TO IGNORE... THEY ARE BUT CHILDREN AND I, THEIR PROTECTIVE PATRIARCH... WHY WILL THEY NOT ACKNOWLEDGE THAT FACT?!
WEIRD-- BUT SO WHAT? IT'S A GOOD THING NO ONE LISTENED TO HIM! WE'D BE WATCHING CABLE TV BY CANDLE LIGHT!
THE DIARY IS FILLED WITH RANTING LIKE THIS-- BUT THERE WAS ALSO A NEWSPAPER CLIPPING...
VAN DERMEULEN WAS TRAINING THE YOUTH OF RIVERDALE IN THE PSYCHIC SCIENCES-- SORCERY TO FIGHT INDUSTRY IN THE 20TH CENTURY!
OCT. 19, 1895
CULT EXPOSED IN POLICE SHOOTOUT!
LEADER CURSES TOWN WITH DYING BREATH!
AN OFFICER WHO RAIDED THE HOUSE IS QUOTED HERE AS SAYING THAT HE SHOT A RAVEN THAT ATTACKED HIM...
THE POLICE COULD FIND NO TRACE OF THE RAVEN -- BUT FOUND A MORTALLY WOUNDED VAN DERMEULEN WHO SWORE HIS SPIRIT WOULD RETURN IN 100 YEARS TO LEAD RIVERDALE INTO THE MILLENNIUM!
ARCHIE, LOOK! LOOK AT WHERE VAN DERMEULEN LIVED!
A BOARDING HOUSE... 23 CROWLEY STREET--- THE HOUSE OF RIVERDALE!
C'MON, BETTY! WHAT ARE YOU TRYING TO SAY? IT'S JUST A COINCIDENCE! JUST BECAUSE THIS VAN DERMEULEN CHARACTER WAS ABLE TO GET SOME KIDS TO JOIN HIS CULT DOESN'T MEAN HE WAS A SORCERER!
I DON'T KNOW, ARCHIE... THERE WAS AN OLD PHOTO OF VAN DERMEULEN TUCKED AWAY IN THE DIARY--- HE LOOKS LIKE HE'S READY TO CONJURE UP SOMETHING BAD!
F-FATHER RIVERDALE!
?
5

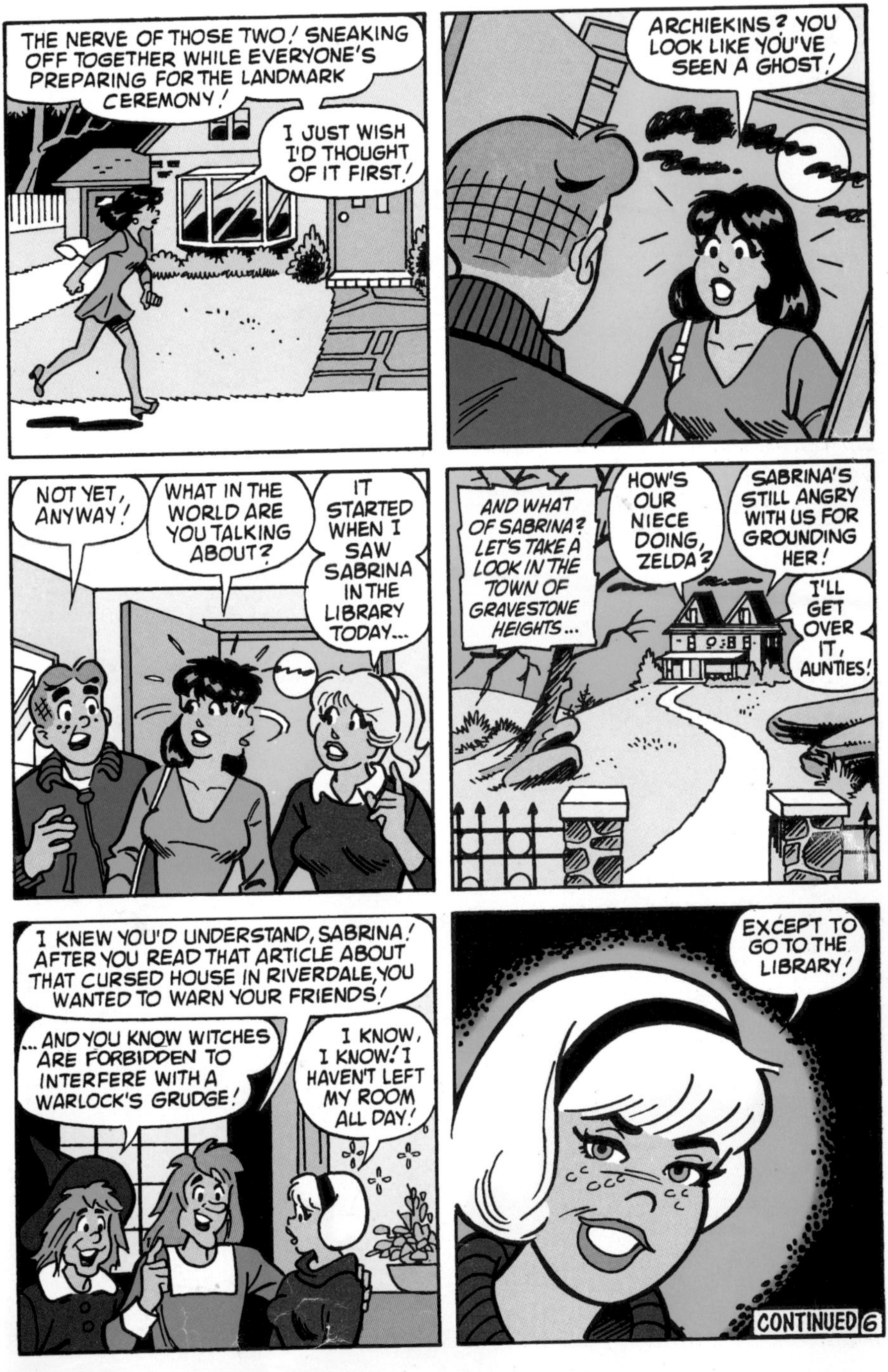
THE NERVE OF THOSE TWO! SNEAKING OFF TOGETHER WHILE EVERYONE'S PREPARING FOR THE LANDMARK CEREMONY!
I JUST WISH I'D THOUGHT OF IT FIRST!
ARCHIEKINS? YOU LOOK LIKE YOU'VE SEEN A GHOST!
NOT YET, ANYWAY!
WHAT IN THE WORLD ARE YOU TALKING ABOUT?
IT STARTED WHEN I SAW SABRINA IN THE LIBRARY TODAY...
AND WHAT OF SABRINA? LET'S TAKE A LOOK IN THE TOWN OF GRAVESTONE HEIGHTS...
HOW'S OUR NIECE DOING, ZELDA?
SABRINA'S STILL ANGRY WITH US FOR GROUNDING HER!
I'LL GET OVER IT, AUNTIES!
I KNEW YOU'D UNDERSTAND, SABRINA! AFTER YOU READ THAT ARTICLE ABOUT THAT CURSED HOUSE IN RIVERDALE, YOU WANTED TO WARN YOUR FRIENDS!
...AND YOU KNOW WITCHES ARE FORBIDDEN TO INTERFERE WITH A WARLOCK'S GRUDGE!
I KNOW, I KNOW! I HAVEN'T LEFT MY ROOM ALL DAY!
EXCEPT TO GO TO THE LIBRARY!
CONTINUED 6

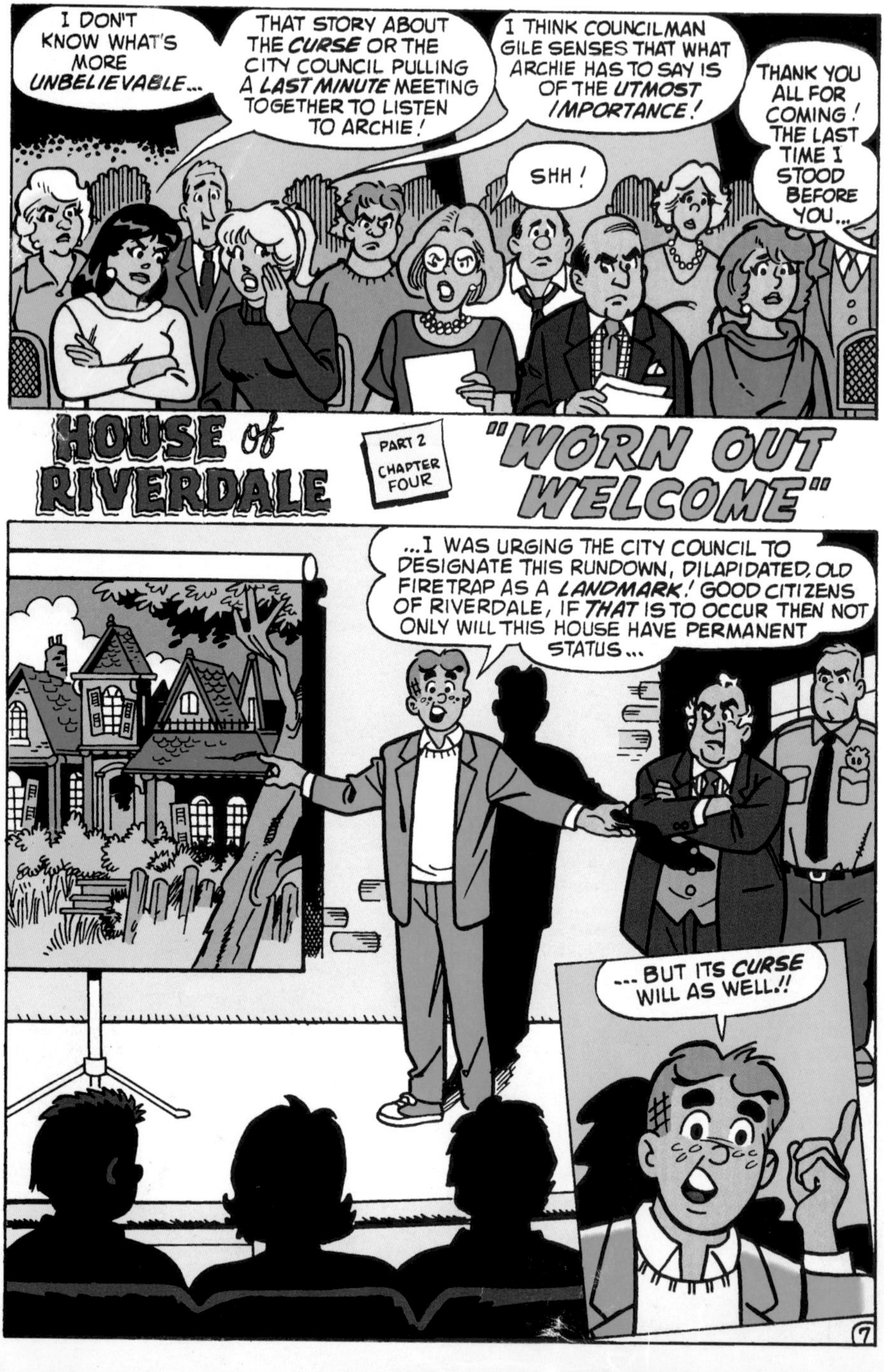
I DON'T KNOW WHAT'S MORE UNBELIEVABLE...
THAT STORY ABOUT THE CURSE OR THE CITY COUNCIL PULLING A LAST MINUTE MEETING TOGETHER TO LISTEN TO ARCHIE!
I THINK COUNCILMAN GILE SENSES THAT WHAT ARCHIE HAS TO SAY IS OF THE UTMOST IMPORTANCE!
SHH!
THANK YOU ALL FOR COMING! THE LAST TIME I STOOD BEFORE YOU...
HOUSE of RIVERDALE
PART 2 CHAPTER FOUR
"WORN OUT WELCOME"
...I WAS URGING THE CITY COUNCIL TO DESIGNATE THIS RUNDOWN, DILAPIDATED, OLD FIRETRAP AS A LANDMARK! GOOD CITIZENS OF RIVERDALE, IF THAT IS TO OCCUR THEN NOT ONLY WILL THIS HOUSE HAVE PERMANENT STATUS...
--- BUT ITS CURSE WILL AS WELL.!!
7

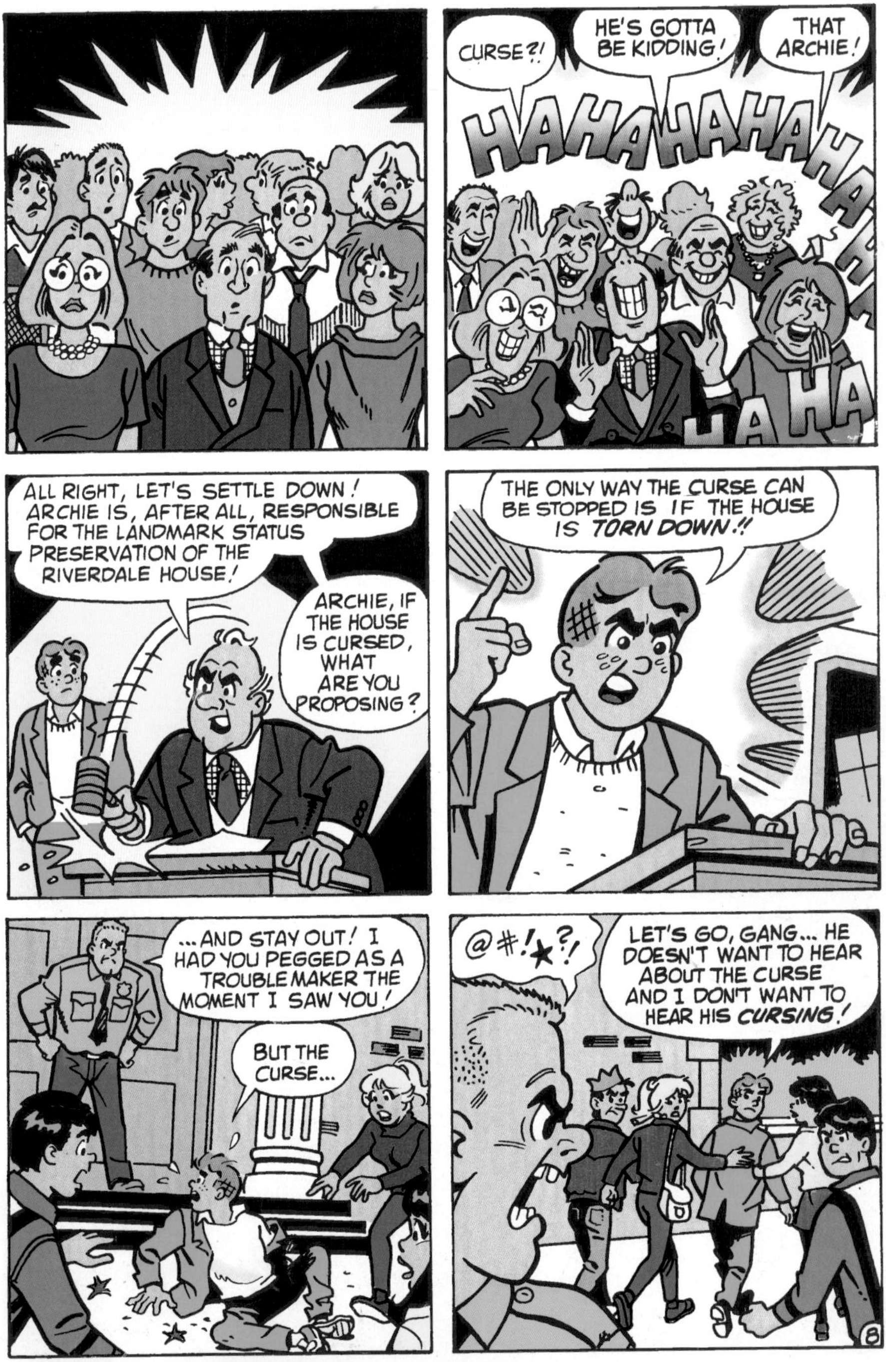
CURSE?!
HE'S GOTTA BE KIDDING!
THAT ARCHIE!
HAHAHAHAHAHAHAHA
HAHA
ALL RIGHT, LET'S SETTLE DOWN! ARCHIE IS, AFTER ALL, RESPONSIBLE FOR THE LANDMARK STATUS PRESERVATION OF THE RIVERDALE HOUSE!
ARCHIE, IF THE HOUSE IS CURSED, WHAT ARE YOU PROPOSING?
THE ONLY WAY THE CURSE CAN BE STOPPED IS IF THE HOUSE IS TORN DOWN!!
...AND STAY OUT! I HAD YOU PEGGED AS A TROUBLEMAKER THE MOMENT I SAW YOU!
BUT THE CURSE...
@#!★?!
LET'S GO, GANG... HE DOESN'T WANT TO HEAR ABOUT THE CURSE AND I DON'T WANT TO HEAR HIS CURSING!
8

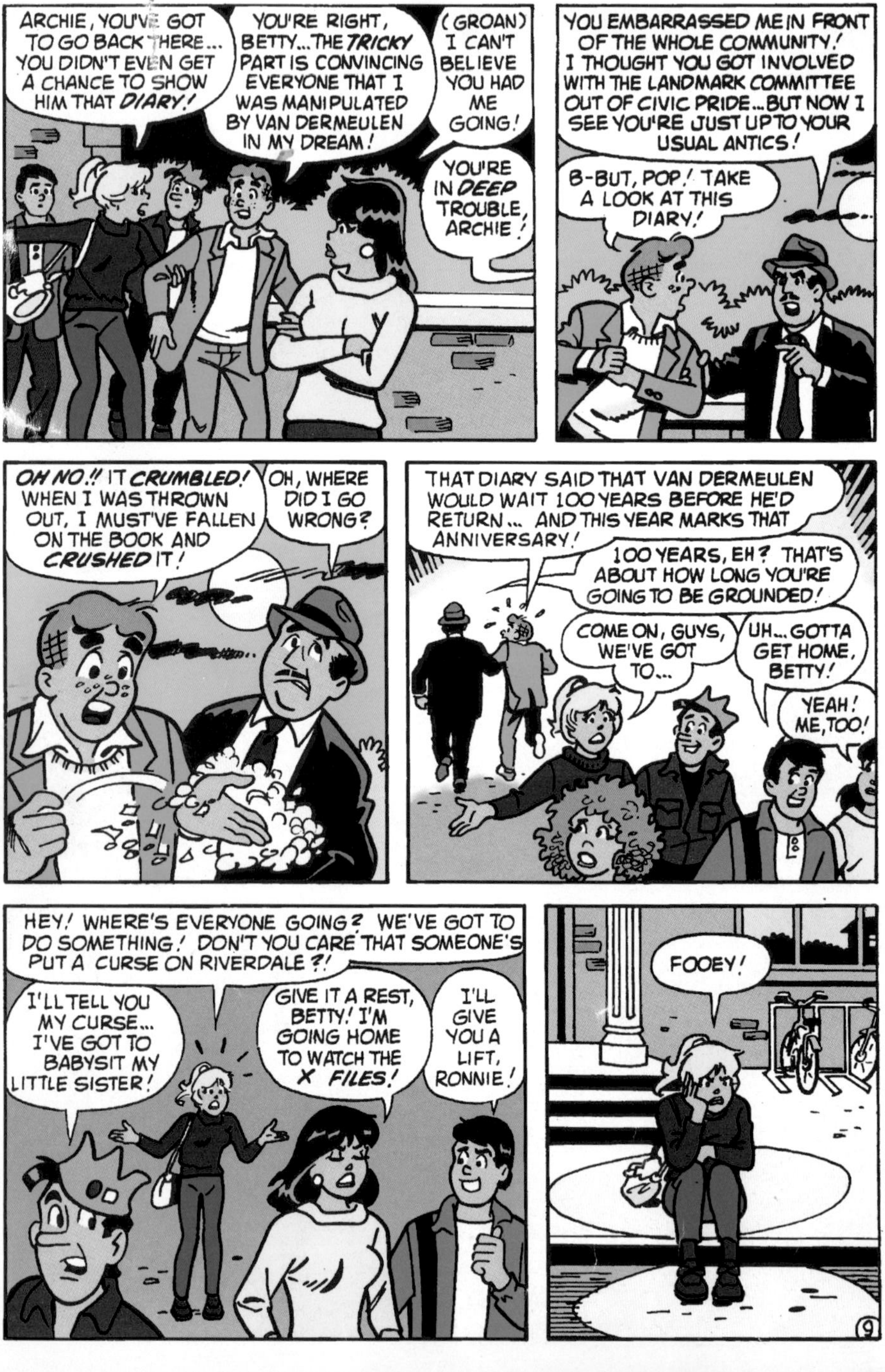
ARCHIE, YOU'VE GOT TO GO BACK THERE... YOU DIDN'T EVEN GET A CHANCE TO SHOW HIM THAT DIARY!
YOU'RE RIGHT, BETTY...THE TRICKY PART IS CONVINCING EVERYONE THAT I WAS MANIPULATED BY VAN DERMEULEN IN MY DREAM!
(GROAN) I CAN'T BELIEVE YOU HAD ME GOING!
YOU'RE IN DEEP TROUBLE, ARCHIE!
YOU EMBARRASSED ME IN FRONT OF THE WHOLE COMMUNITY! I THOUGHT YOU GOT INVOLVED WITH THE LANDMARK COMMITTEE OUT OF CIVIC PRIDE...BUT NOW I SEE YOU'RE JUST UP TO YOUR USUAL ANTICS!
B-BUT, POP! TAKE A LOOK AT THIS DIARY!
OH NO!! IT CRUMBLED! WHEN I WAS THROWN OUT, I MUST'VE FALLEN ON THE BOOK AND CRUSHED IT!
OH, WHERE DID I GO WRONG?
THAT DIARY SAID THAT VAN DERMEULEN WOULD WAIT 100 YEARS BEFORE HE'D RETURN... AND THIS YEAR MARKS THAT ANNIVERSARY!
100 YEARS, EH? THAT'S ABOUT HOW LONG YOU'RE GOING TO BE GROUNDED!
COME ON, GUYS, WE'VE GOT TO...
UH...GOTTA GET HOME, BETTY!
YEAH! ME, TOO!
HEY! WHERE'S EVERYONE GOING? WE'VE GOT TO DO SOMETHING! DON'T YOU CARE THAT SOMEONE'S PUT A CURSE ON RIVERDALE?!
I'LL TELL YOU MY CURSE... I'VE GOT TO BABYSIT MY LITTLE SISTER!
GIVE IT A REST, BETTY! I'M GOING HOME TO WATCH THE X FILES!
I'LL GIVE YOU A LIFT, RONNIE!
FOOEY!
9

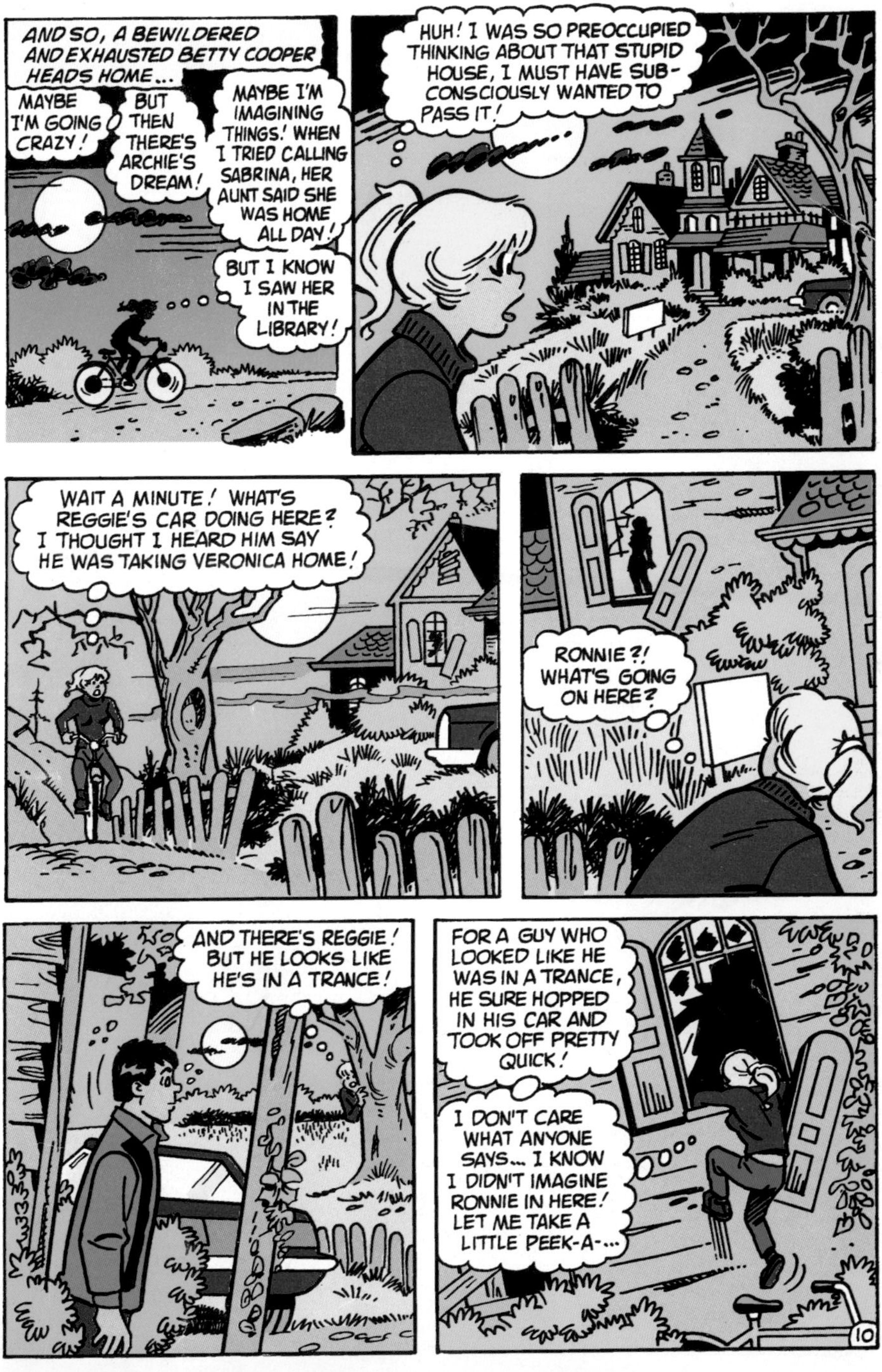
AND SO, A BEWILDERED AND EXHAUSTED BETTY COOPER HEADS HOME...
MAYBE I'M GOING CRAZY!
BUT THEN THERE'S ARCHIE'S DREAM!
MAYBE I'M IMAGINING THINGS! WHEN I TRIED CALLING SABRINA, HER AUNT SAID SHE WAS HOME ALL DAY!
BUT I KNOW I SAW HER IN THE LIBRARY!
HUH! I WAS SO PREOCCUPIED THINKING ABOUT THAT STUPID HOUSE, I MUST HAVE SUB-CONSCIOUSLY WANTED TO PASS IT!
WAIT A MINUTE! WHAT'S REGGIE'S CAR DOING HERE? I THOUGHT I HEARD HIM SAY HE WAS TAKING VERONICA HOME!
RONNIE?! WHAT'S GOING ON HERE?
AND THERE'S REGGIE! BUT HE LOOKS LIKE HE'S IN A TRANCE!
FOR A GUY WHO LOOKED LIKE HE WAS IN A TRANCE, HE SURE HOPPED IN HIS CAR AND TOOK OFF PRETTY QUICK!
I DON'T CARE WHAT ANYONE SAYS... I KNOW I DIDN'T IMAGINE RONNIE IN HERE! LET ME TAKE A LITTLE PEEK-A-...
10

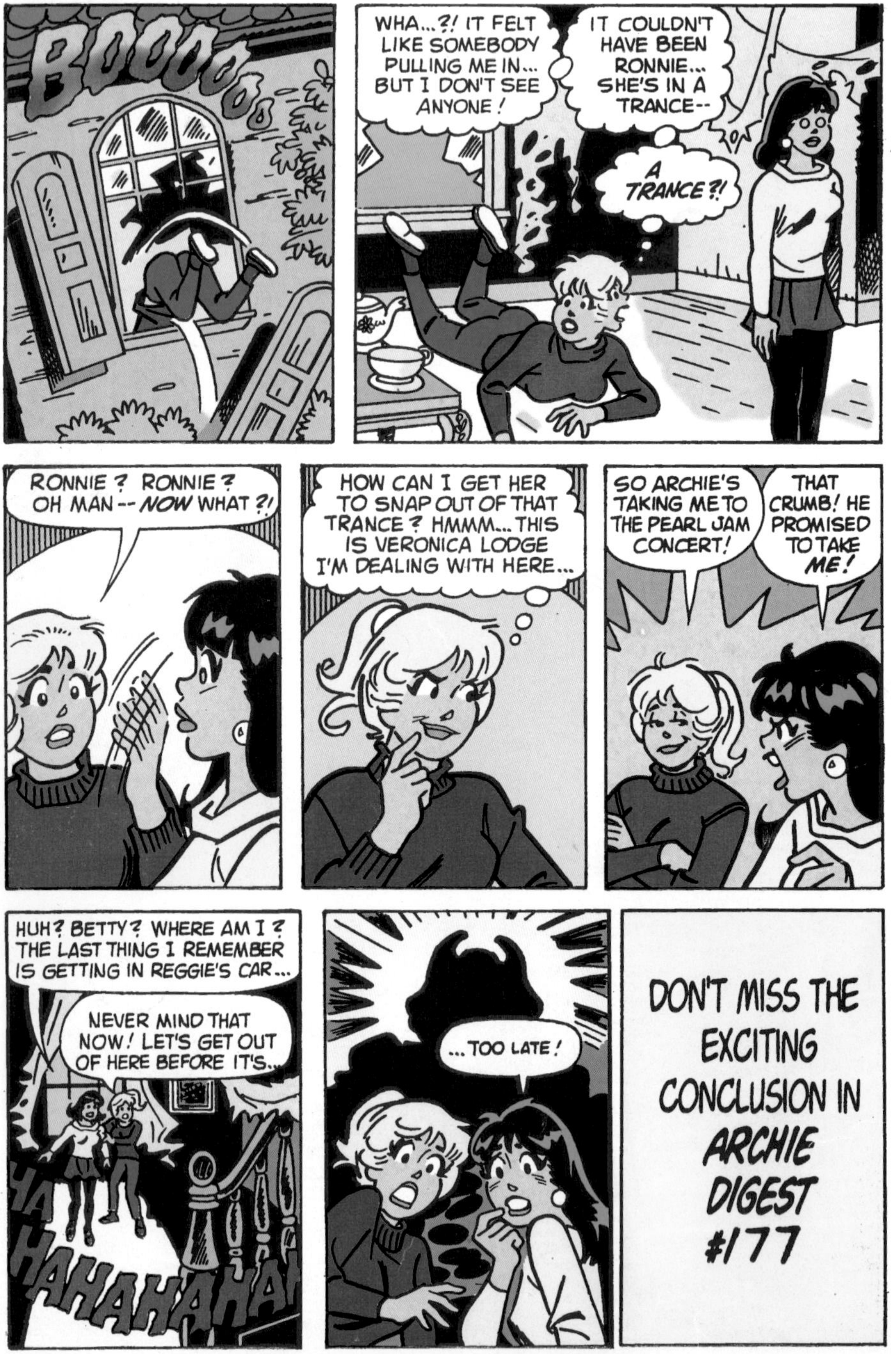
BOOOOO
WHA...?! IT FELT LIKE SOMEBODY PULLING ME IN... BUT I DON'T SEE ANYONE!
IT COULDN'T HAVE BEEN RONNIE... SHE'S IN A TRANCE--
A TRANCE?!
RONNIE? RONNIE? OH MAN -- NOW WHAT?!
HOW CAN I GET HER TO SNAP OUT OF THAT TRANCE? HMMM... THIS IS VERONICA LODGE I'M DEALING WITH HERE...
SO ARCHIE'S TAKING ME TO THE PEARL JAM CONCERT!
THAT CRUMB! HE PROMISED TO TAKE ME!
HUH? BETTY? WHERE AM I? THE LAST THING I REMEMBER IS GETTING IN REGGIE'S CAR...
NEVER MIND THAT NOW! LET'S GET OUT OF HERE BEFORE IT'S...
HAHAHAHAHAHA
...TOO LATE!
DON'T MISS THE EXCITING CONCLUSION IN ARCHIE DIGEST #177

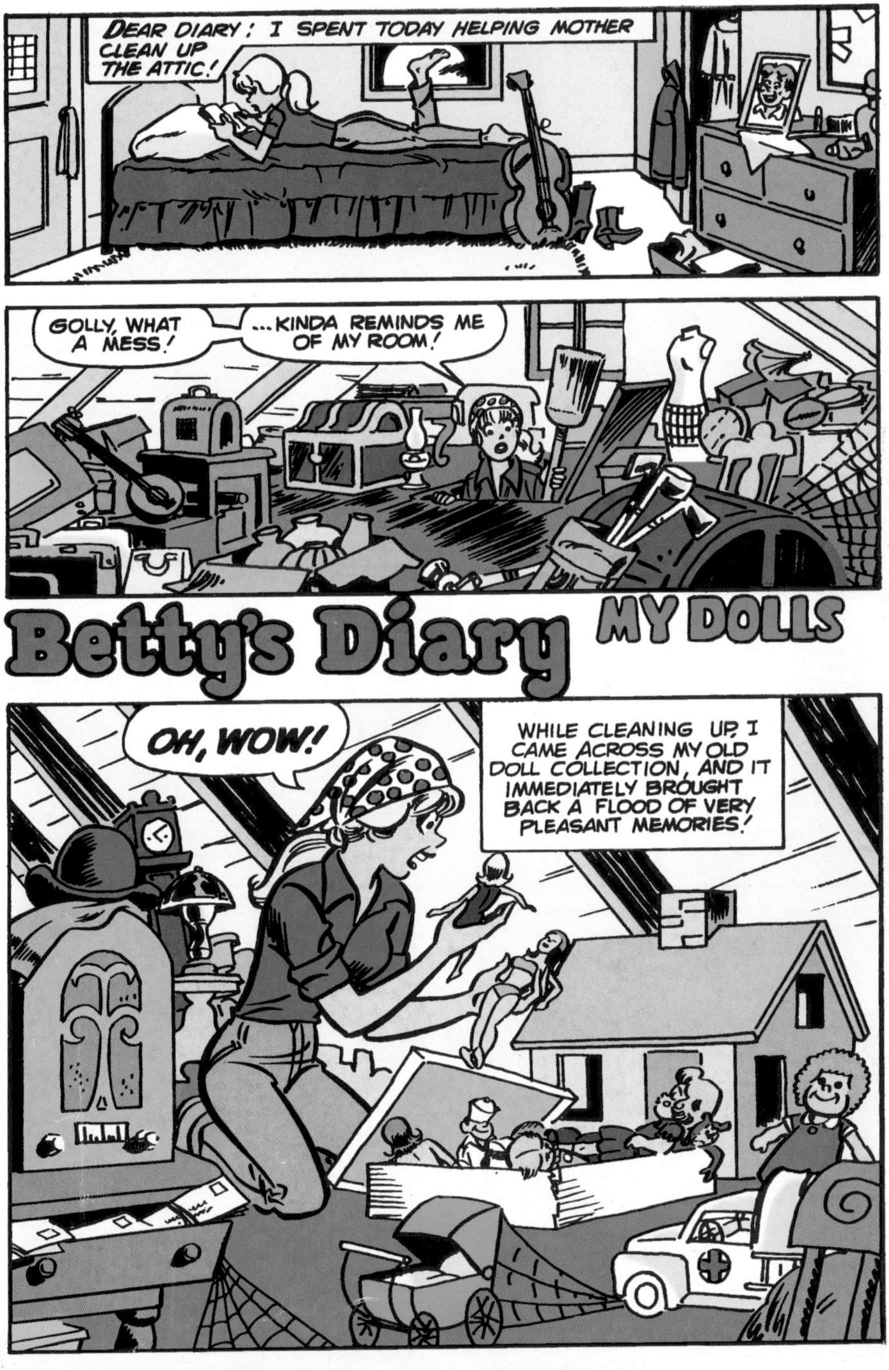
DEAR DIARY: I SPENT TODAY HELPING MOTHER CLEAN UP THE ATTIC!
GOLLY, WHAT A MESS!
...KINDA REMINDS ME OF MY ROOM!
Betty's Diary
MY DOLLS
OH, WOW!
WHILE CLEANING UP, I CAME ACROSS MY OLD DOLL COLLECTION, AND IT IMMEDIATELY BROUGHT BACK A FLOOD OF VERY PLEASANT MEMORIES!

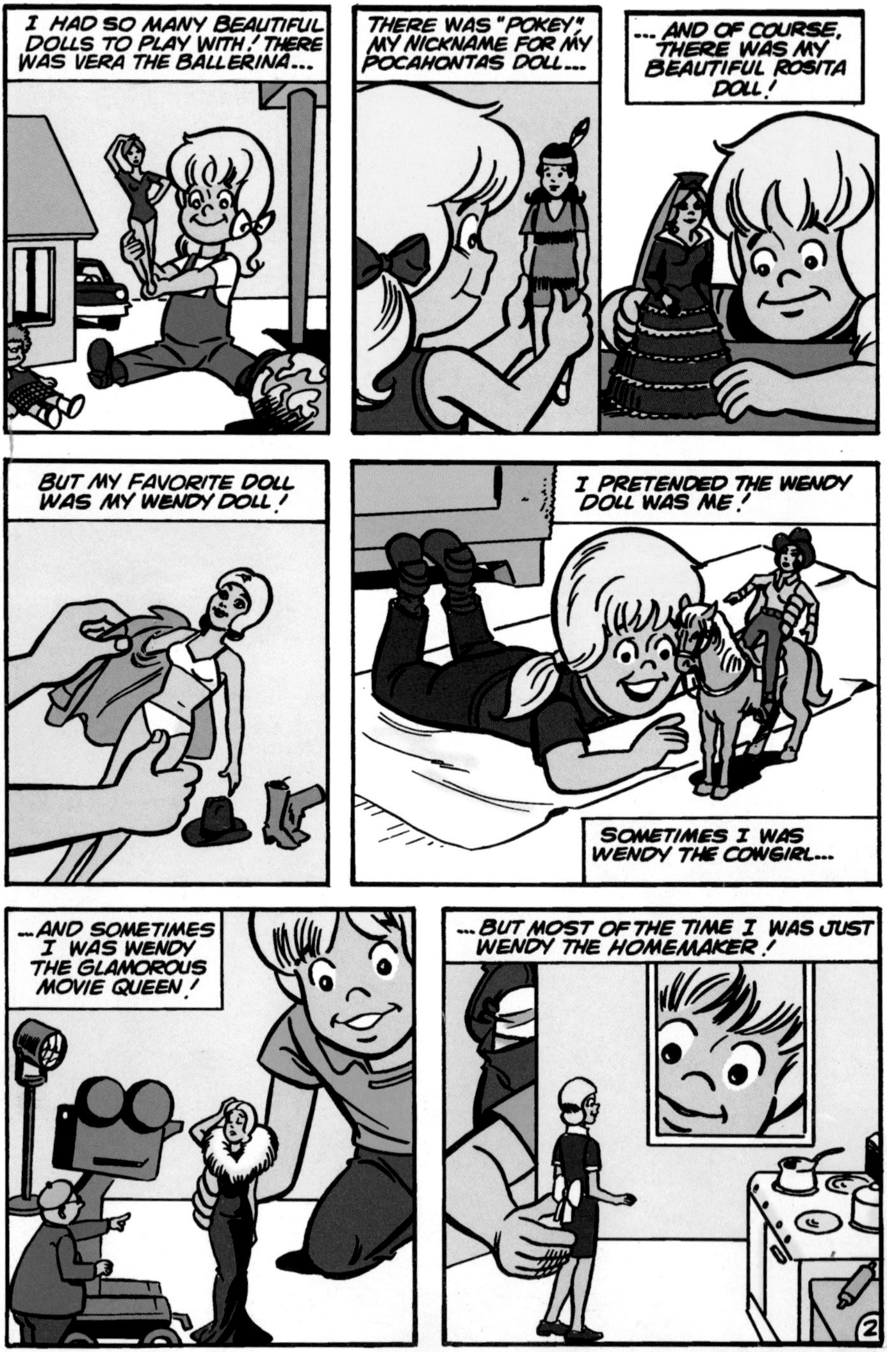
I HAD SO MANY BEAUTIFUL DOLLS TO PLAY WITH! THERE WAS VERA THE BALLERINA...
THERE WAS "POKEY," MY NICKNAME FOR MY POCAHONTAS DOLL...
...AND OF COURSE, THERE WAS MY BEAUTIFUL ROSITA DOLL!
BUT MY FAVORITE DOLL WAS MY WENDY DOLL!
I PRETENDED THE WENDY DOLL WAS ME!
SOMETIMES I WAS WENDY THE COWGIRL...
...AND SOMETIMES I WAS WENDY THE GLAMOROUS MOVIE QUEEN!
...BUT MOST OF THE TIME I WAS JUST WENDY THE HOMEMAKER!
2

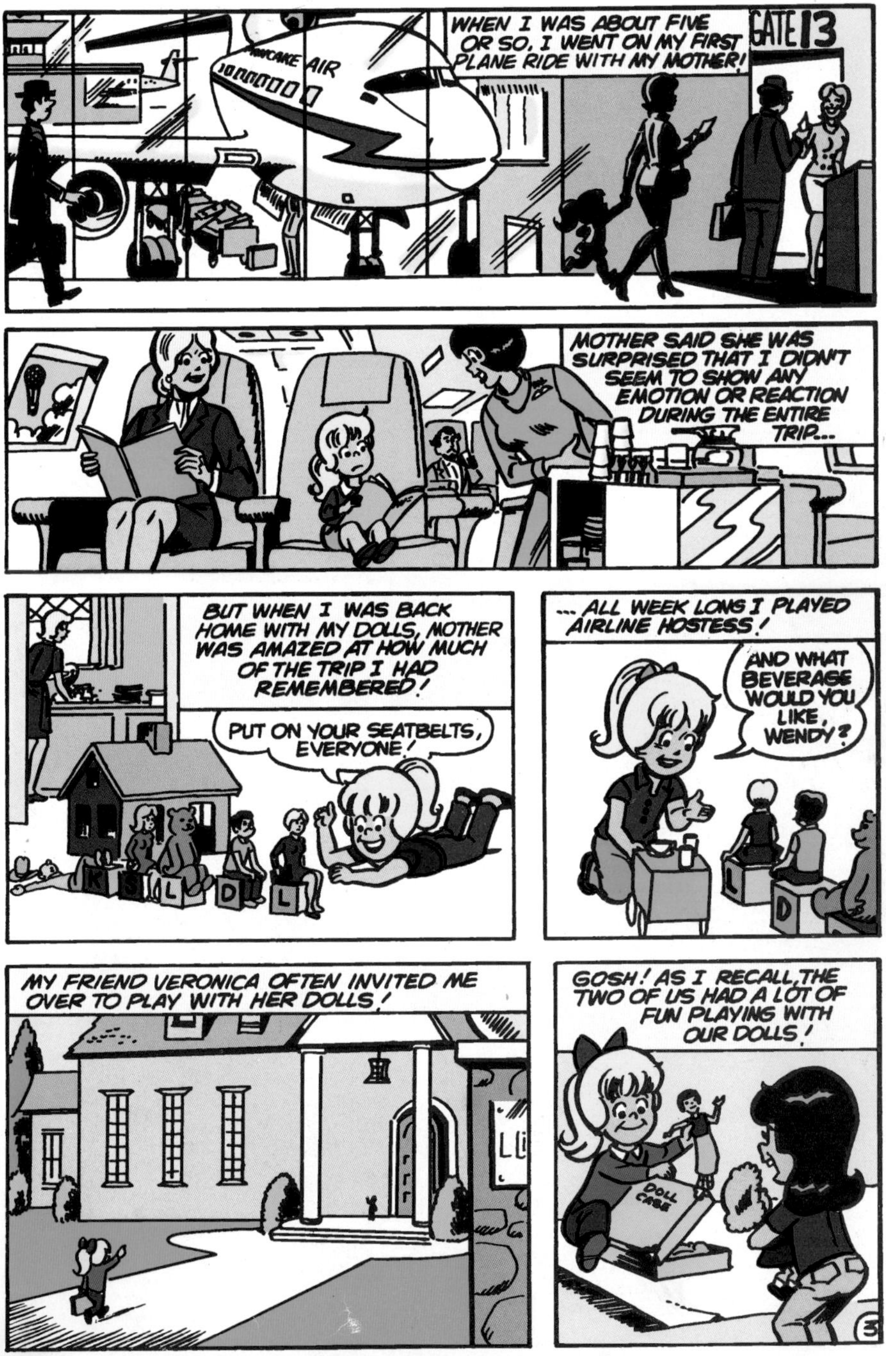
WHEN I WAS ABOUT FIVE OR SO, I WENT ON MY FIRST PLANE RIDE WITH MY MOTHER!
GATE 13
AIR
MOTHER SAID SHE WAS SURPRISED THAT I DIDN'T SEEM TO SHOW ANY EMOTION OR REACTION DURING THE ENTIRE TRIP...
BUT WHEN I WAS BACK HOME WITH MY DOLLS, MOTHER WAS AMAZED AT HOW MUCH OF THE TRIP I HAD REMEMBERED!
PUT ON YOUR SEATBELTS, EVERYONE!
...ALL WEEK LONG I PLAYED AIRLINE HOSTESS!
AND WHAT BEVERAGE WOULD YOU LIKE, WENDY?
MY FRIEND VERONICA OFTEN INVITED ME OVER TO PLAY WITH HER DOLLS!
GOSH! AS I RECALL, THE TWO OF US HAD A LOT OF FUN PLAYING WITH OUR DOLLS!
DOLL CASE
3

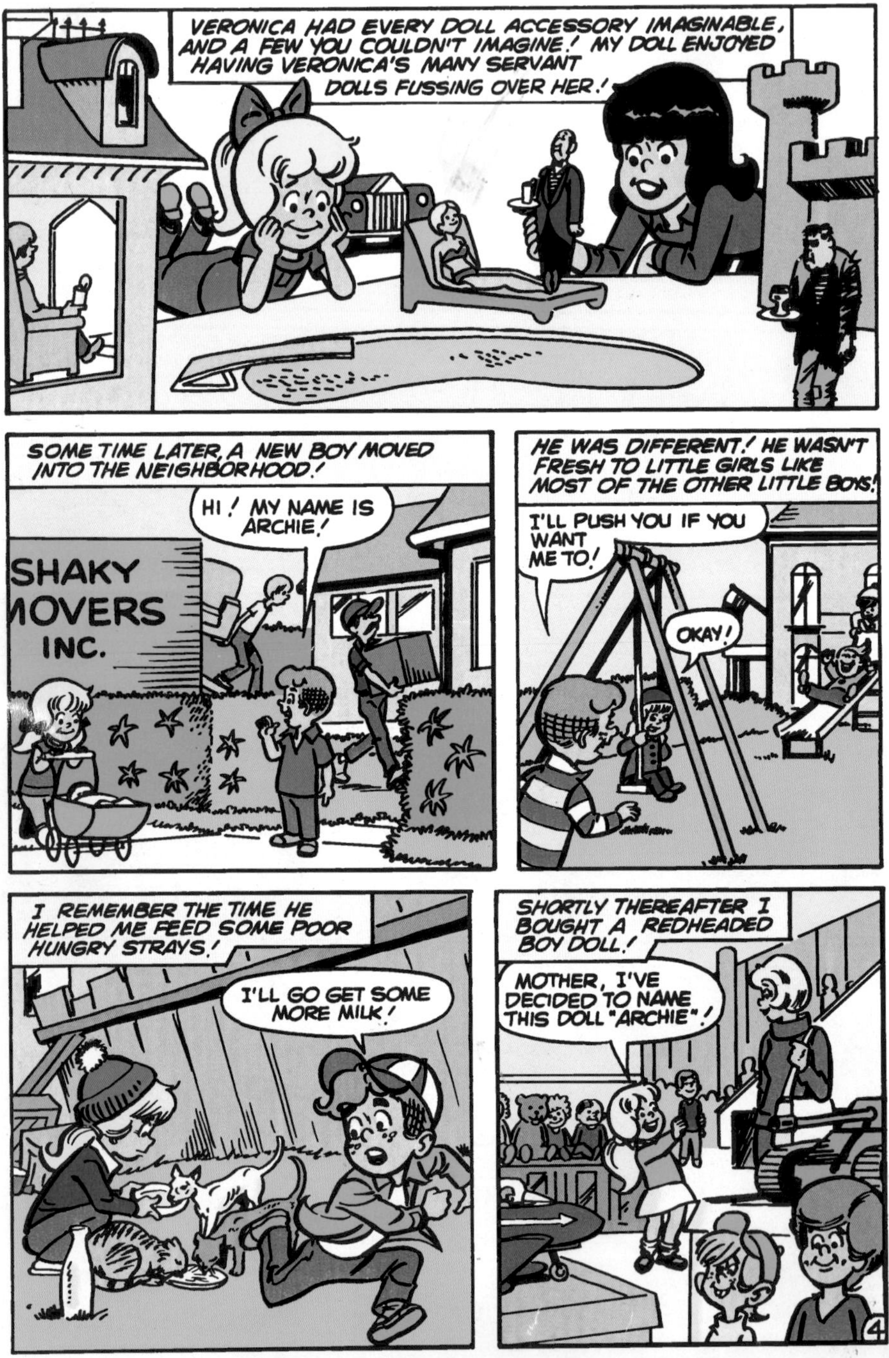
VERONICA HAD EVERY DOLL ACCESSORY IMAGINABLE, AND A FEW YOU COULDN'T IMAGINE! MY DOLL ENJOYED HAVING VERONICA'S MANY SERVANT DOLLS FUSSING OVER HER!
SOME TIME LATER, A NEW BOY MOVED INTO THE NEIGHBORHOOD!
HI! MY NAME IS ARCHIE!
SHAKY MOVERS INC.
HE WAS DIFFERENT! HE WASN'T FRESH TO LITTLE GIRLS LIKE MOST OF THE OTHER LITTLE BOYS!
I'LL PUSH YOU IF YOU WANT ME TO!
OKAY!
I REMEMBER THE TIME HE HELPED ME FEED SOME POOR HUNGRY STRAYS!
I'LL GO GET SOME MORE MILK!
SHORTLY THEREAFTER I BOUGHT A REDHEADED BOY DOLL!
MOTHER, I'VE DECIDED TO NAME THIS DOLL "ARCHIE"!
4

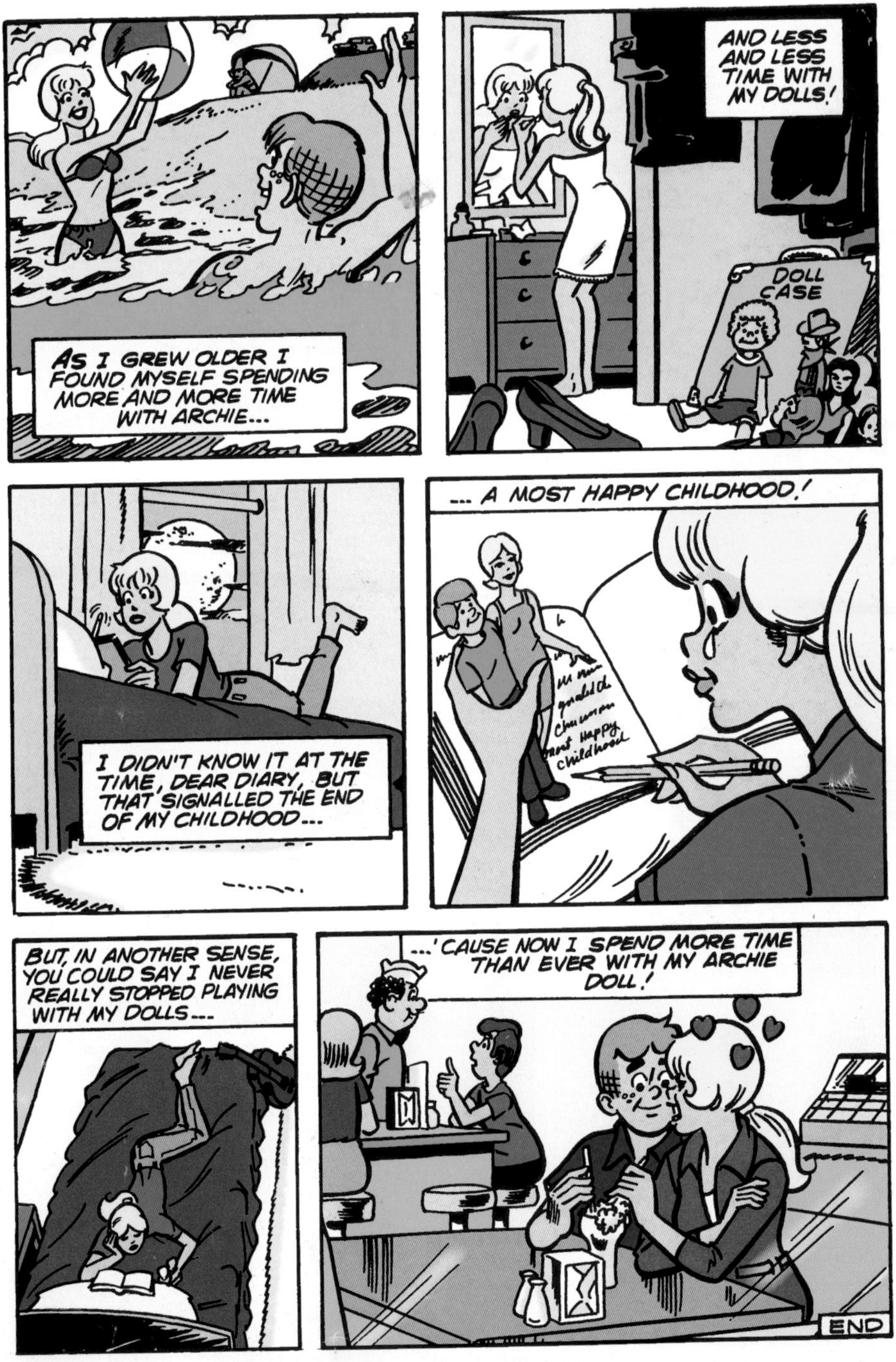
AS I GREW OLDER I FOUND MYSELF SPENDING MORE AND MORE TIME WITH ARCHIE...
AND LESS AND LESS TIME WITH MY DOLLS!
DOLL CASE
I DIDN'T KNOW IT AT THE TIME, DEAR DIARY, BUT THAT SIGNALLED THE END OF MY CHILDHOOD...
... A MOST HAPPY CHILDHOOD!
BUT, IN ANOTHER SENSE, YOU COULD SAY I NEVER REALLY STOPPED PLAYING WITH MY DOLLS...
...'CAUSE NOW I SPEND MORE TIME THAN EVER WITH MY ARCHIE DOLL!
END

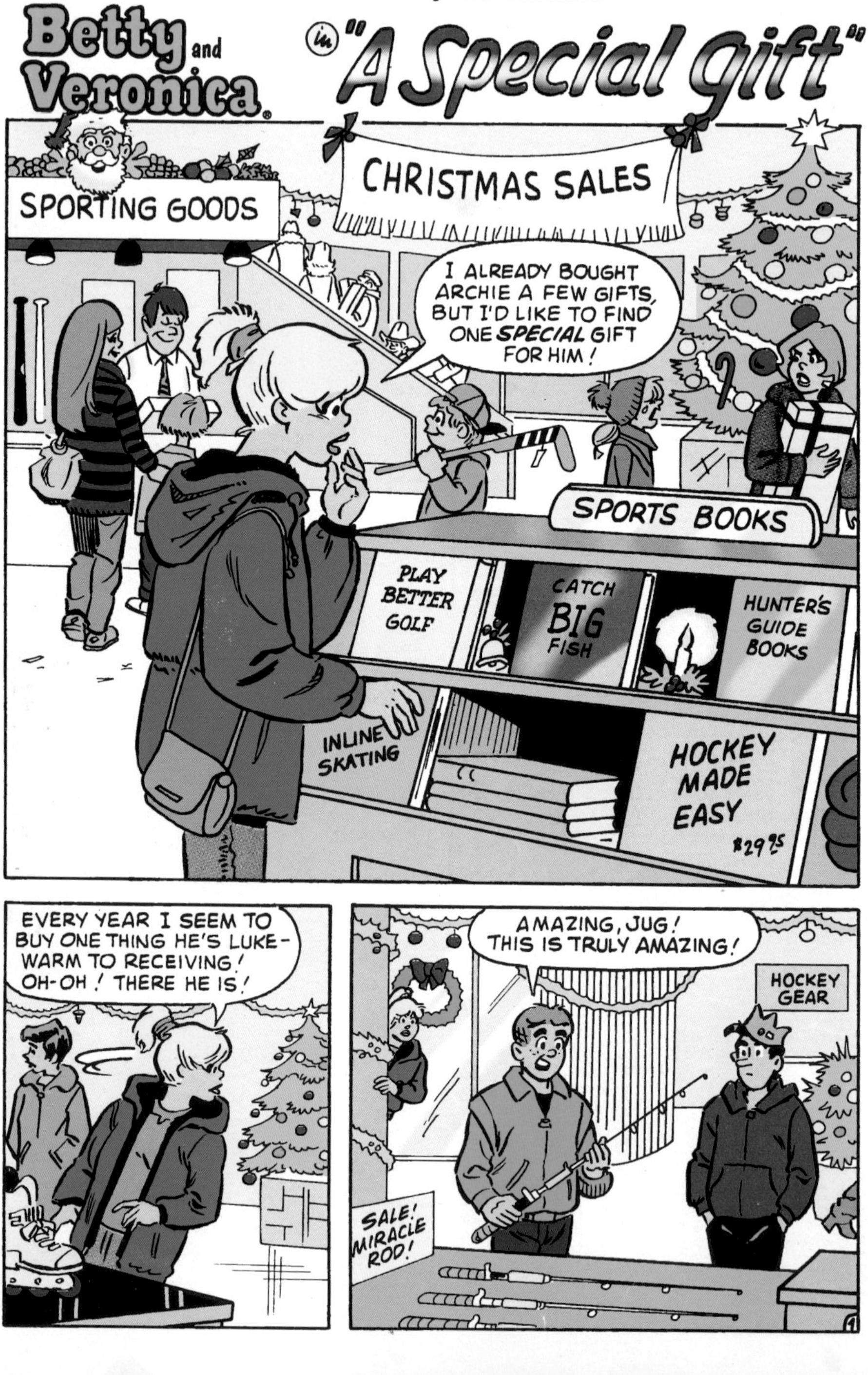
Betty and Veronica
in "A Special gift"
SPORTING GOODS
CHRISTMAS SALES
I ALREADY BOUGHT ARCHIE A FEW GIFTS, BUT I'D LIKE TO FIND ONE SPECIAL GIFT FOR HIM!
SPORTS BOOKS
PLAY BETTER GOLF
CATCH BIG FISH
HUNTER'S GUIDE BOOKS
INLINE SKATING
HOCKEY MADE EASY
$29.95
EVERY YEAR I SEEM TO BUY ONE THING HE'S LUKE-WARM TO RECEIVING! OH-OH! THERE HE IS!
AMAZING, JUG! THIS IS TRULY AMAZING!
HOCKEY GEAR
SALE! MIRACLE ROD!
1

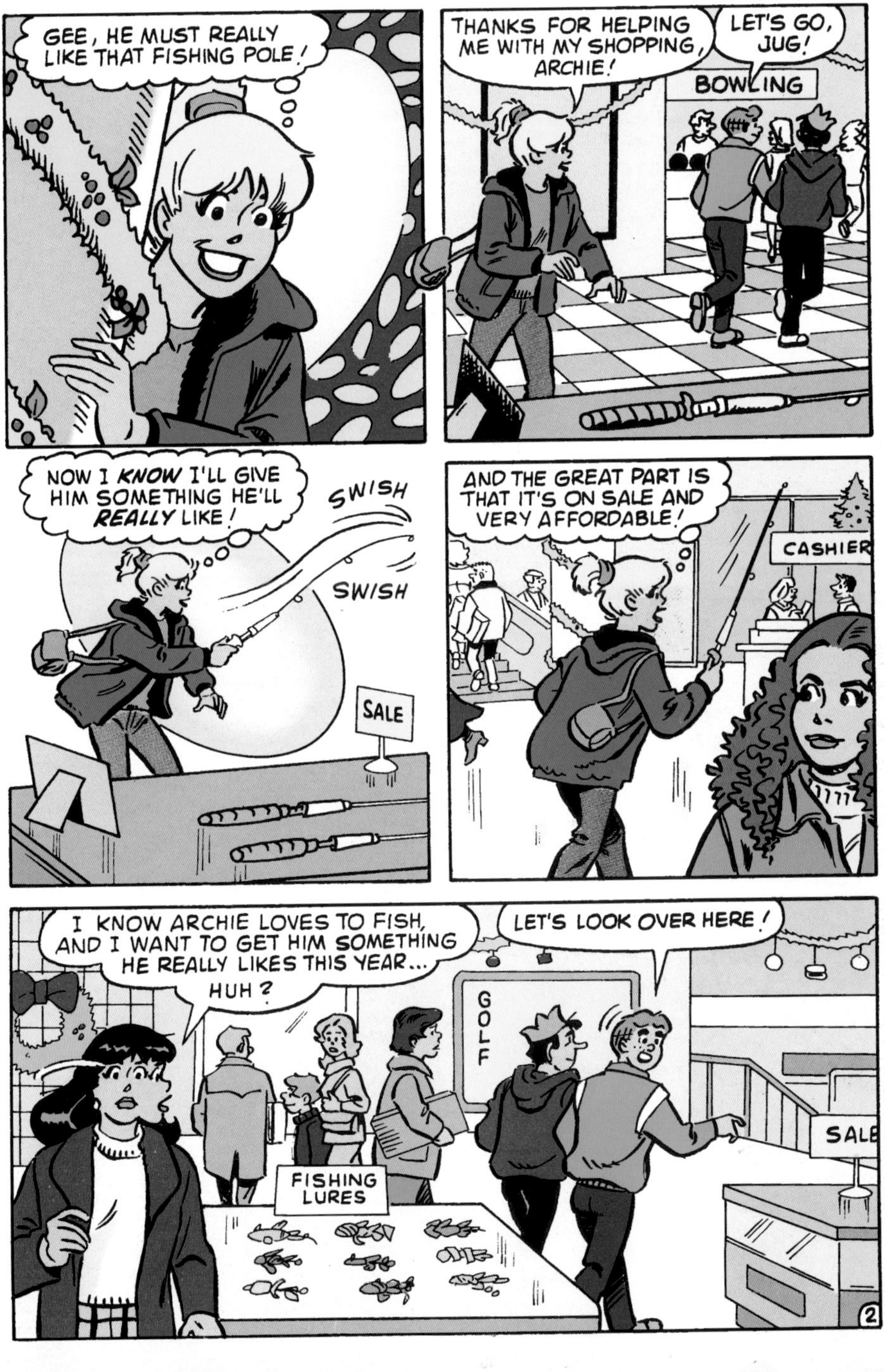
GEE, HE MUST REALLY LIKE THAT FISHING POLE!
THANKS FOR HELPING ME WITH MY SHOPPING, ARCHIE!
LET'S GO, JUG!
BOWLING
NOW I KNOW I'LL GIVE HIM SOMETHING HE'LL REALLY LIKE!
SWISH
SWISH
SALE
AND THE GREAT PART IS THAT IT'S ON SALE AND VERY AFFORDABLE!
CASHIER
I KNOW ARCHIE LOVES TO FISH, AND I WANT TO GET HIM SOMETHING HE REALLY LIKES THIS YEAR...
HUH?
LET'S LOOK OVER HERE!
GOLF
FISHING LURES
SALE
2

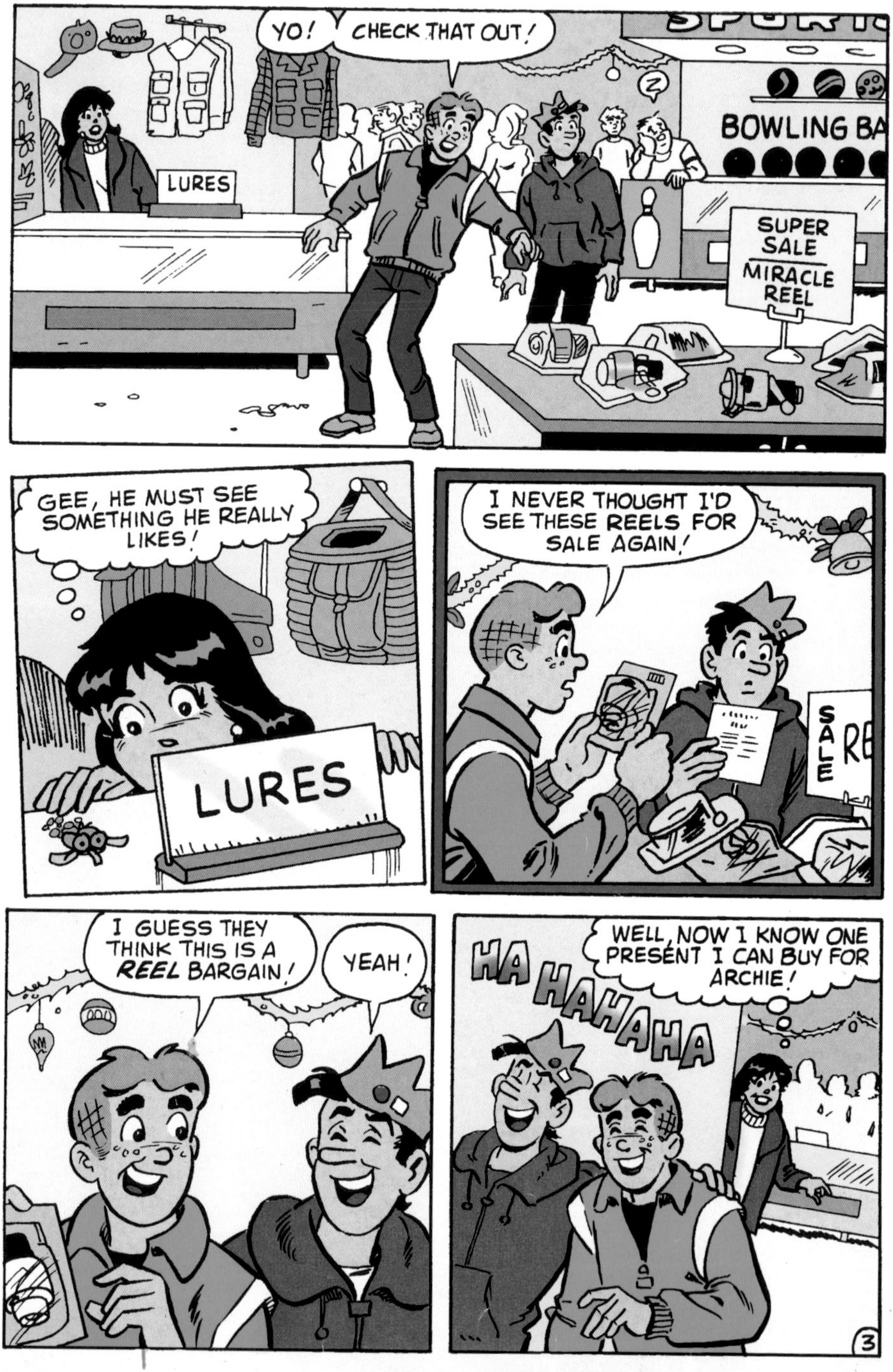
YO!
CHECK THAT OUT!
LURES
BOWLING BA
SUPER SALE MIRACLE REEL
GEE, HE MUST SEE SOMETHING HE REALLY LIKES!
LURES
I NEVER THOUGHT I'D SEE THESE REELS FOR SALE AGAIN!
SALE
I GUESS THEY THINK THIS IS A REEL BARGAIN!
YEAH!
HA HA HAHAHA
WELL, NOW I KNOW ONE PRESENT I CAN BUY FOR ARCHIE!
3

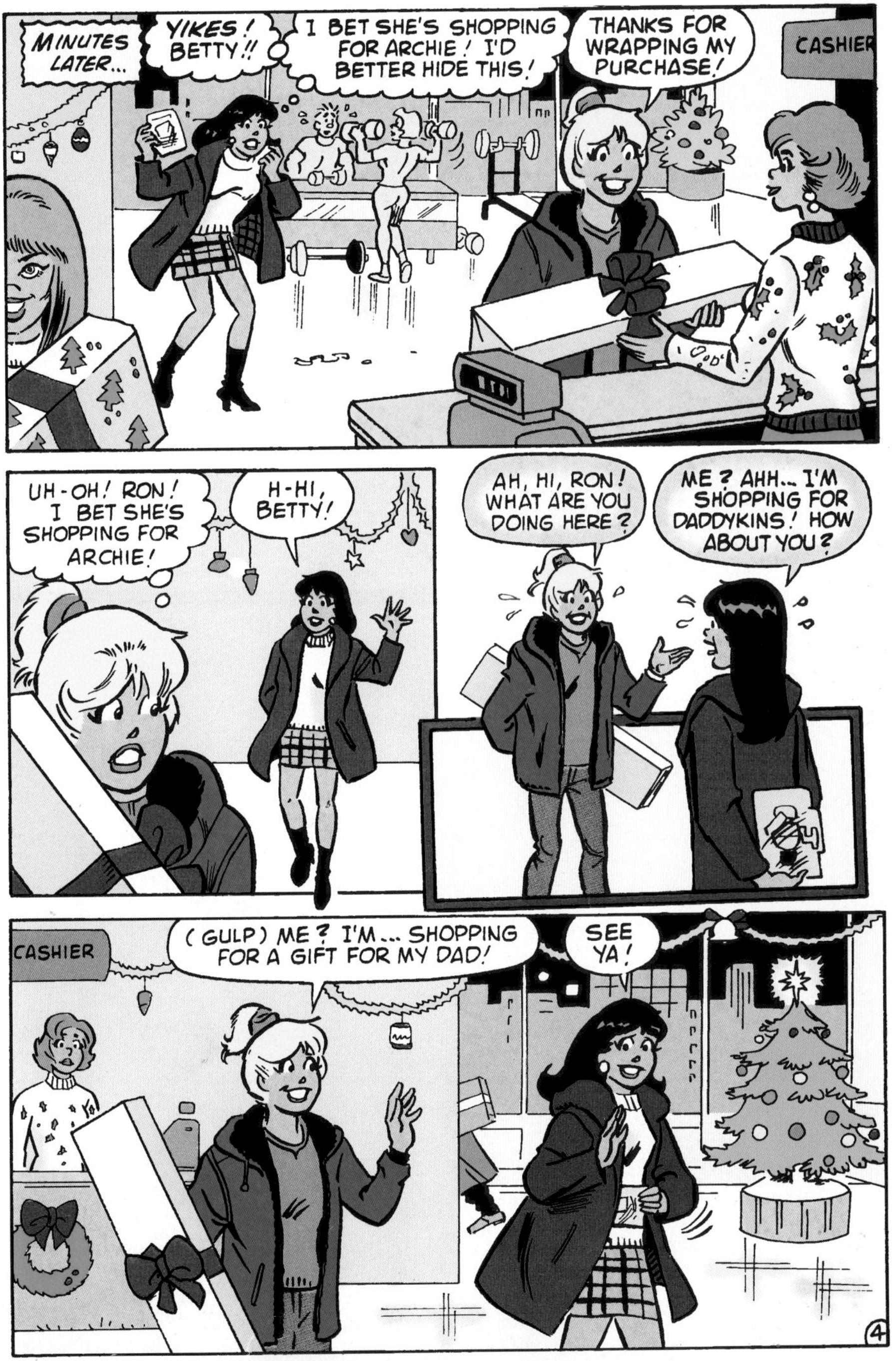
MINUTES LATER...
YIKES! BETTY!!
I BET SHE'S SHOPPING FOR ARCHIE! I'D BETTER HIDE THIS!
THANKS FOR WRAPPING MY PURCHASE!
CASHIER
UH-OH! RON! I BET SHE'S SHOPPING FOR ARCHIE!
H-HI, BETTY!
AH, HI, RON! WHAT ARE YOU DOING HERE?
ME? AHH... I'M SHOPPING FOR DADDYKINS! HOW ABOUT YOU?
CASHIER
(GULP) ME? I'M... SHOPPING FOR A GIFT FOR MY DAD!
SEE YA!
4

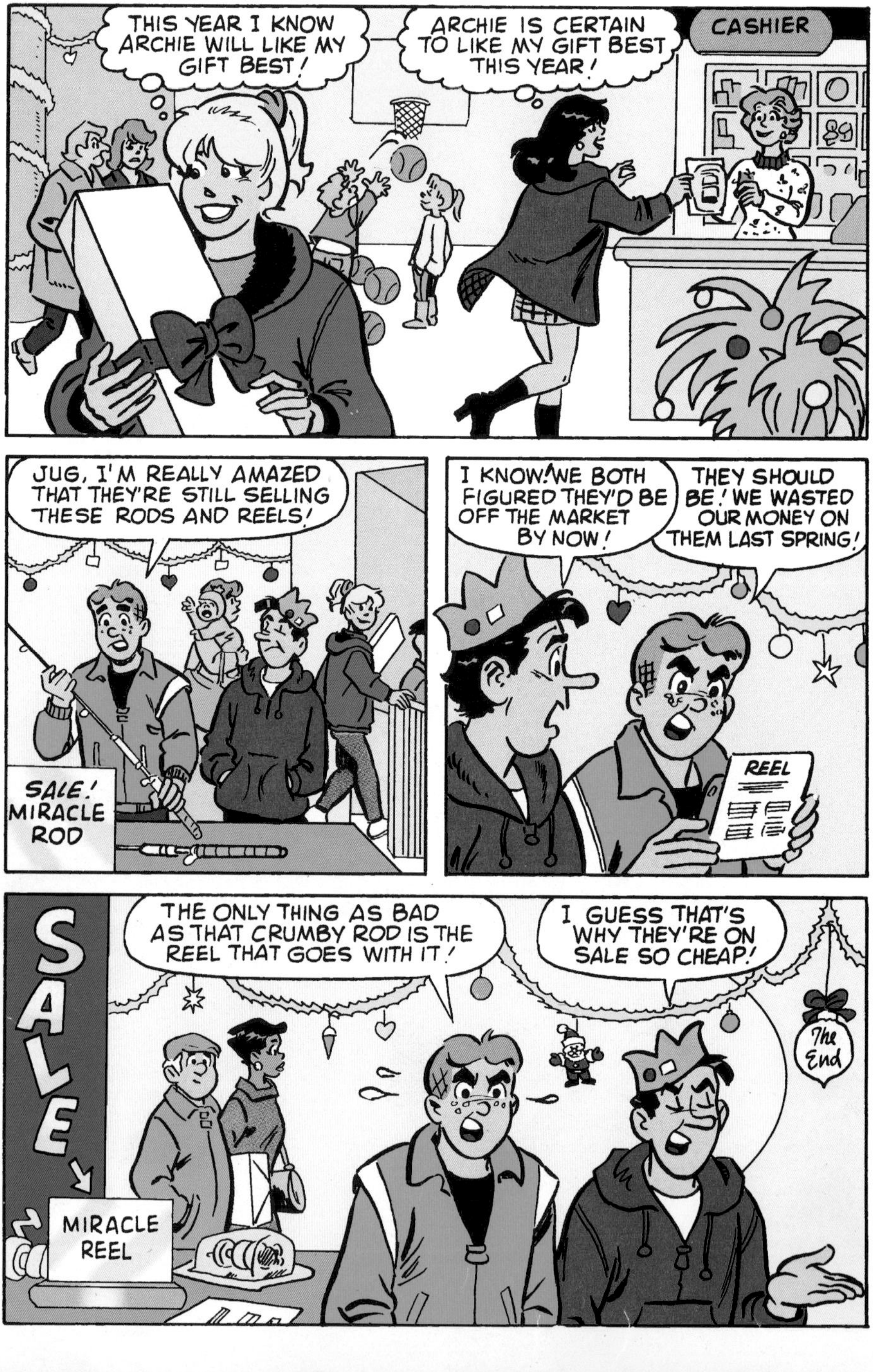
THIS YEAR I KNOW ARCHIE WILL LIKE MY GIFT BEST!
ARCHIE IS CERTAIN TO LIKE MY GIFT BEST THIS YEAR!
CASHIER
JUG, I'M REALLY AMAZED THAT THEY'RE STILL SELLING THESE RODS AND REELS!
SALE! MIRACLE ROD
I KNOW! WE BOTH FIGURED THEY'D BE OFF THE MARKET BY NOW!
THEY SHOULD BE! WE WASTED OUR MONEY ON THEM LAST SPRING!
REEL
SALE
THE ONLY THING AS BAD AS THAT CRUMBY ROD IS THE REEL THAT GOES WITH IT!
I GUESS THAT'S WHY THEY'RE ON SALE SO CHEAP!
MIRACLE REEL
The End

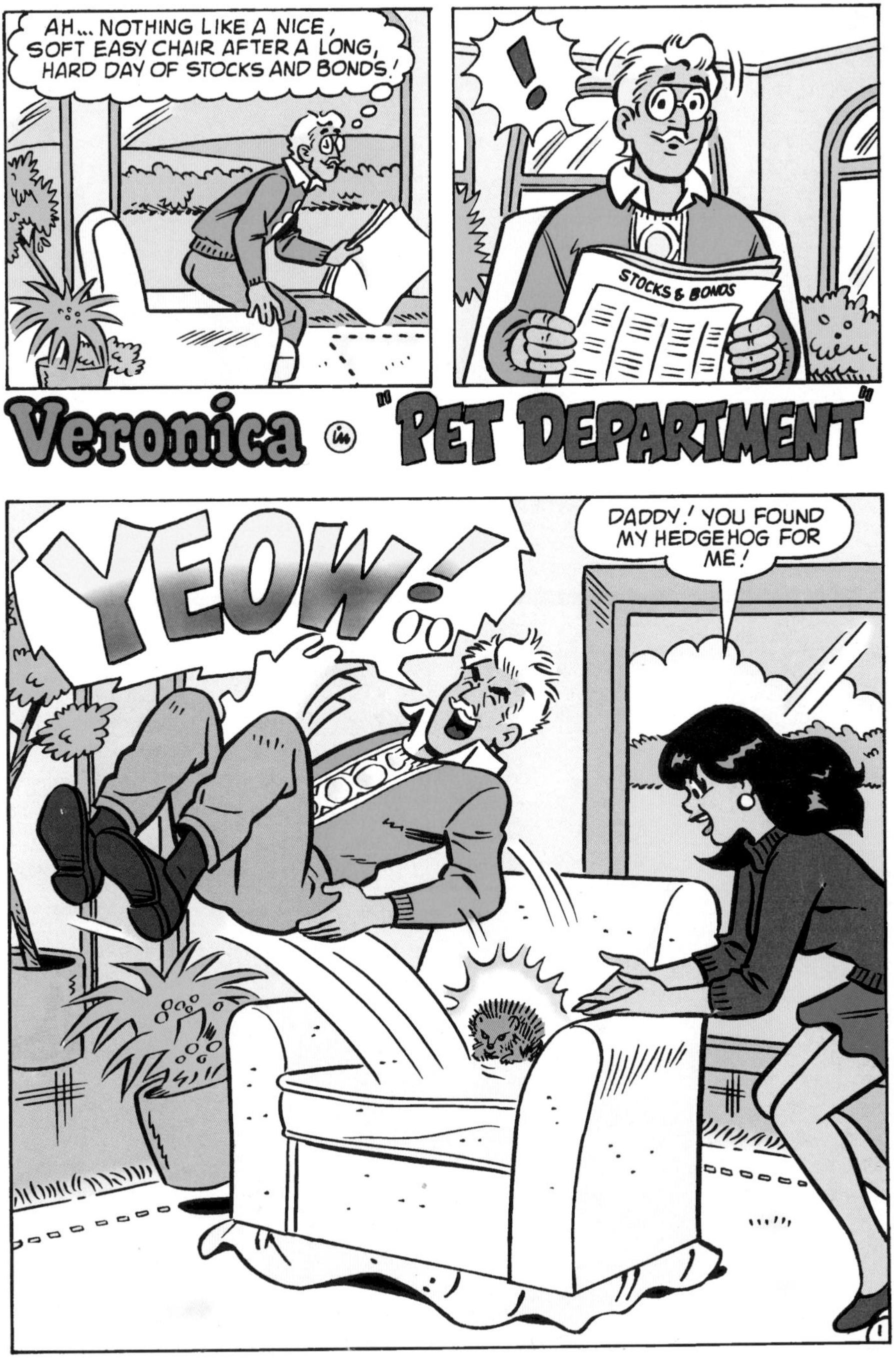
AH... NOTHING LIKE A NICE, SOFT EASY CHAIR AFTER A LONG, HARD DAY OF STOCKS AND BONDS!
!
STOCKS & BONDS
Veronica in "PET DEPARTMENT"
YEOW!
DADDY! YOU FOUND MY HEDGEHOG FOR ME!

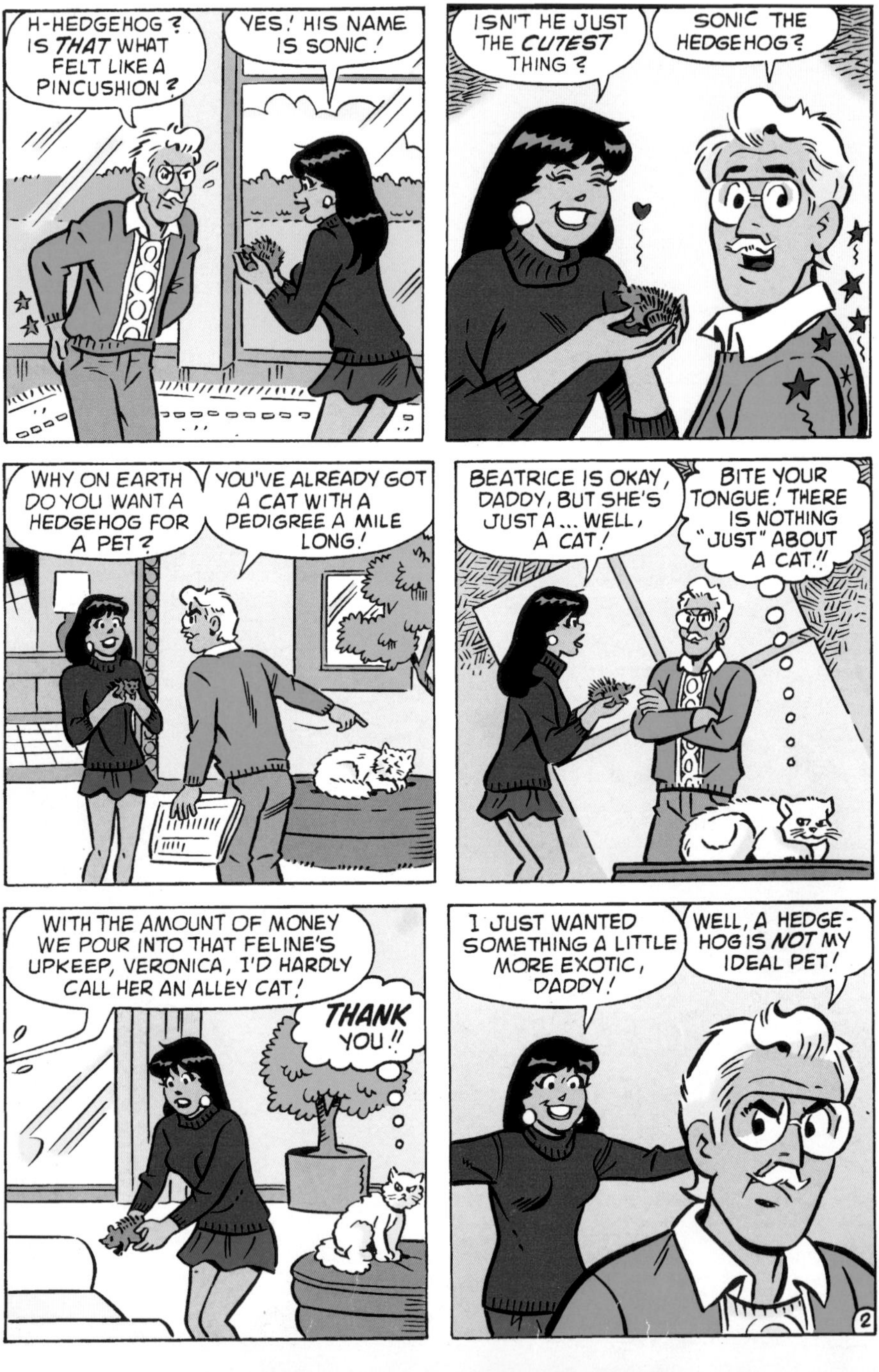
H-HEDGEHOG? IS THAT WHAT FELT LIKE A PINCUSHION?
YES! HIS NAME IS SONIC!
ISN'T HE JUST THE CUTEST THING?
SONIC THE HEDGEHOG?
WHY ON EARTH DO YOU WANT A HEDGEHOG FOR A PET?
YOU'VE ALREADY GOT A CAT WITH A PEDIGREE A MILE LONG!
BEATRICE IS OKAY, DADDY, BUT SHE'S JUST A ... WELL, A CAT!
BITE YOUR TONGUE! THERE IS NOTHING "JUST" ABOUT A CAT!!
WITH THE AMOUNT OF MONEY WE POUR INTO THAT FELINE'S UPKEEP, VERONICA, I'D HARDLY CALL HER AN ALLEY CAT!
THANK YOU!!
I JUST WANTED SOMETHING A LITTLE MORE EXOTIC, DADDY!
WELL, A HEDGE-HOG IS NOT MY IDEAL PET!
2

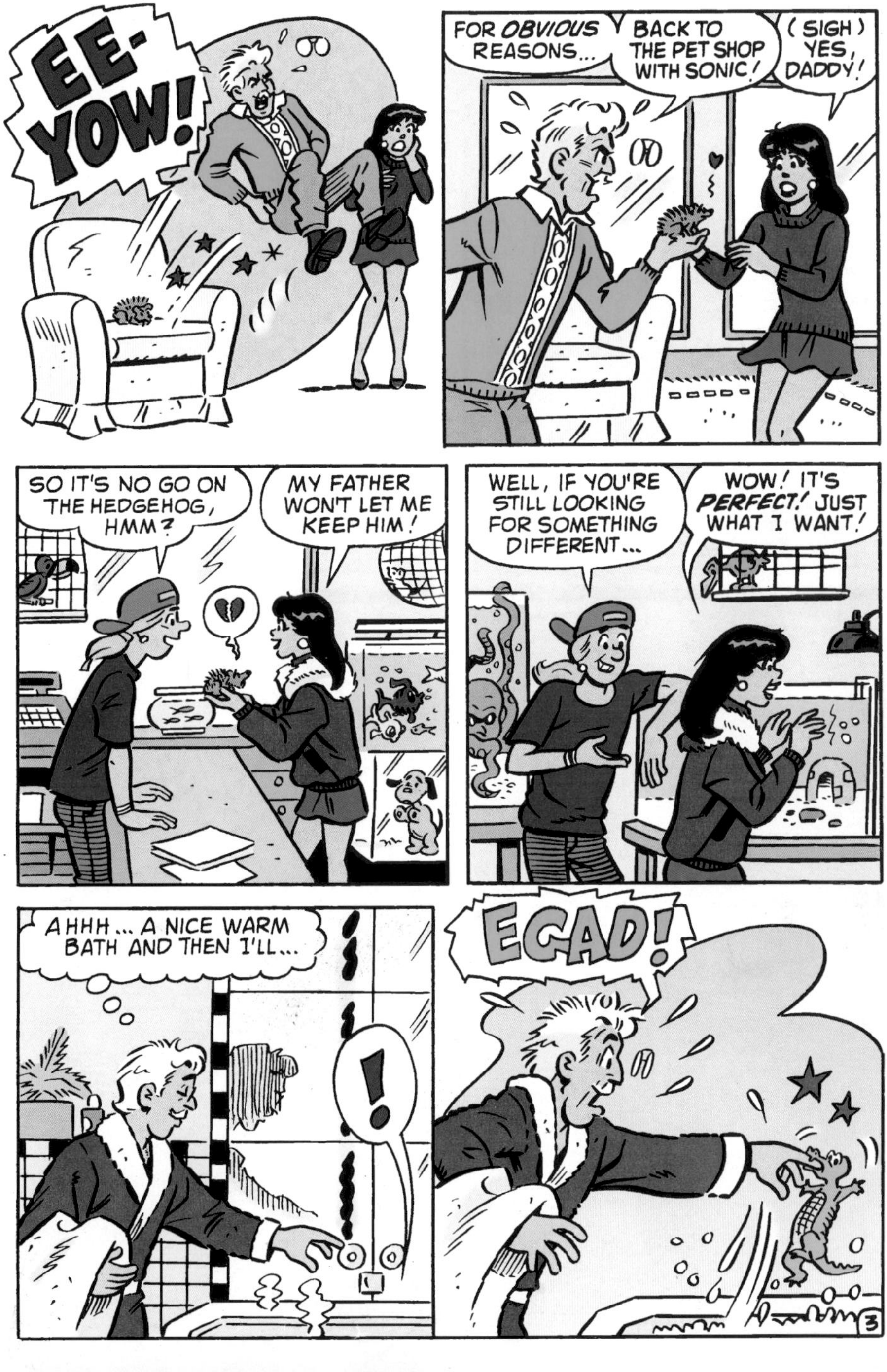
EE-YOW!
FOR OBVIOUS REASONS...
BACK TO THE PET SHOP WITH SONIC!
(SIGH) YES, DADDY!
SO IT'S NO GO ON THE HEDGEHOG, HMM?
MY FATHER WON'T LET ME KEEP HIM!
WELL, IF YOU'RE STILL LOOKING FOR SOMETHING DIFFERENT...
WOW! IT'S PERFECT! JUST WHAT I WANT!
AHHH ... A NICE WARM BATH AND THEN I'LL...
!
EGAD!
3

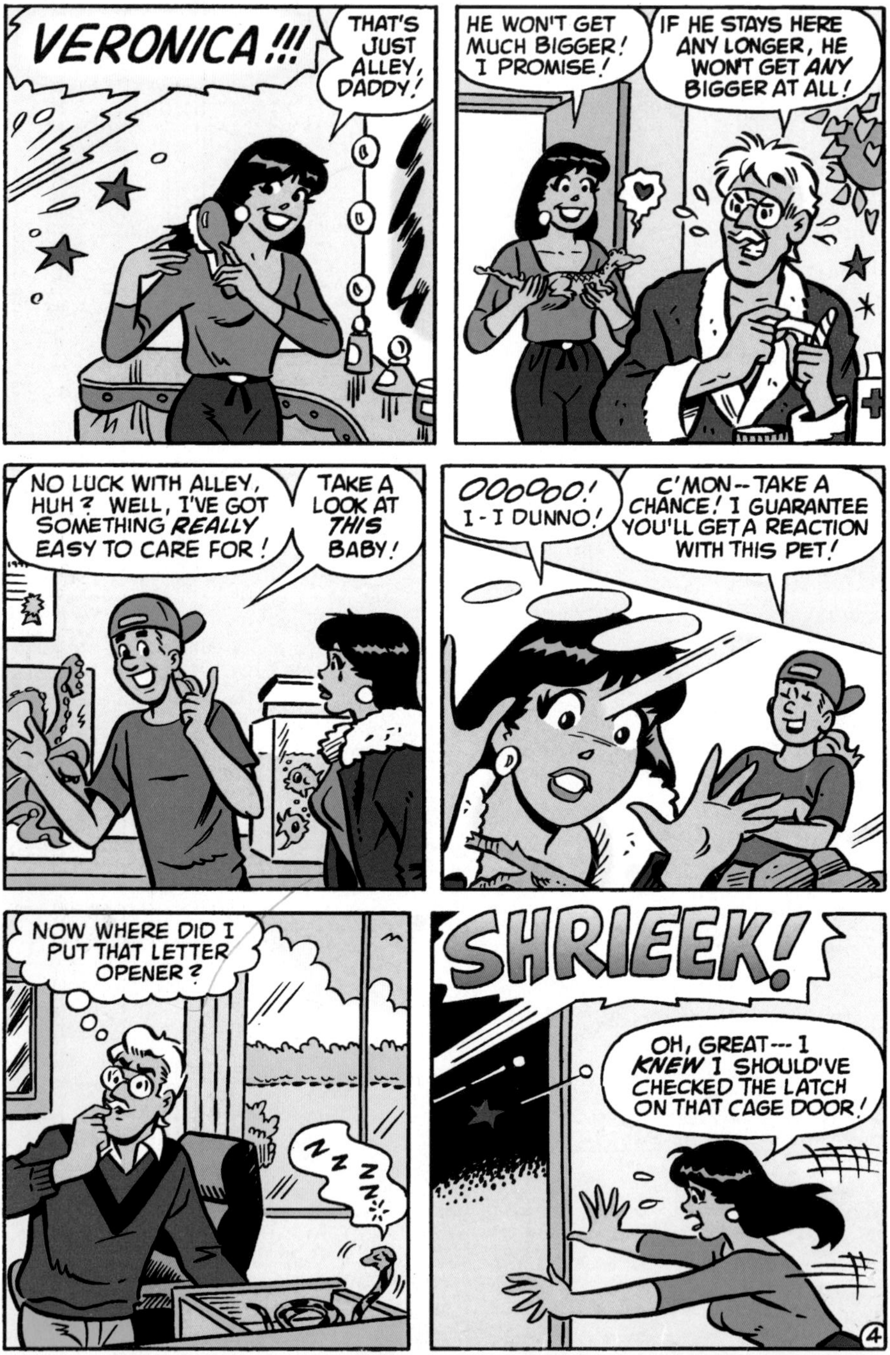
VERONICA!!!
THAT'S JUST ALLEY, DADDY!
HE WON'T GET MUCH BIGGER! I PROMISE!
IF HE STAYS HERE ANY LONGER, HE WON'T GET ANY BIGGER AT ALL!
NO LUCK WITH ALLEY, HUH? WELL, I'VE GOT SOMETHING REALLY EASY TO CARE FOR!
TAKE A LOOK AT THIS BABY!
OOOOOO! I - I DUNNO!
C'MON -- TAKE A CHANCE! I GUARANTEE YOU'LL GET A REACTION WITH THIS PET!
NOW WHERE DID I PUT THAT LETTER OPENER?
Z Z Z
SHRIEEK!
OH, GREAT --- I KNEW I SHOULD'VE CHECKED THE LATCH ON THAT CAGE DOOR!
4

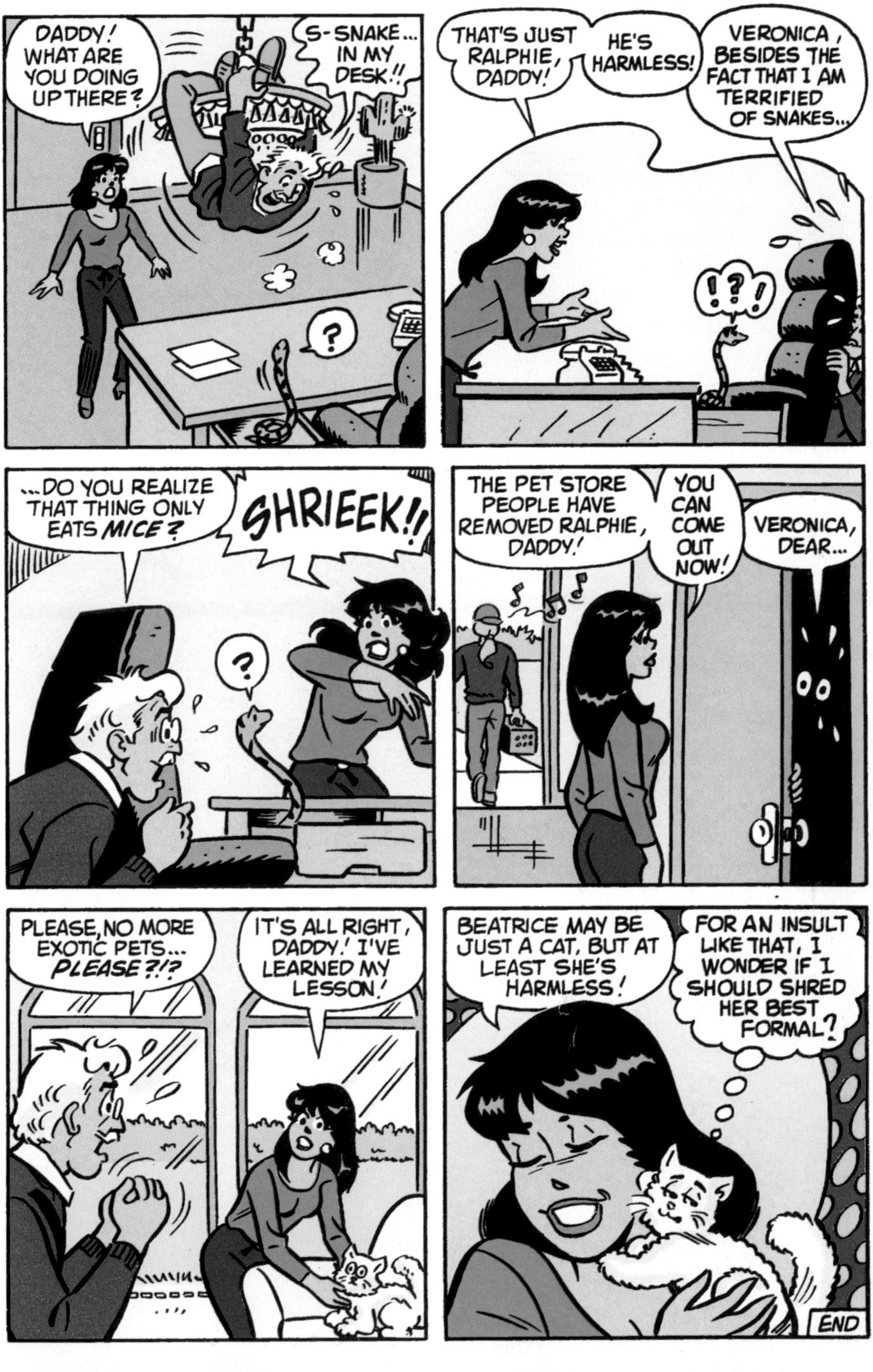
DADDY! WHAT ARE YOU DOING UP THERE?
S-SNAKE... IN MY DESK!!
?
THAT'S JUST RALPHIE, DADDY!
HE'S HARMLESS!
VERONICA, BESIDES THE FACT THAT I AM TERRIFIED OF SNAKES...
!?!
...DO YOU REALIZE THAT THING ONLY EATS MICE?
SHRIEEK!!
?
THE PET STORE PEOPLE HAVE REMOVED RALPHIE, DADDY!
YOU CAN COME OUT NOW!
VERONICA, DEAR...
PLEASE, NO MORE EXOTIC PETS... PLEASE?!?
IT'S ALL RIGHT, DADDY! I'VE LEARNED MY LESSON!
BEATRICE MAY BE JUST A CAT, BUT AT LEAST SHE'S HARMLESS!
FOR AN INSULT LIKE THAT, I WONDER IF I SHOULD SHRED HER BEST FORMAL?
END

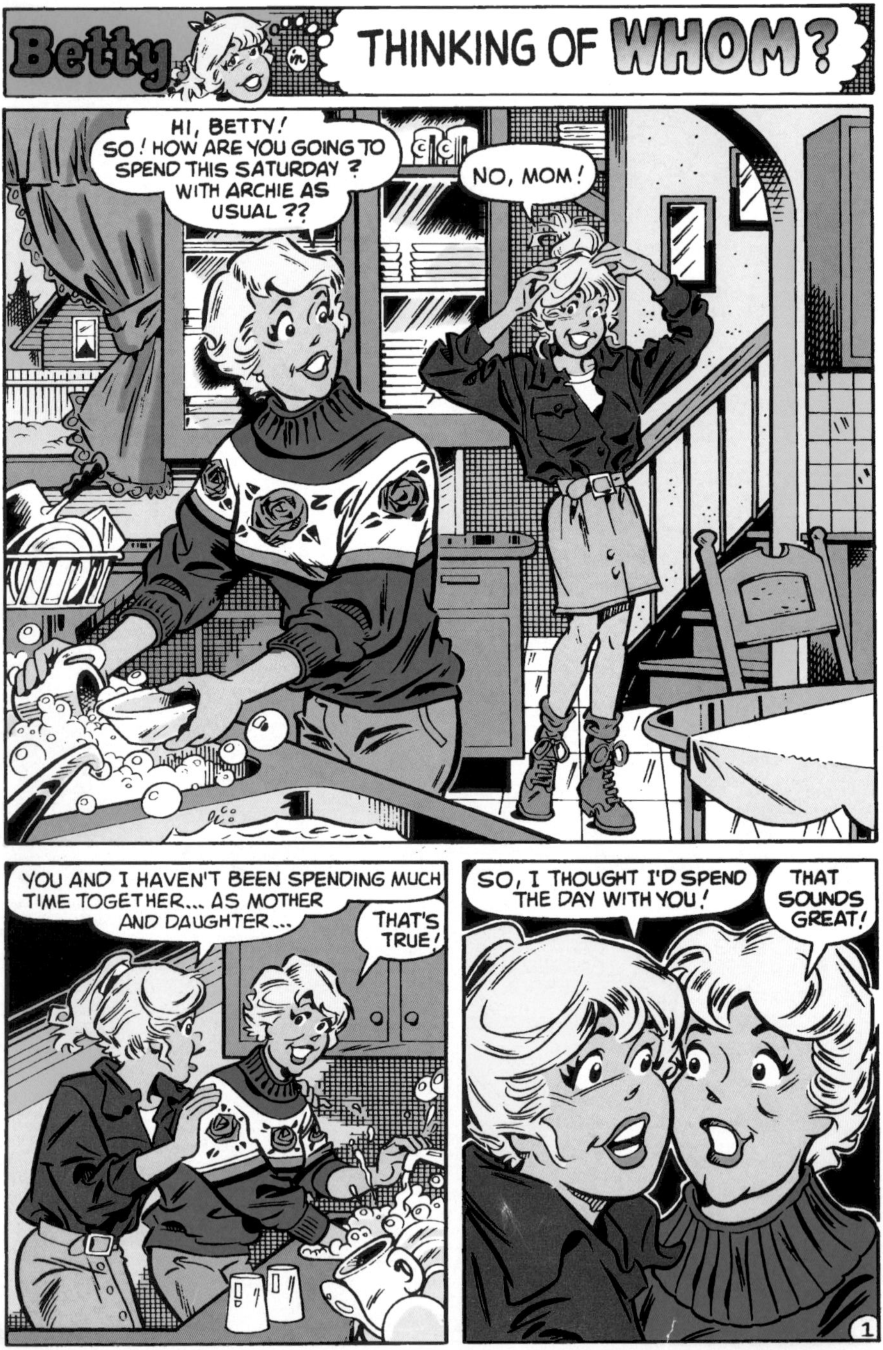
Betty
in
THINKING OF WHOM?
HI, BETTY! SO! HOW ARE YOU GOING TO SPEND THIS SATURDAY? WITH ARCHIE AS USUAL??
NO, MOM!
YOU AND I HAVEN'T BEEN SPENDING MUCH TIME TOGETHER... AS MOTHER AND DAUGHTER...
THAT'S TRUE!
SO, I THOUGHT I'D SPEND THE DAY WITH YOU!
THAT SOUNDS GREAT!
1

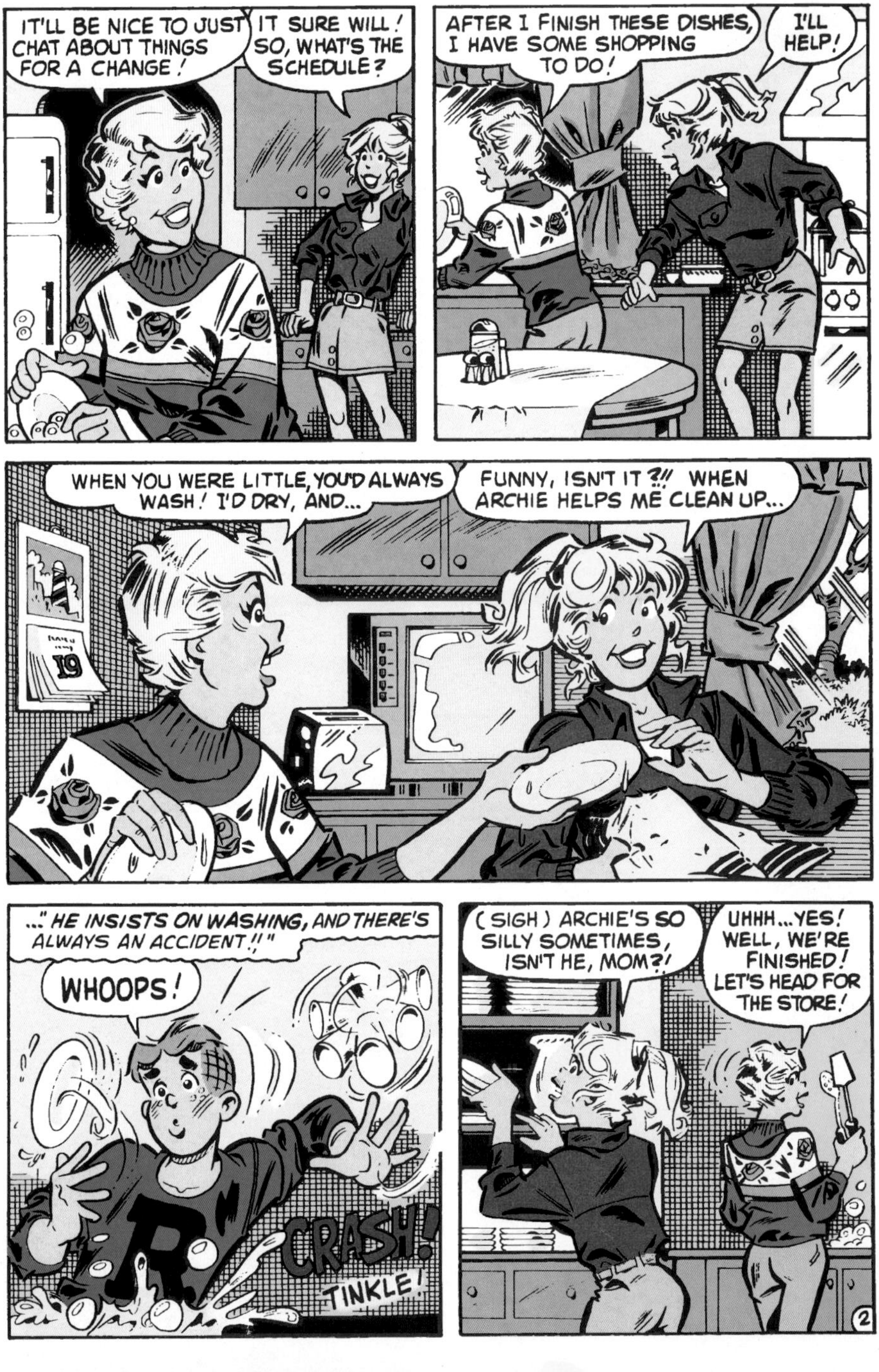
IT'LL BE NICE TO JUST CHAT ABOUT THINGS FOR A CHANGE!
IT SURE WILL! SO, WHAT'S THE SCHEDULE?
AFTER I FINISH THESE DISHES, I HAVE SOME SHOPPING TO DO!
I'LL HELP!
WHEN YOU WERE LITTLE, YOU'D ALWAYS WASH! I'D DRY, AND...
FUNNY, ISN'T IT?!! WHEN ARCHIE HELPS ME CLEAN UP...
..."HE INSISTS ON WASHING, AND THERE'S ALWAYS AN ACCIDENT!!"
WHOOPS!
CRASH!
TINKLE!
(SIGH) ARCHIE'S SO SILLY SOMETIMES, ISN'T HE, MOM?!
UHHH...YES! WELL, WE'RE FINISHED! LET'S HEAD FOR THE STORE!
2

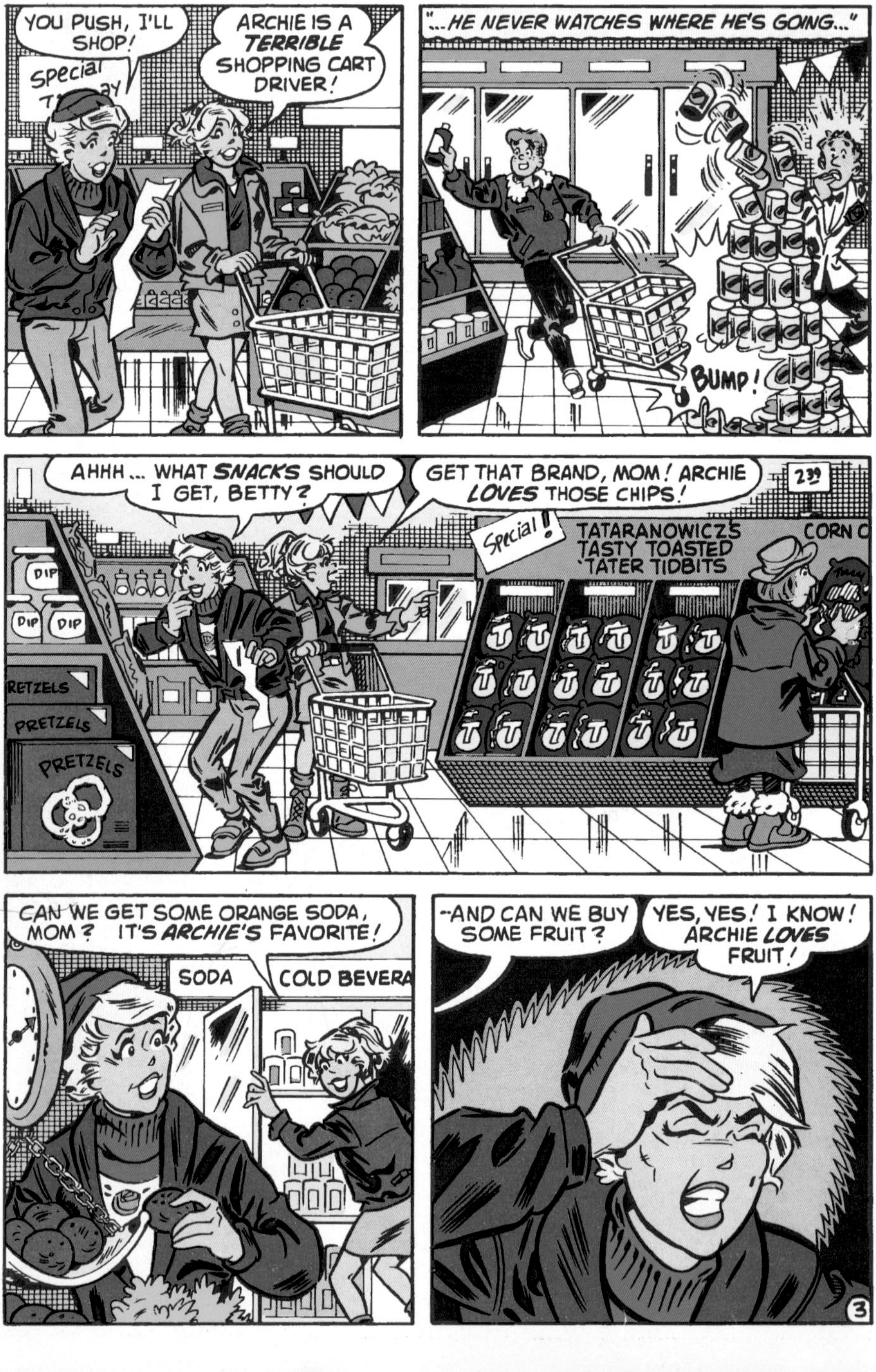
YOU PUSH, I'LL SHOP!
ARCHIE IS A *TERRIBLE* SHOPPING CART DRIVER!
"...HE NEVER WATCHES WHERE HE'S GOING..."
BUMP!
AHHH... WHAT *SNACKS* SHOULD I GET, BETTY?
GET THAT BRAND, MOM! ARCHIE *LOVES* THOSE CHIPS!
2.39
Special!
TATARANOWICZS TASTY TOASTED 'TATER TIDBITS
DIP
DIP
DIP
PRETZELS
PRETZELS
PRETZELS
CAN WE GET SOME ORANGE SODA, MOM? IT'S *ARCHIE'S* FAVORITE!
SODA
--AND CAN WE BUY SOME FRUIT?
YES, YES! I KNOW! ARCHIE *LOVES* FRUIT!
3

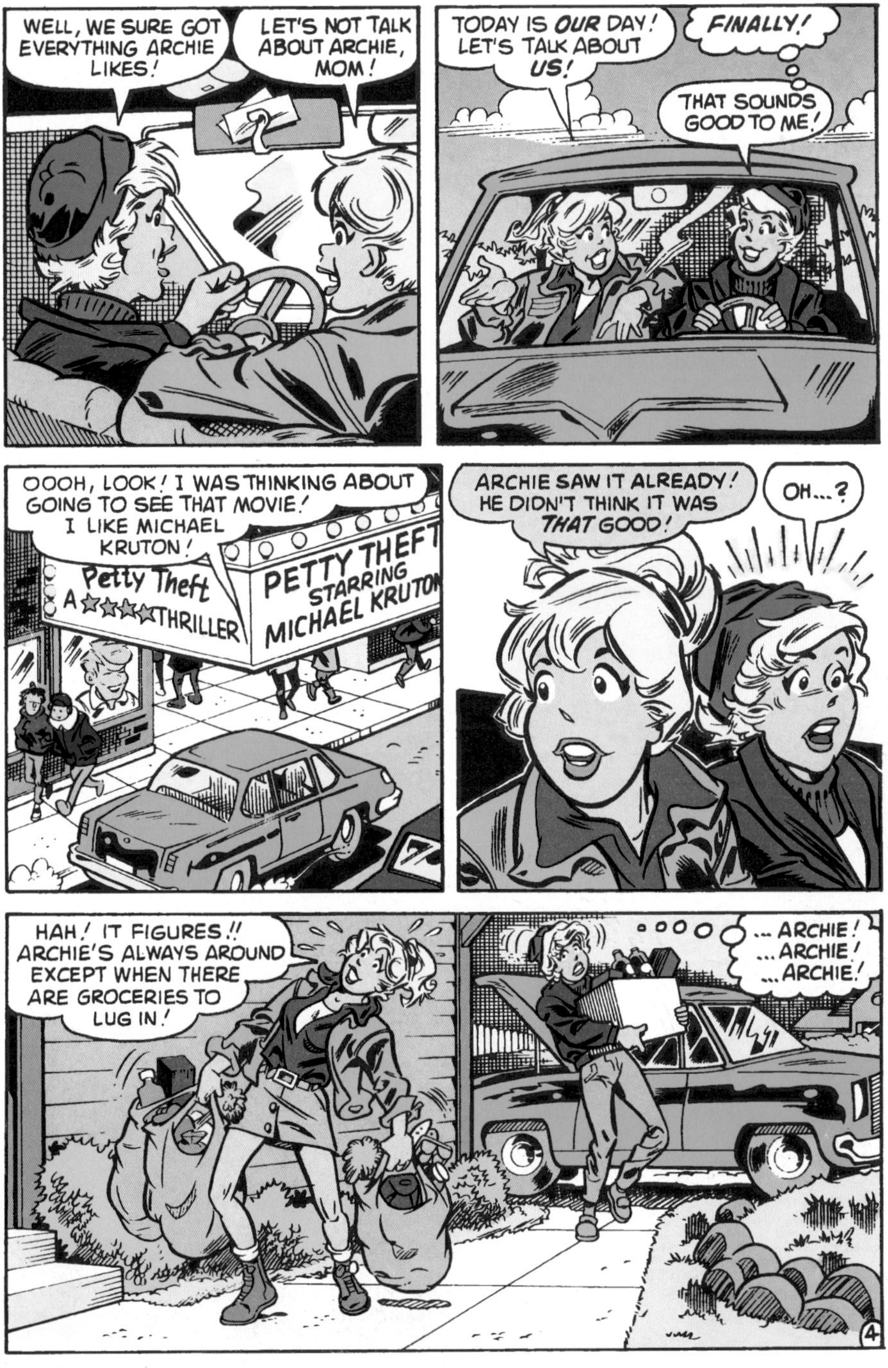
WELL, WE SURE GOT EVERYTHING ARCHIE LIKES!
LET'S NOT TALK ABOUT ARCHIE, MOM!
TODAY IS OUR DAY! LET'S TALK ABOUT US!
FINALLY!
THAT SOUNDS GOOD TO ME!
OOOH, LOOK! I WAS THINKING ABOUT GOING TO SEE THAT MOVIE! I LIKE MICHAEL KRUTON!
Petty Theft A ★★★★ THRILLER
PETTY THEFT STARRING MICHAEL KRUTON
ARCHIE SAW IT ALREADY! HE DIDN'T THINK IT WAS THAT GOOD!
OH...?
HAH! IT FIGURES!! ARCHIE'S ALWAYS AROUND EXCEPT WHEN THERE ARE GROCERIES TO LUG IN!
...ARCHIE! ...ARCHIE! ...ARCHIE!
4

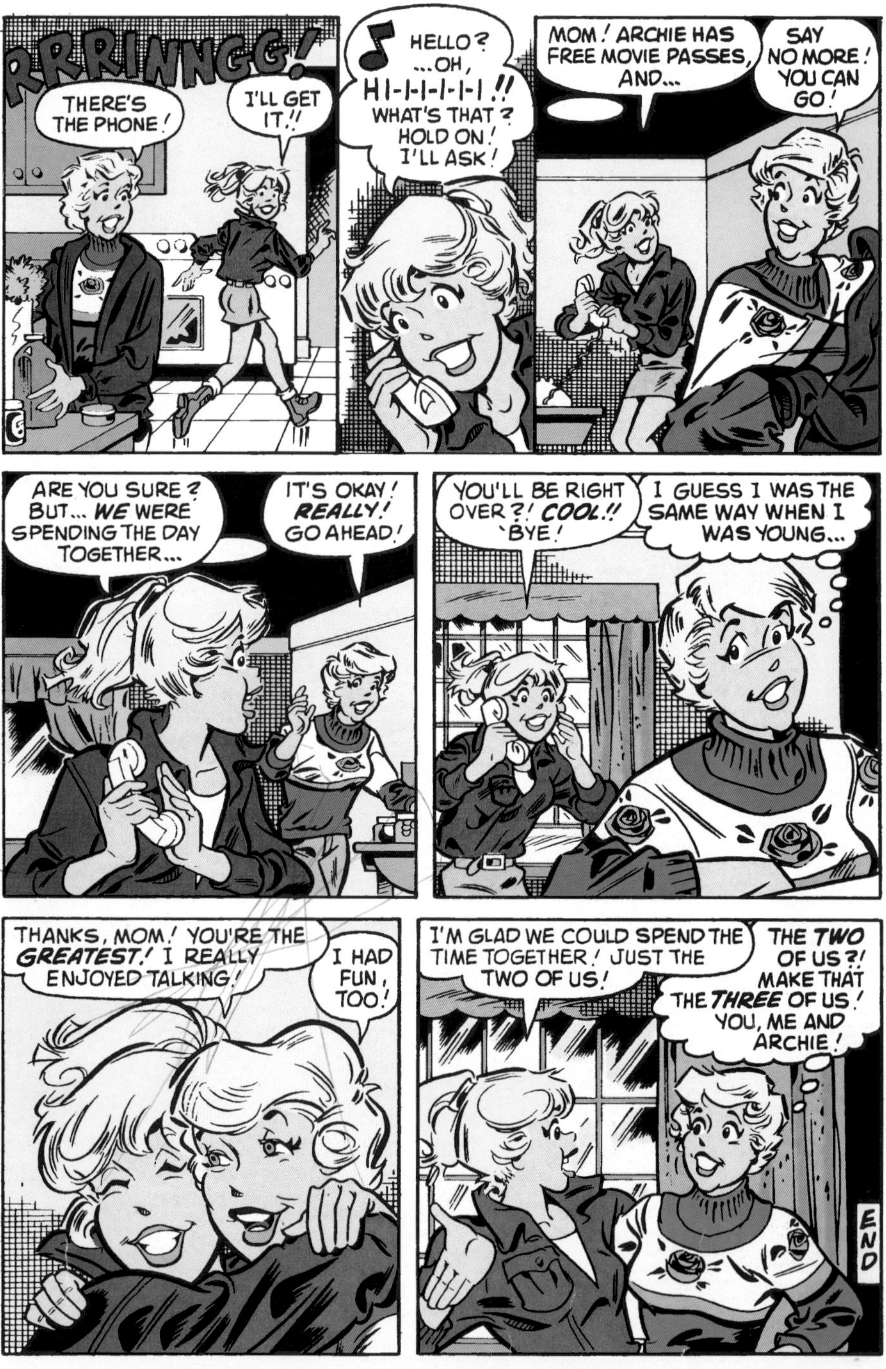
RRRINNGG!
THERE'S THE PHONE!
I'LL GET IT!!
HELLO? ...OH, HI-I-I-I-I-I!! WHAT'S THAT? HOLD ON! I'LL ASK!
MOM! ARCHIE HAS FREE MOVIE PASSES, AND...
SAY NO MORE! YOU CAN GO!
ARE YOU SURE? BUT... WE WERE SPENDING THE DAY TOGETHER...
IT'S OKAY! REALLY! GO AHEAD!
YOU'LL BE RIGHT OVER?! COOL!! 'BYE!
I GUESS I WAS THE SAME WAY WHEN I WAS YOUNG...
THANKS, MOM! YOU'RE THE GREATEST! I REALLY ENJOYED TALKING!
I HAD FUN, TOO!
I'M GLAD WE COULD SPEND THE TIME TOGETHER! JUST THE TWO OF US!
THE TWO OF US?! MAKE THAT THE THREE OF US! YOU, ME AND ARCHIE!
END

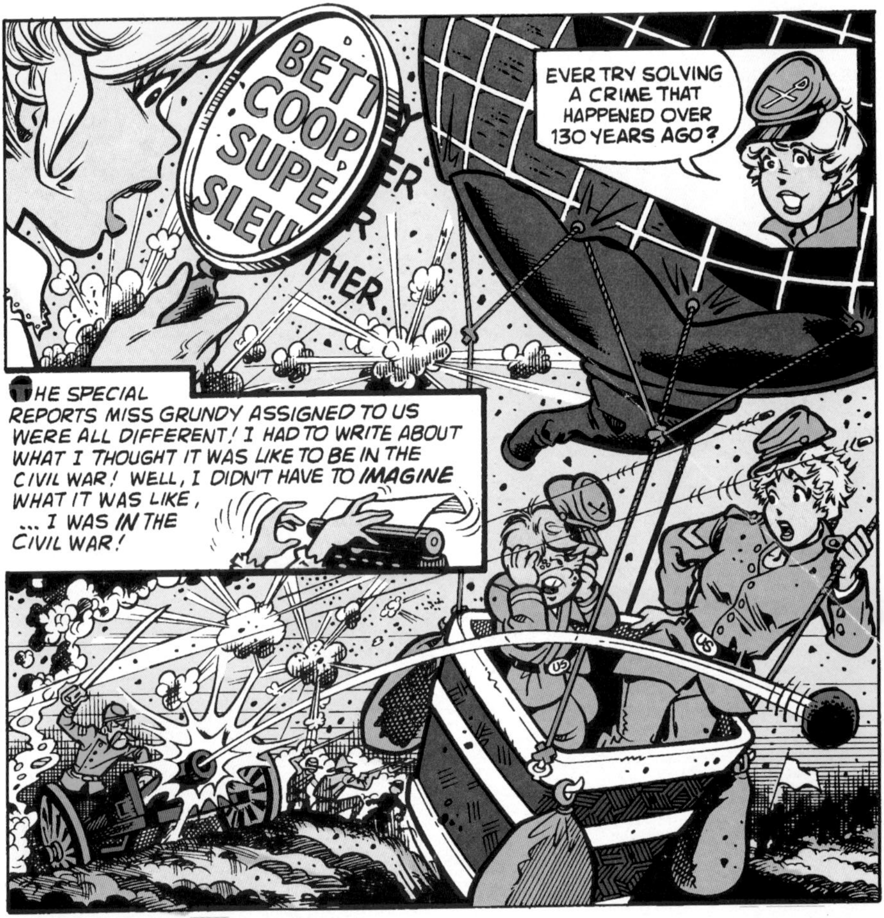
EVER TRY SOLVING A CRIME THAT HAPPENED OVER 130 YEARS AGO?
THE SPECIAL REPORTS MISS GRUNDY ASSIGNED TO US WERE ALL DIFFERENT! I HAD TO WRITE ABOUT WHAT I THOUGHT IT WAS LIKE TO BE IN THE CIVIL WAR! WELL, I DIDN'T HAVE TO IMAGINE WHAT IT WAS LIKE, ... I WAS IN THE CIVIL WAR!
US
US

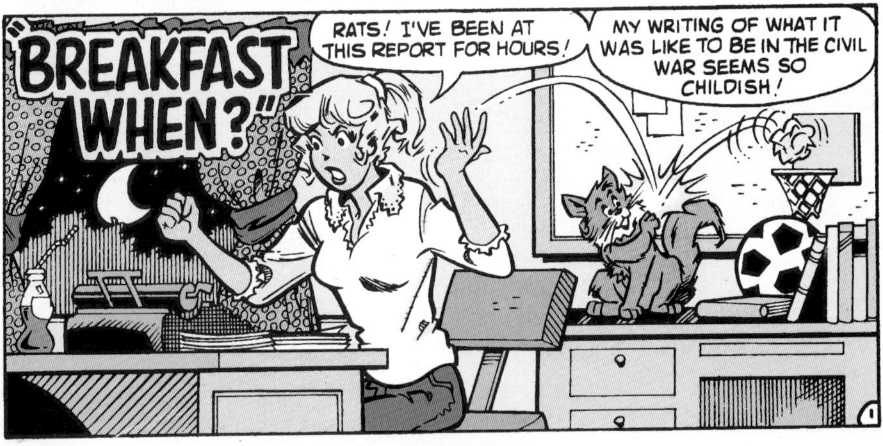
"BREAKFAST WHEN?"
RATS! I'VE BEEN AT THIS REPORT FOR HOURS!
MY WRITING OF WHAT IT WAS LIKE TO BE IN THE CIVIL WAR SEEMS SO CHILDISH!
1

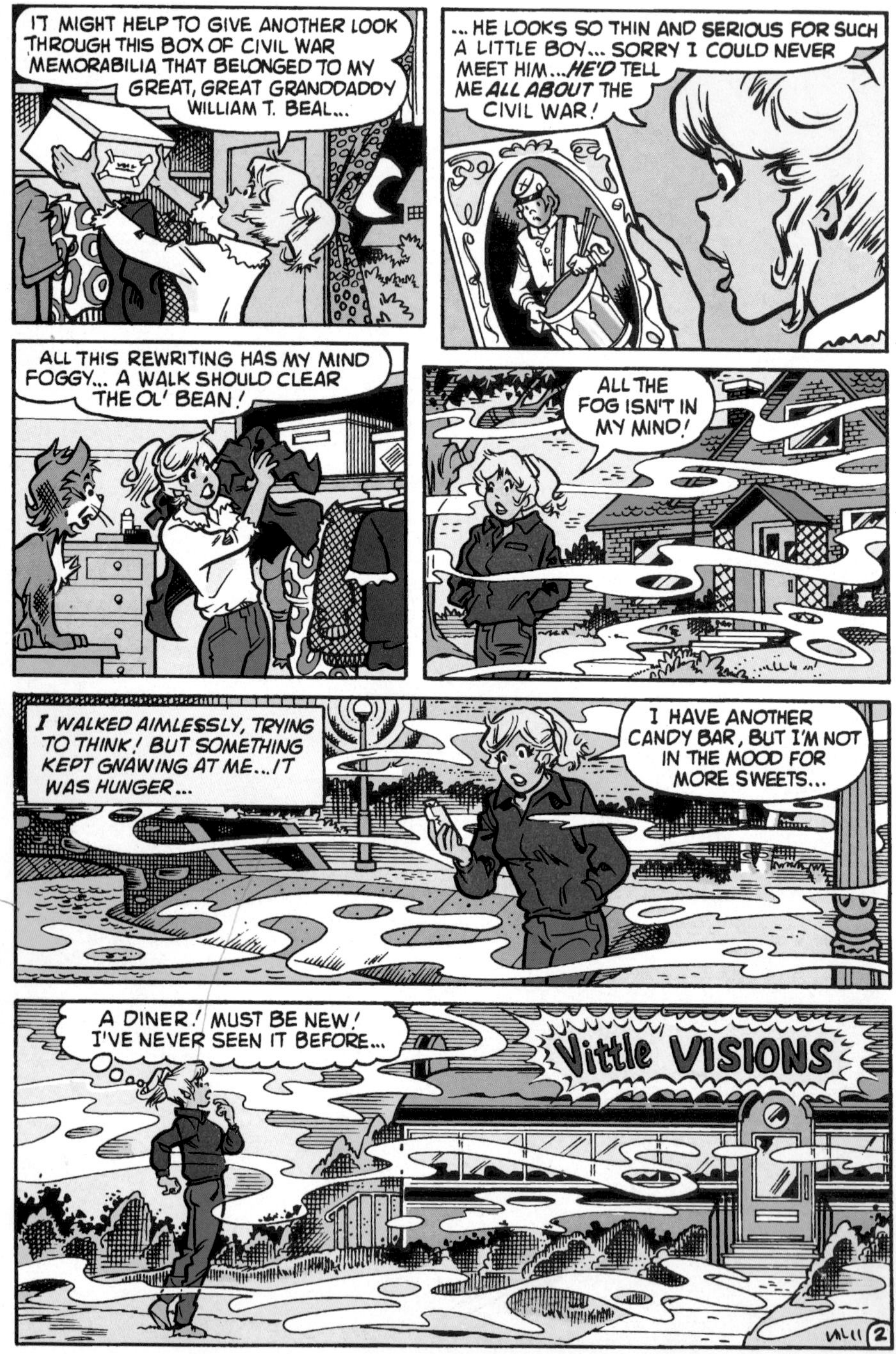
IT MIGHT HELP TO GIVE ANOTHER LOOK THROUGH THIS BOX OF CIVIL WAR MEMORABILIA THAT BELONGED TO MY GREAT, GREAT GRANDDADDY WILLIAM T. BEAL...
... HE LOOKS SO THIN AND SERIOUS FOR SUCH A LITTLE BOY... SORRY I COULD NEVER MEET HIM... HE'D TELL ME ALL ABOUT THE CIVIL WAR!
ALL THIS REWRITING HAS MY MIND FOGGY... A WALK SHOULD CLEAR THE OL' BEAN!
ALL THE FOG ISN'T IN MY MIND!
I WALKED AIMLESSLY, TRYING TO THINK! BUT SOMETHING KEPT GNAWING AT ME... IT WAS HUNGER...
I HAVE ANOTHER CANDY BAR, BUT I'M NOT IN THE MOOD FOR MORE SWEETS...
A DINER! MUST BE NEW! I'VE NEVER SEEN IT BEFORE...
Vittle VISIONS
2

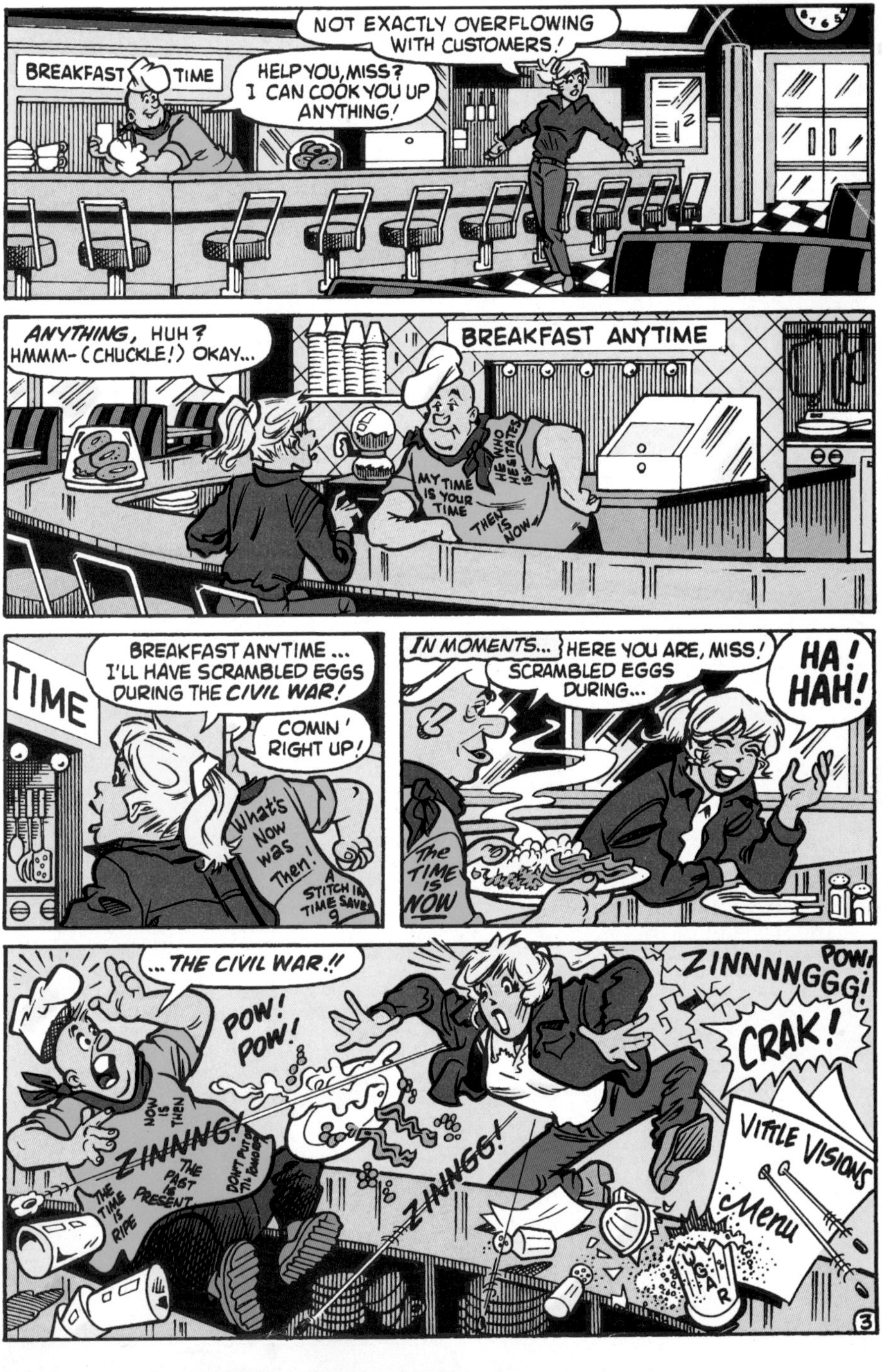
BREAKFAST TIME
NOT EXACTLY OVERFLOWING WITH CUSTOMERS!
HELP YOU, MISS? I CAN COOK YOU UP ANYTHING!
BREAKFAST ANYTIME
ANYTHING, HUH? HMMM- (CHUCKLE!) OKAY...
MY TIME IS YOUR TIME
HE WHO HESITATES IS...
THEN IS NOW
TIME
BREAKFAST ANYTIME ... I'LL HAVE SCRAMBLED EGGS DURING THE CIVIL WAR!
COMIN' RIGHT UP!
What's Now was Then!
A STITCH IN TIME SAVES 9
IN MOMENTS...
HERE YOU ARE, MISS! SCRAMBLED EGGS DURING...
HA! HAH!
The TIME IS NOW
... THE CIVIL WAR!!
POW! POW!
ZINNNNGGG!
POW!
CRAK!
NOW IS THEN
ZINNNG!
THE PAST IS PRESENT
THE TIME IS RIPE
ZINNGG!
VITTLE VISIONS
Menu
SUGAR
3

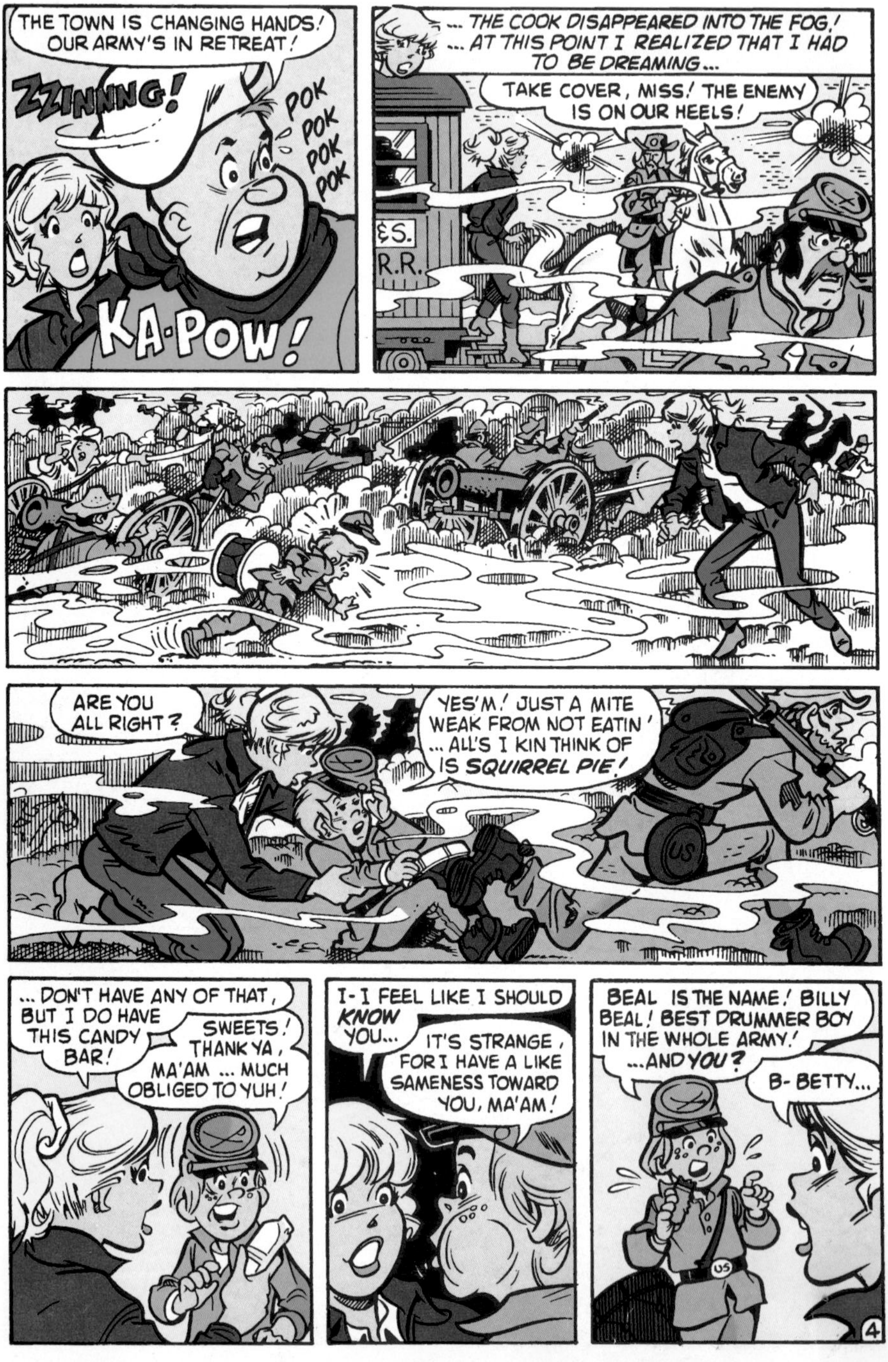
THE TOWN IS CHANGING HANDS! OUR ARMY'S IN RETREAT!
ZZINNNG!
POK POK POK POK
KA-POW!
... THE COOK DISAPPEARED INTO THE FOG! ... AT THIS POINT I REALIZED THAT I HAD TO BE DREAMING...
TAKE COVER, MISS! THE ENEMY IS ON OUR HEELS!
ARE YOU ALL RIGHT?
YES'M! JUST A MITE WEAK FROM NOT EATIN' ... ALL'S I KIN THINK OF IS SQUIRREL PIE!
... DON'T HAVE ANY OF THAT, BUT I DO HAVE THIS CANDY BAR!
SWEETS! THANK YA, MA'AM ... MUCH OBLIGED TO YUH!
I-I FEEL LIKE I SHOULD KNOW YOU...
IT'S STRANGE, FOR I HAVE A LIKE SAMENESS TOWARD YOU, MA'AM!
BEAL IS THE NAME! BILLY BEAL! BEST DRUMMER BOY IN THE WHOLE ARMY! ...AND YOU?
B- BETTY...
4

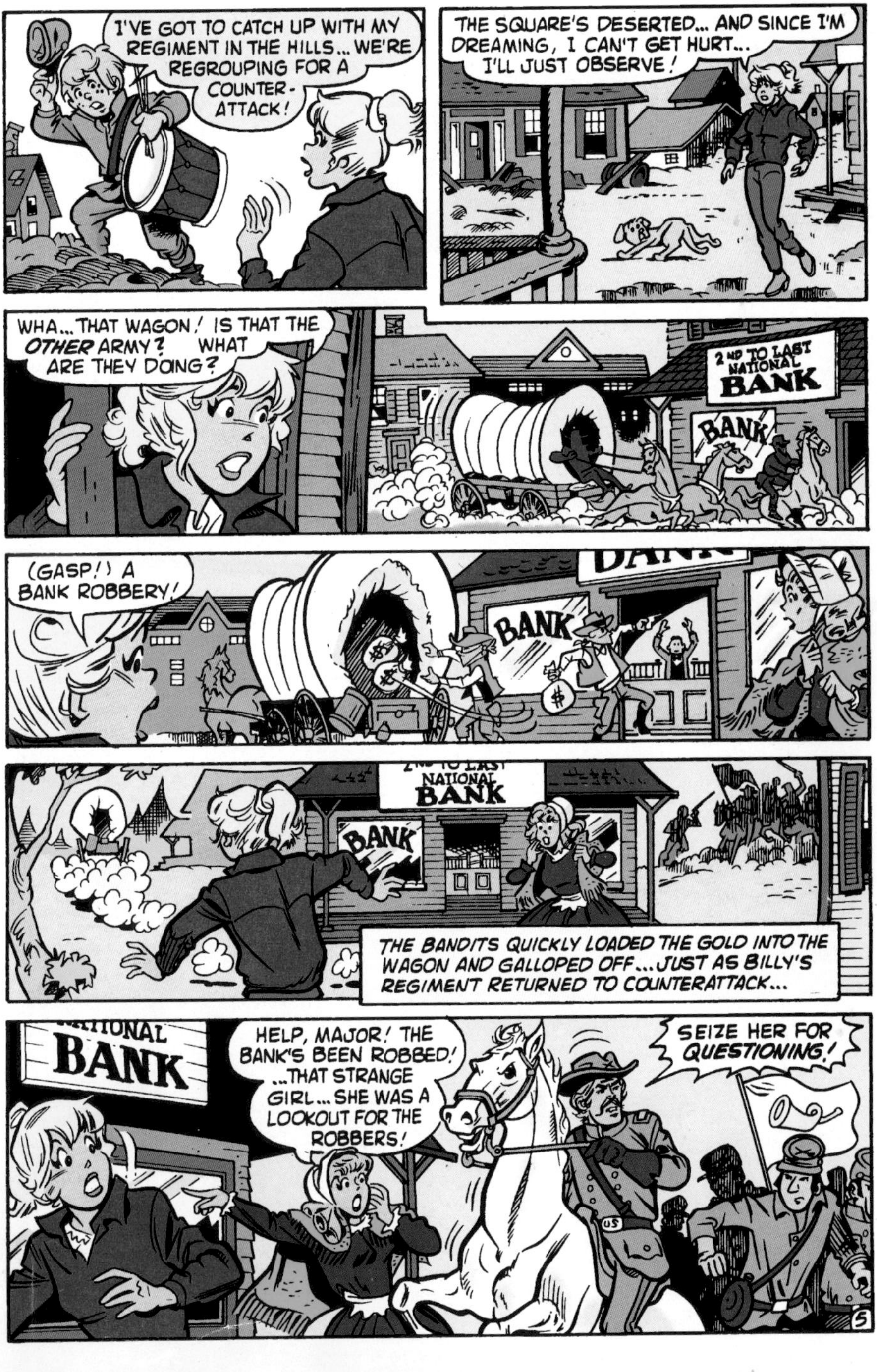
I'VE GOT TO CATCH UP WITH MY REGIMENT IN THE HILLS... WE'RE REGROUPING FOR A COUNTER-ATTACK!
THE SQUARE'S DESERTED... AND SINCE I'M DREAMING, I CAN'T GET HURT... I'LL JUST OBSERVE!
WHA... THAT WAGON! IS THAT THE OTHER ARMY? WHAT ARE THEY DOING?
2ND TO LAST NATIONAL BANK
BANK
(GASP!) A BANK ROBBERY!
BANK
NATIONAL BANK
BANK
THE BANDITS QUICKLY LOADED THE GOLD INTO THE WAGON AND GALLOPED OFF... JUST AS BILLY'S REGIMENT RETURNED TO COUNTERATTACK...
BANK
HELP, MAJOR! THE BANK'S BEEN ROBBED! ...THAT STRANGE GIRL... SHE WAS A LOOKOUT FOR THE ROBBERS!
SEIZE HER FOR QUESTIONING!
US
5

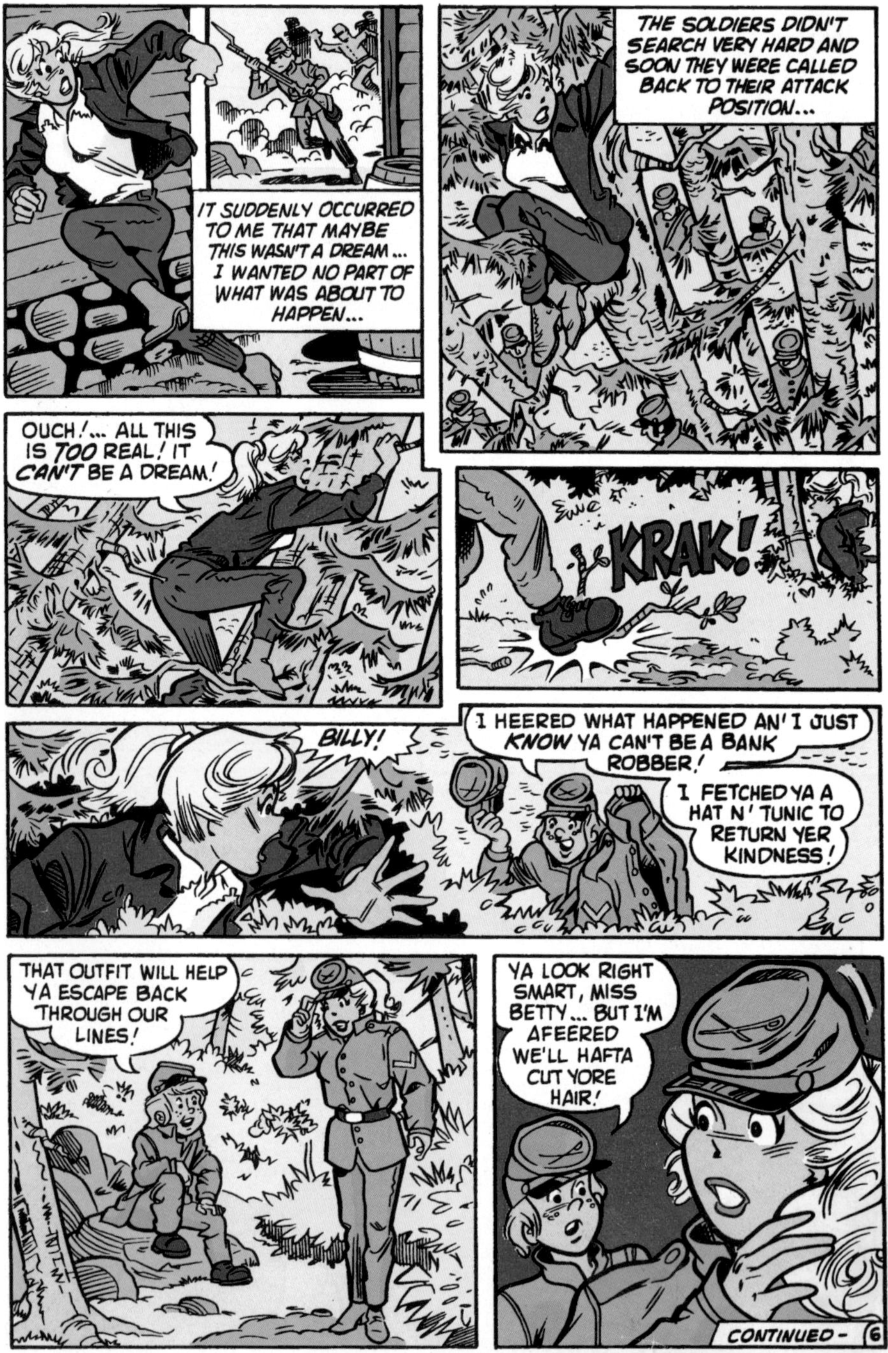
IT SUDDENLY OCCURRED TO ME THAT MAYBE THIS WASN'T A DREAM ... I WANTED NO PART OF WHAT WAS ABOUT TO HAPPEN...
THE SOLDIERS DIDN'T SEARCH VERY HARD AND SOON THEY WERE CALLED BACK TO THEIR ATTACK POSITION...
OUCH!... ALL THIS IS TOO REAL! IT CAN'T BE A DREAM!
KRAK!
BILLY!
I HEERED WHAT HAPPENED AN' I JUST KNOW YA CAN'T BE A BANK ROBBER!
I FETCHED YA A HAT N' TUNIC TO RETURN YER KINDNESS!
THAT OUTFIT WILL HELP YA ESCAPE BACK THROUGH OUR LINES!
YA LOOK RIGHT SMART, MISS BETTY... BUT I'M AFEERED WE'LL HAFTA CUT YORE HAIR!
CONTINUED- 6

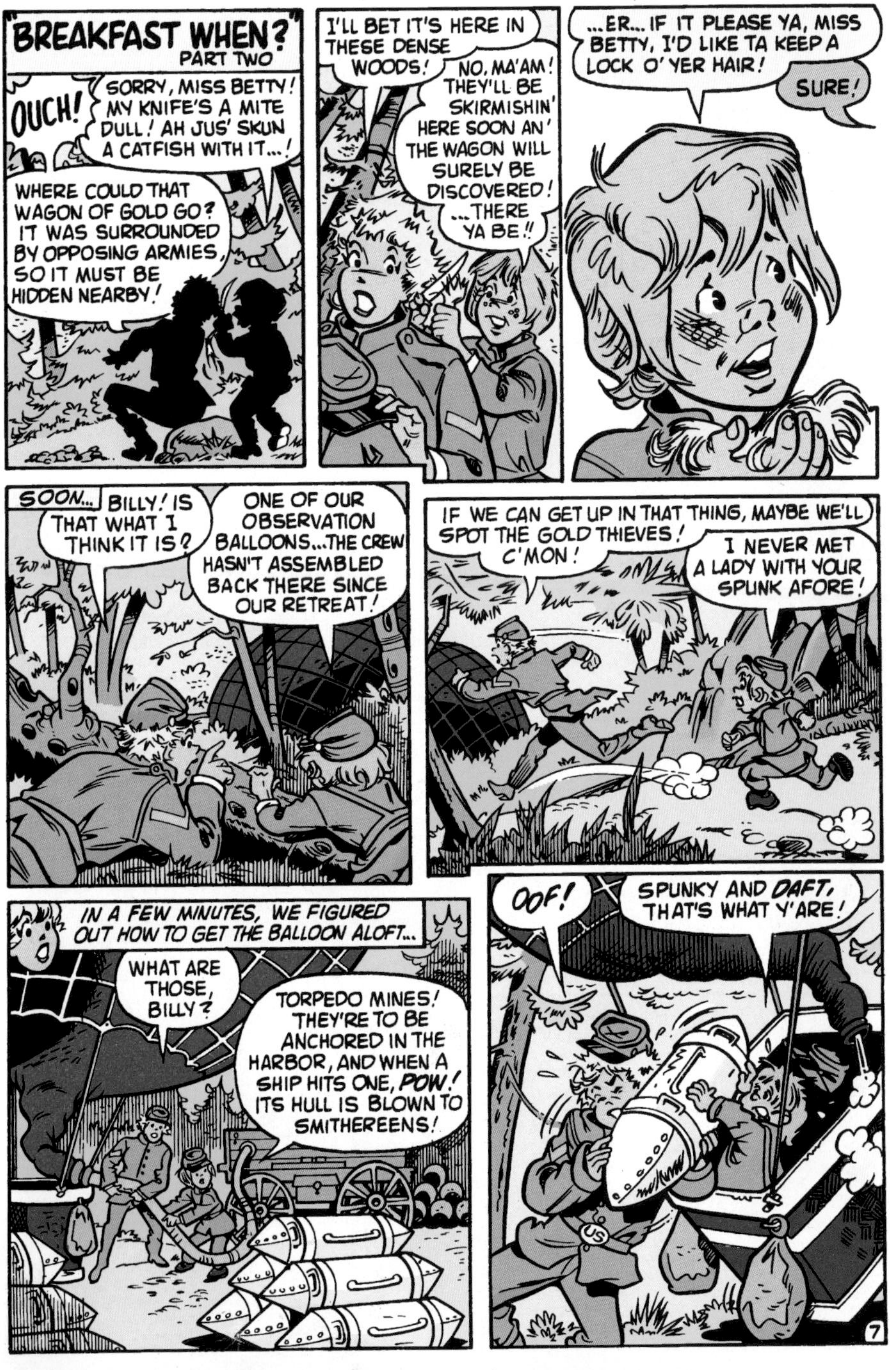
"BREAKFAST WHEN?" PART TWO
OUCH!
SORRY, MISS BETTY! MY KNIFE'S A MITE DULL! AH JUS' SKUN A CATFISH WITH IT...!
WHERE COULD THAT WAGON OF GOLD GO? IT WAS SURROUNDED BY OPPOSING ARMIES, SO IT MUST BE HIDDEN NEARBY!
I'LL BET IT'S HERE IN THESE DENSE WOODS!
NO, MA'AM! THEY'LL BE SKIRMISHIN' HERE SOON AN' THE WAGON WILL SURELY BE DISCOVERED! ...THERE YA BE!!
...ER... IF IT PLEASE YA, MISS BETTY, I'D LIKE TA KEEP A LOCK O' YER HAIR!
SURE!
SOON...
BILLY! IS THAT WHAT I THINK IT IS?
ONE OF OUR OBSERVATION BALLOONS... THE CREW HASN'T ASSEMBLED BACK THERE SINCE OUR RETREAT!
IF WE CAN GET UP IN THAT THING, MAYBE WE'LL SPOT THE GOLD THIEVES! C'MON!
I NEVER MET A LADY WITH YOUR SPUNK AFORE!
IN A FEW MINUTES, WE FIGURED OUT HOW TO GET THE BALLOON ALOFT...
WHAT ARE THOSE, BILLY?
TORPEDO MINES! THEY'RE TO BE ANCHORED IN THE HARBOR, AND WHEN A SHIP HITS ONE, POW! ITS HULL IS BLOWN TO SMITHEREENS!
OOF!
SPUNKY AND DAFT, THAT'S WHAT Y'ARE!
US
7

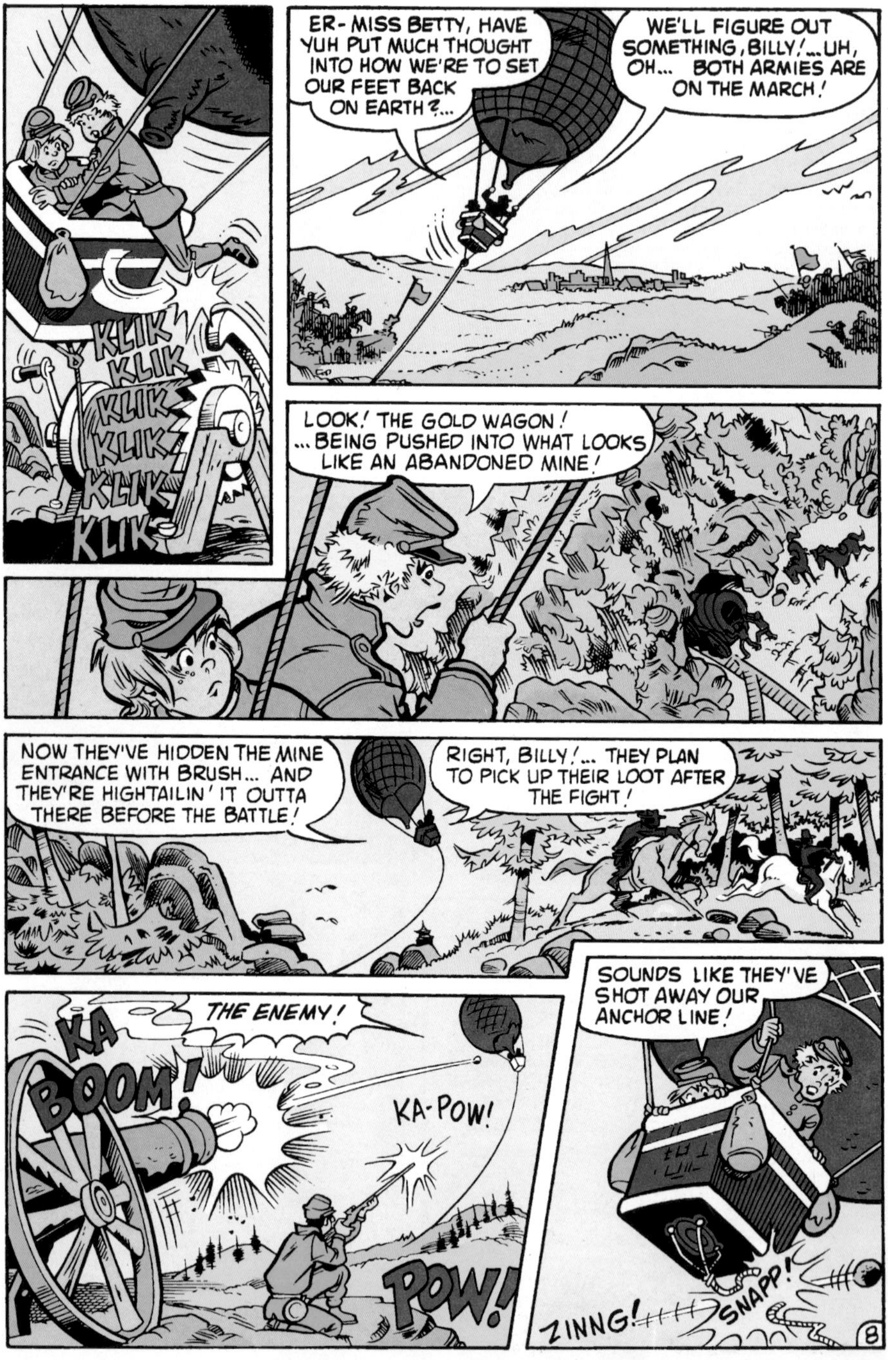
KLIK
KLIK
KLIK
KLIK
KLIK
KLIK
ER- MISS BETTY, HAVE YUH PUT MUCH THOUGHT INTO HOW WE'RE TO SET OUR FEET BACK ON EARTH?...
WE'LL FIGURE OUT SOMETHING, BILLY!... UH, OH... BOTH ARMIES ARE ON THE MARCH!
LOOK! THE GOLD WAGON! ...BEING PUSHED INTO WHAT LOOKS LIKE AN ABANDONED MINE!
NOW THEY'VE HIDDEN THE MINE ENTRANCE WITH BRUSH... AND THEY'RE HIGHTAILIN' IT OUTTA THERE BEFORE THE BATTLE!
RIGHT, BILLY!... THEY PLAN TO PICK UP THEIR LOOT AFTER THE FIGHT!
KA BOOM!
THE ENEMY!
KA-POW!
POW!
SOUNDS LIKE THEY'VE SHOT AWAY OUR ANCHOR LINE!
ZINNG!
SNAPP!
8

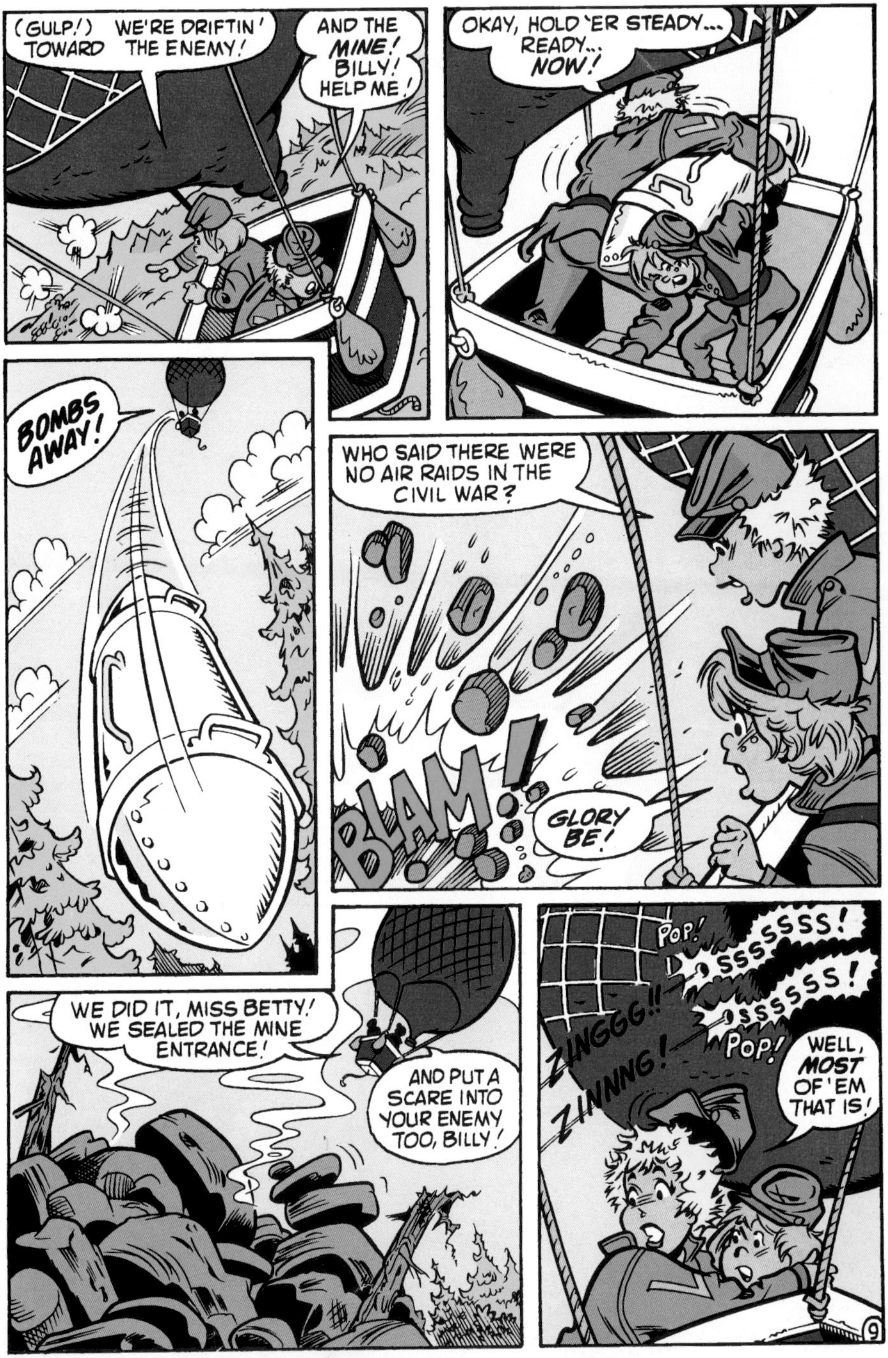
(GULP!) WE'RE DRIFTIN' TOWARD THE ENEMY!
AND THE MINE! BILLY! HELP ME!
OKAY, HOLD 'ER STEADY... READY... NOW!
BOMBS AWAY!
WHO SAID THERE WERE NO AIR RAIDS IN THE CIVIL WAR?
BLAM!
GLORY BE!
WE DID IT, MISS BETTY! WE SEALED THE MINE ENTRANCE!
AND PUT A SCARE INTO YOUR ENEMY TOO, BILLY!
POP!
SSSSSSS!
SSSSSSS!
ZINGGG!!
ZINNNG!
POP!
WELL, MOST OF 'EM THAT IS!
9

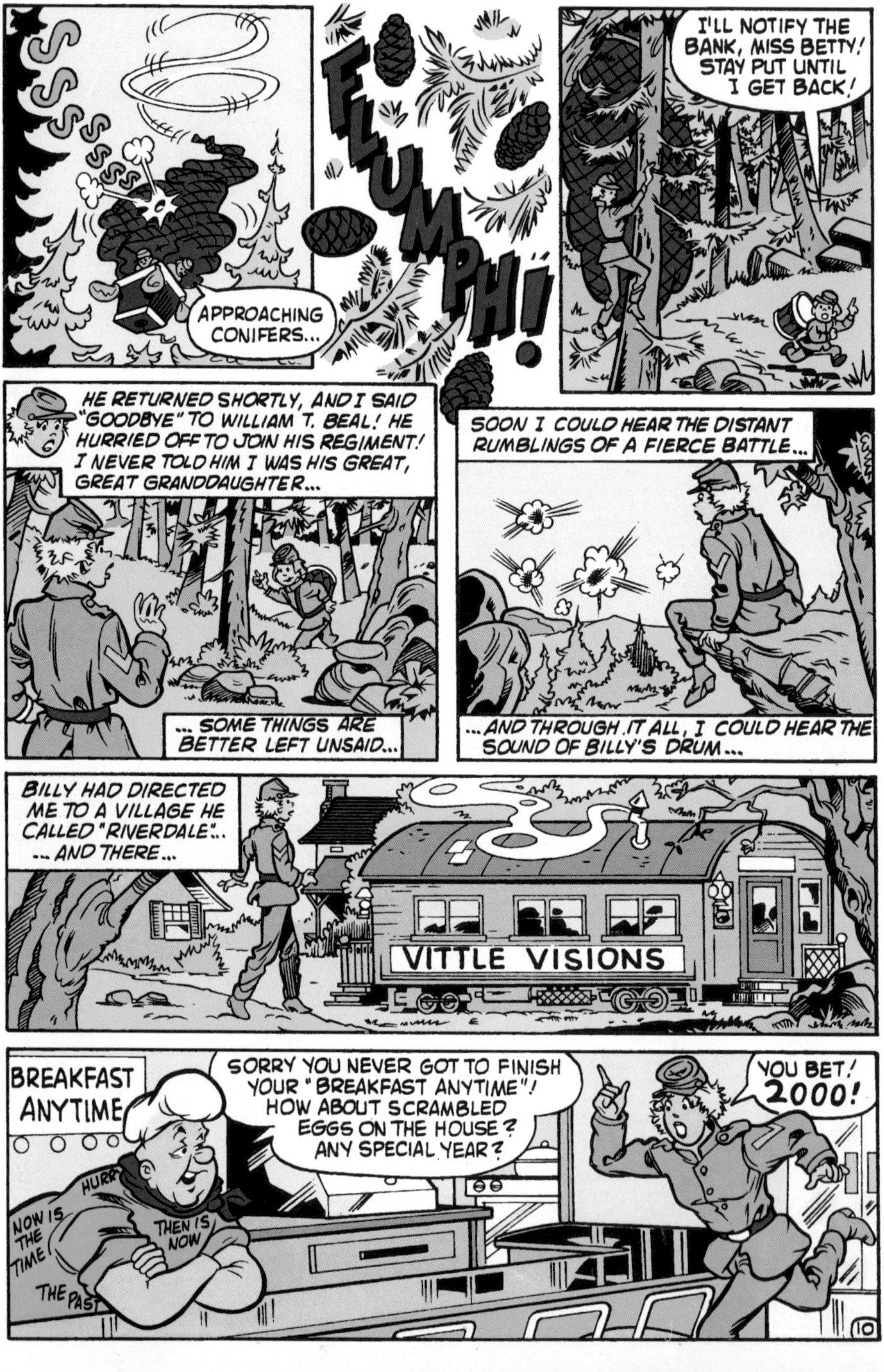
SSSSSSS
APPROACHING CONIFERS...
FLUMPH!
I'LL NOTIFY THE BANK, MISS BETTY! STAY PUT UNTIL I GET BACK!
HE RETURNED SHORTLY, AND I SAID "GOODBYE" TO WILLIAM T. BEAL! HE HURRIED OFF TO JOIN HIS REGIMENT! I NEVER TOLD HIM I WAS HIS GREAT, GREAT GRANDDAUGHTER...
... SOME THINGS ARE BETTER LEFT UNSAID...
SOON I COULD HEAR THE DISTANT RUMBLINGS OF A FIERCE BATTLE...
...AND THROUGH IT ALL, I COULD HEAR THE SOUND OF BILLY'S DRUM...
BILLY HAD DIRECTED ME TO A VILLAGE HE CALLED "RIVERDALE"... ... AND THERE...
VITTLE VISIONS
BREAKFAST ANYTIME
SORRY YOU NEVER GOT TO FINISH YOUR "BREAKFAST ANYTIME"! HOW ABOUT SCRAMBLED EGGS ON THE HOUSE? ANY SPECIAL YEAR?
YOU BET! 2000!
HURR
NOW IS THE TIME
THEN IS NOW
THE PAST
10

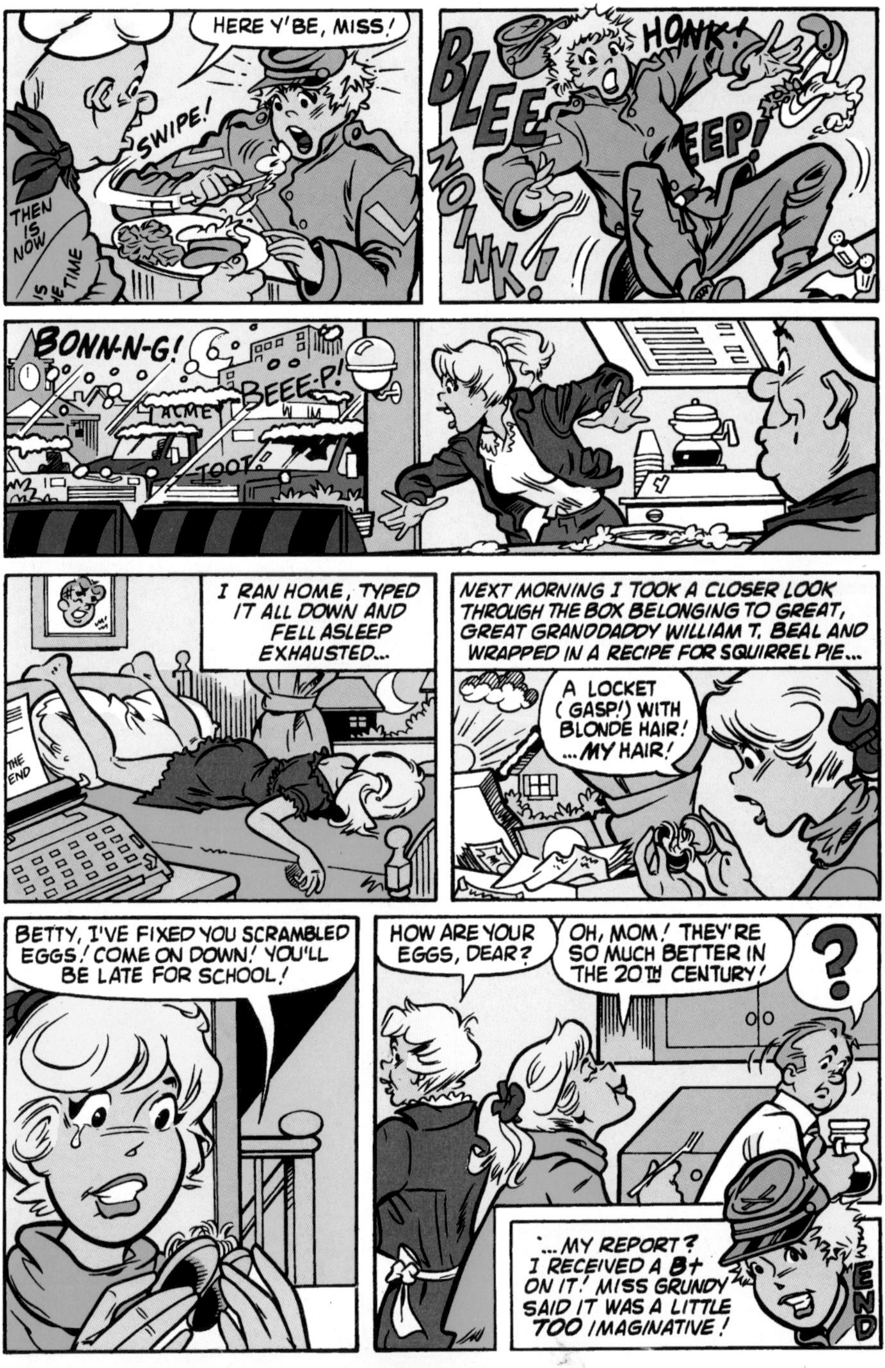
HERE Y'BE, MISS!
SWIPE!
THEN IS NOW
BLEE
NOINK!
HONK!
EEEP!
BONN-N-G!
BEEE-P!
ACME
TOOT
I RAN HOME, TYPED IT ALL DOWN AND FELL ASLEEP EXHAUSTED...
THE END
NEXT MORNING I TOOK A CLOSER LOOK THROUGH THE BOX BELONGING TO GREAT, GREAT GRANDDADDY WILLIAM T. BEAL AND WRAPPED IN A RECIPE FOR SQUIRREL PIE...
A LOCKET (GASP!) WITH BLONDE HAIR! ...MY HAIR!
BETTY, I'VE FIXED YOU SCRAMBLED EGGS! COME ON DOWN! YOU'LL BE LATE FOR SCHOOL!
HOW ARE YOUR EGGS, DEAR?
OH, MOM! THEY'RE SO MUCH BETTER IN THE 20TH CENTURY!
?
"...MY REPORT? I RECEIVED A B+ ON IT! MISS GRUNDY SAID IT WAS A LITTLE TOO IMAGINATIVE!
END

Veronica's GAG BAG

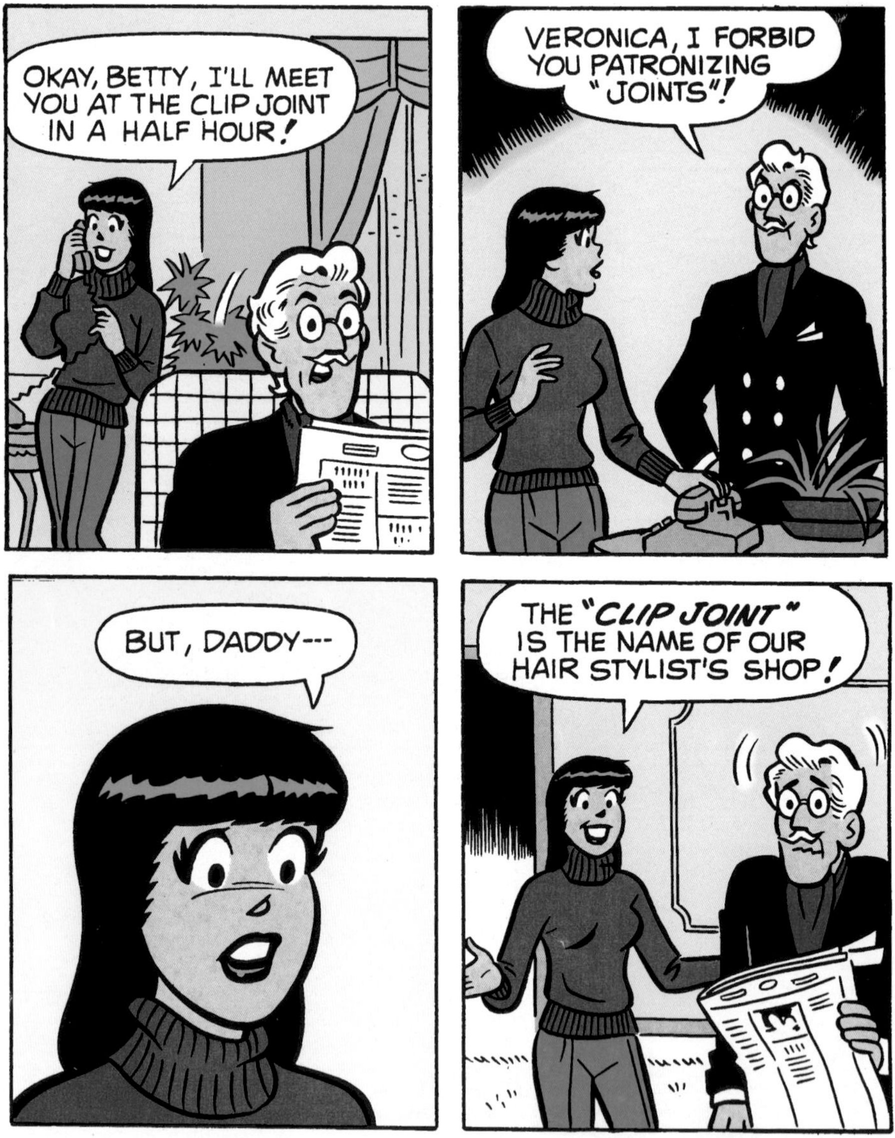
OKAY, BETTY, I'LL MEET YOU AT THE CLIP JOINT IN A HALF HOUR!
VERONICA, I FORBID YOU PATRONIZING "JOINTS"!
BUT, DADDY---
THE "CLIP JOINT" IS THE NAME OF OUR HAIR STYLIST'S SHOP!

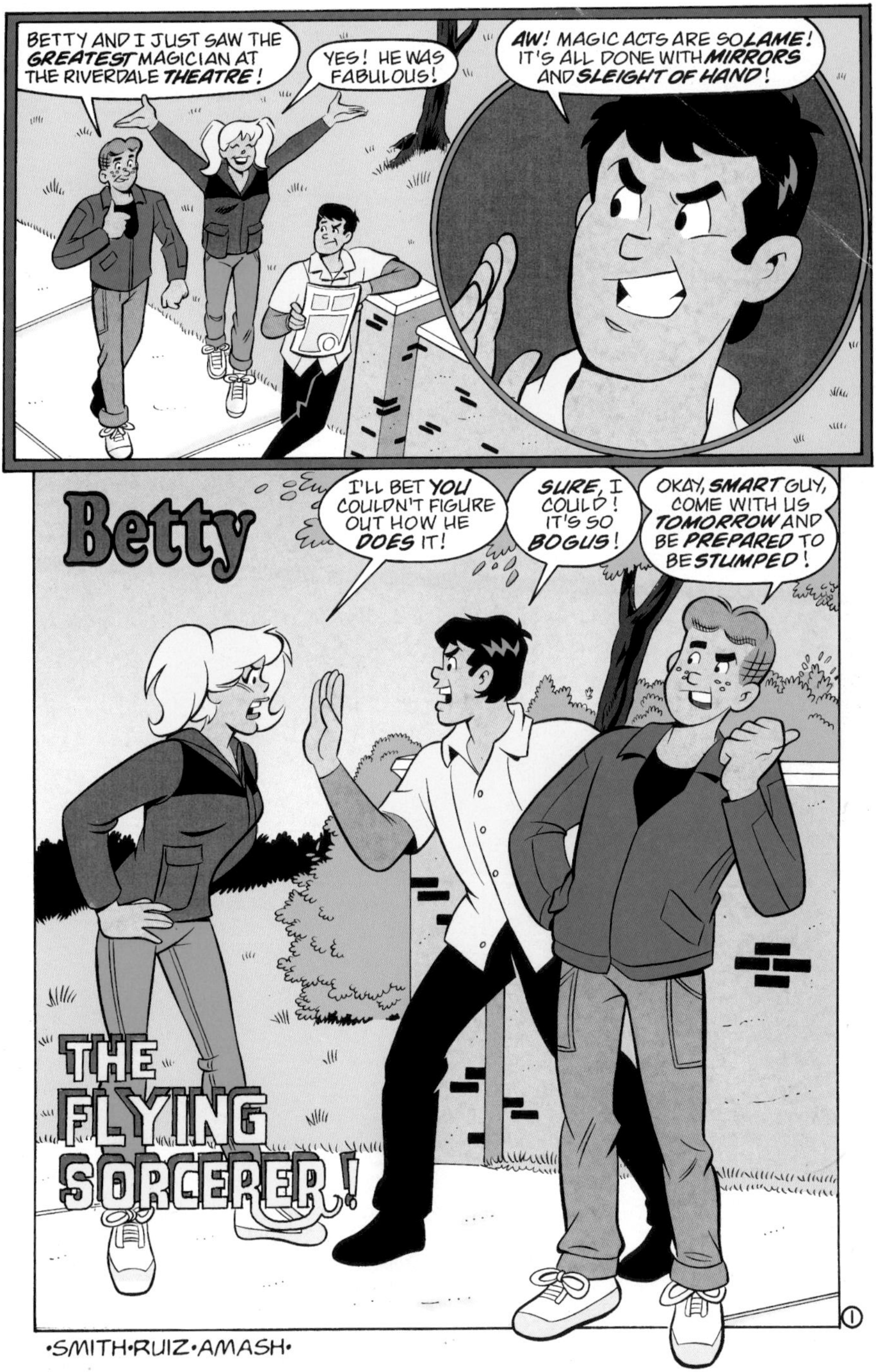
BETTY AND I JUST SAW THE GREATEST MAGICIAN AT THE RIVERDALE THEATRE!
YES! HE WAS FABULOUS!
AW! MAGIC ACTS ARE SO LAME! IT'S ALL DONE WITH MIRRORS AND SLEIGHT OF HAND!
Betty
I'LL BET YOU COULDN'T FIGURE OUT HOW HE DOES IT!
SURE, I COULD! IT'S SO BOGUS!
OKAY, SMART GUY, COME WITH US TOMORROW AND BE PREPARED TO BE STUMPED!
THE FLYING SORCERER!
1

•SMITH•RUIZ•AMASH•

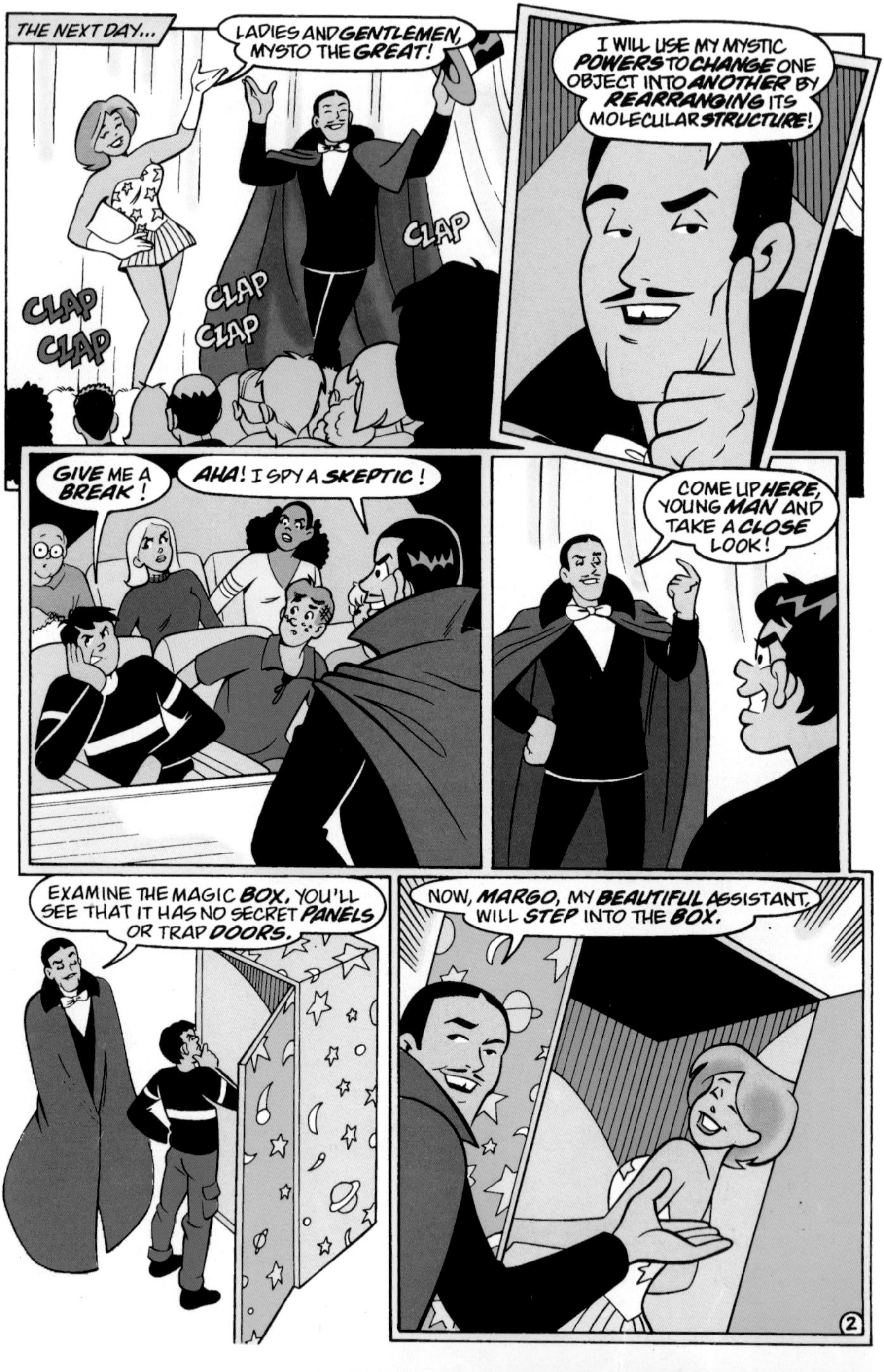
THE NEXT DAY...
LADIES AND GENTLEMEN, MYSTO THE GREAT!
CLAP
CLAP
CLAP
CLAP
CLAP
I WILL USE MY MYSTIC POWERS TO CHANGE ONE OBJECT INTO ANOTHER BY REARRANGING ITS MOLECULAR STRUCTURE!
GIVE ME A BREAK!
AHA! I SPY A SKEPTIC!
COME UP HERE, YOUNG MAN AND TAKE A CLOSE LOOK!
EXAMINE THE MAGIC BOX. YOU'LL SEE THAT IT HAS NO SECRET PANELS OR TRAP DOORS.
NOW, MARGO, MY BEAUTIFUL ASSISTANT, WILL STEP INTO THE BOX.
2

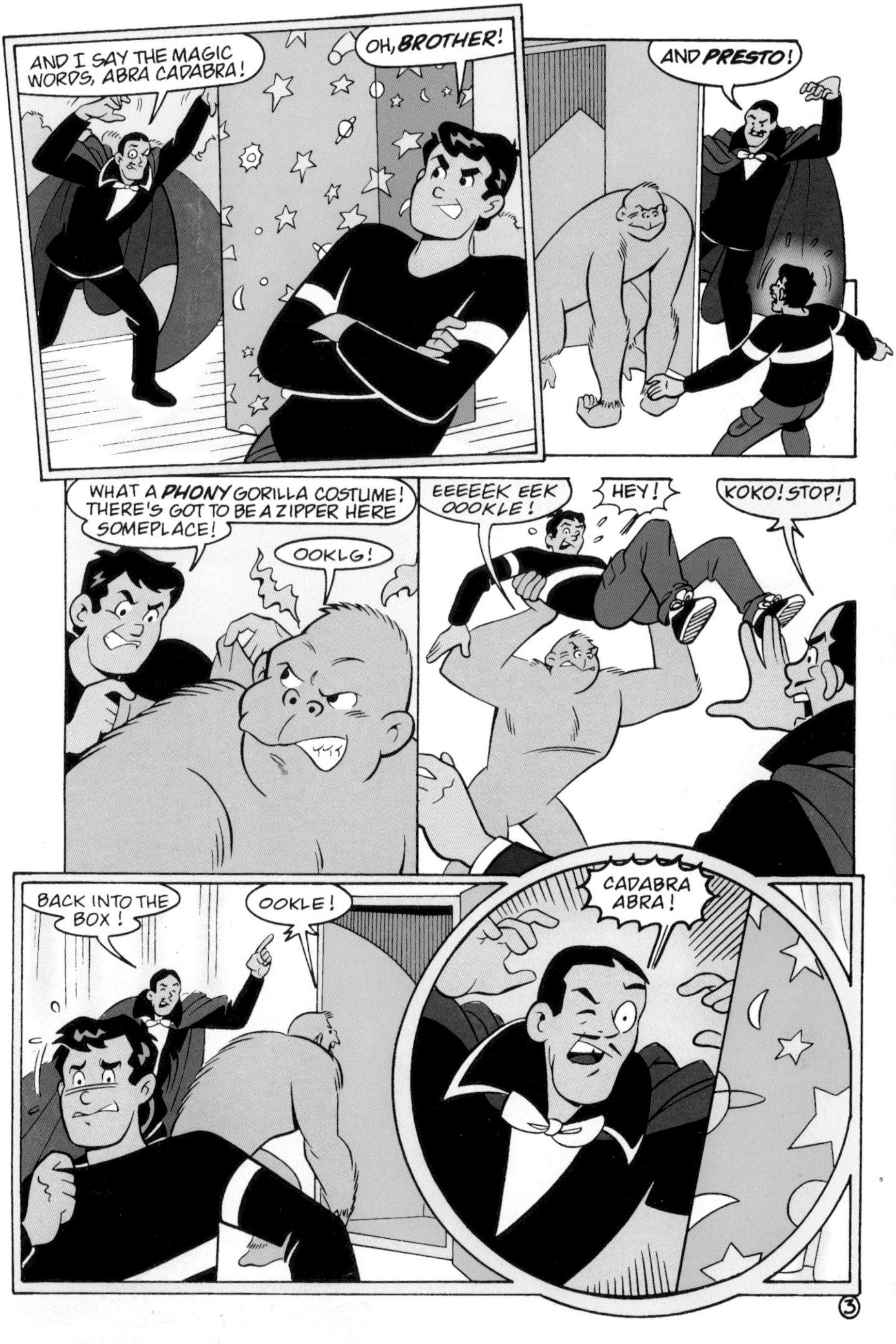
AND I SAY THE MAGIC WORDS, ABRA CADABRA!
OH, BROTHER!
AND PRESTO!
WHAT A PHONY GORILLA COSTUME! THERE'S GOT TO BE A ZIPPER HERE SOMEPLACE!
OOKLG!
EEEEEK EEK OOOKLE!
HEY!
KOKO! STOP!
BACK INTO THE BOX!
OOKLE!
CADABRA ABRA!

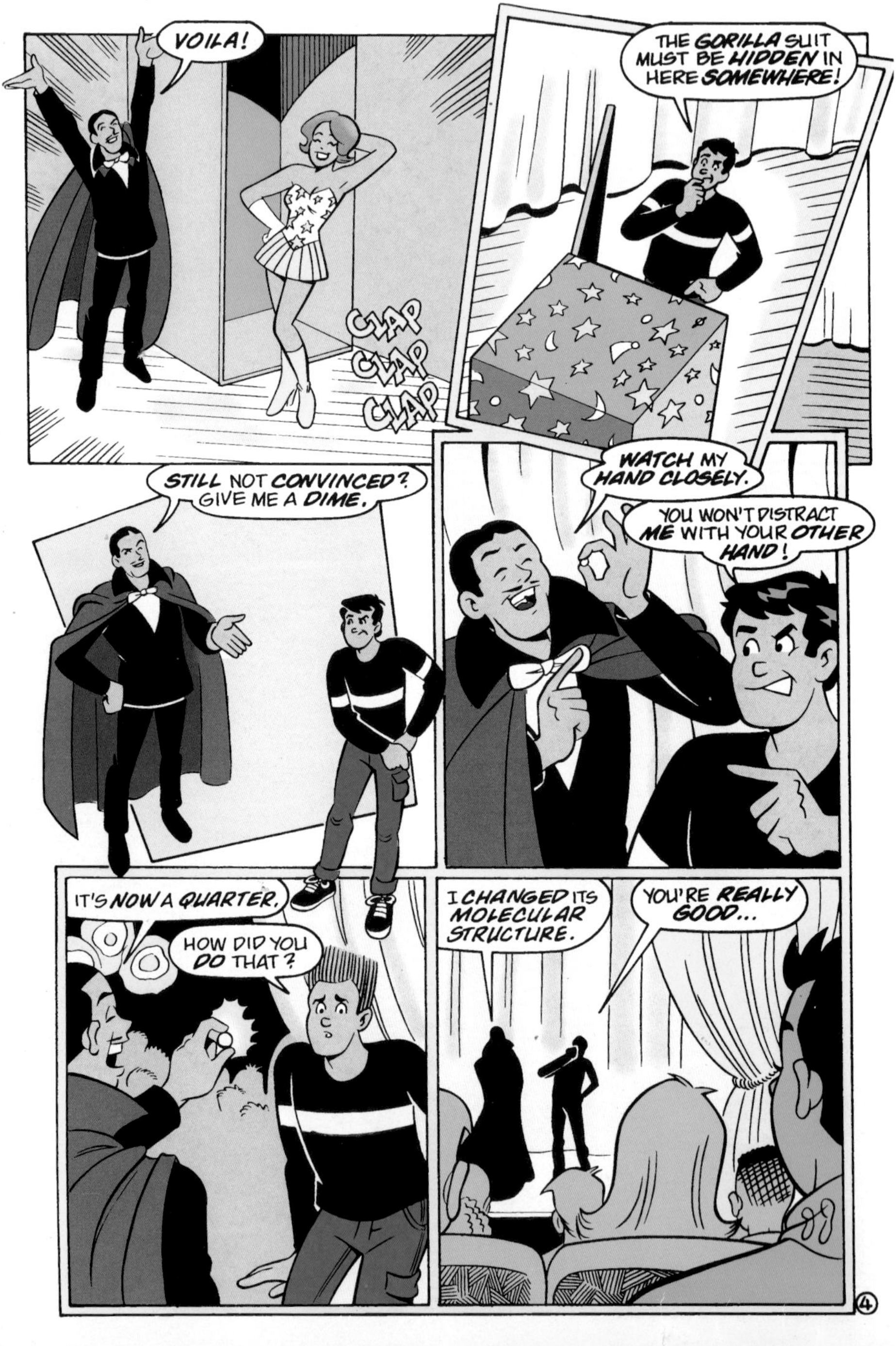
VOILA!
CLAP
CLAP
CLAP
THE GORILLA SUIT MUST BE HIDDEN IN HERE SOMEWHERE!
STILL NOT CONVINCED? GIVE ME A DIME.
WATCH MY HAND CLOSELY.
YOU WON'T DISTRACT ME WITH YOUR OTHER HAND!
IT'S NOW A QUARTER.
HOW DID YOU DO THAT?
I CHANGED ITS MOLECULAR STRUCTURE.
YOU'RE REALLY GOOD...
4

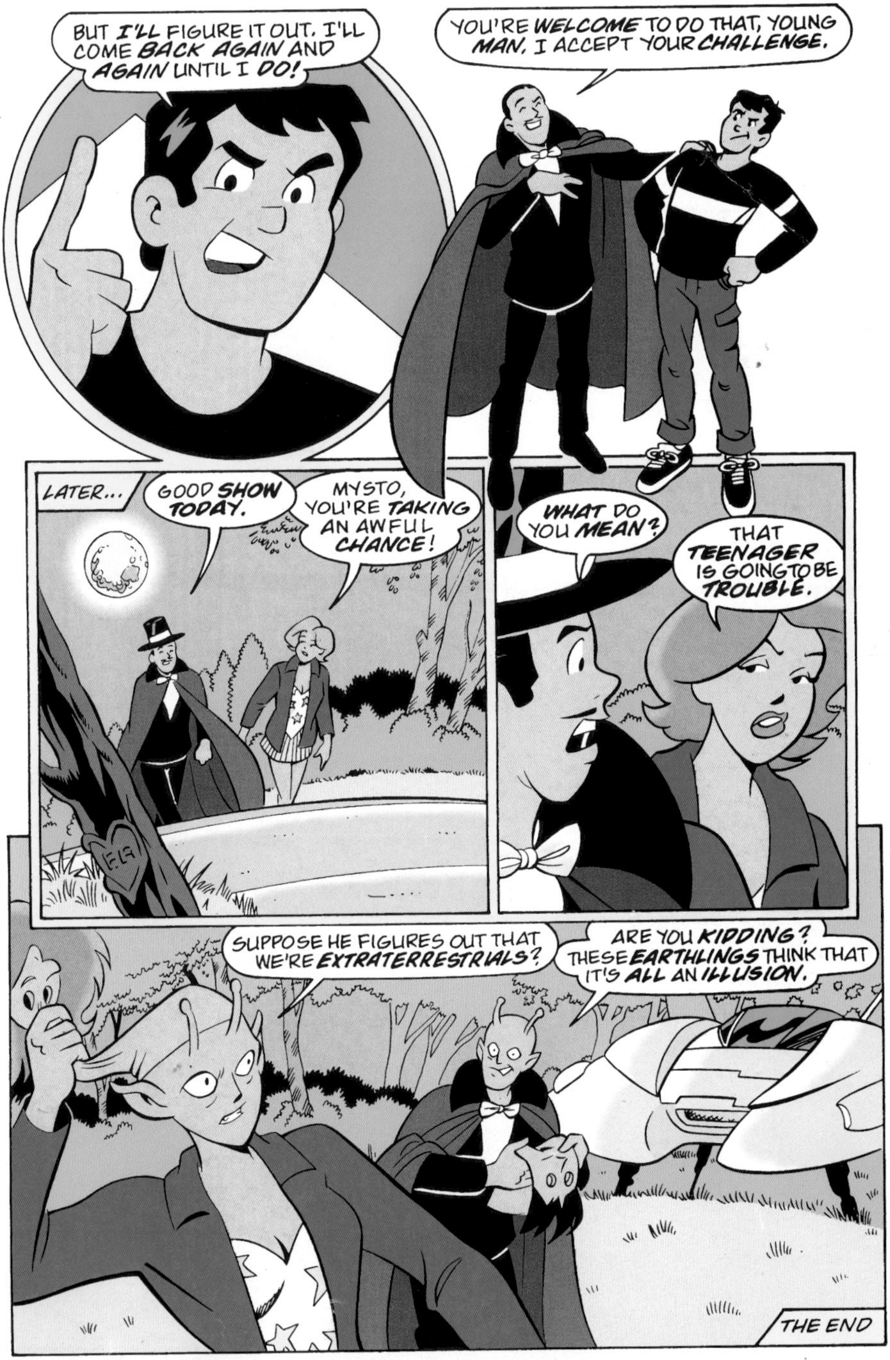
BUT I'LL FIGURE IT OUT. I'LL COME BACK AGAIN AND AGAIN UNTIL I DO!
YOU'RE WELCOME TO DO THAT, YOUNG MAN. I ACCEPT YOUR CHALLENGE.
LATER...
GOOD SHOW TODAY.
MYSTO, YOU'RE TAKING AN AWFUL CHANCE!
WHAT DO YOU MEAN?
THAT TEENAGER IS GOING TO BE TROUBLE.
SUPPOSE HE FIGURES OUT THAT WE'RE EXTRATERRESTRIALS?
ARE YOU KIDDING? THESE EARTHLINGS THINK THAT IT'S ALL AN ILLUSION.
THE END

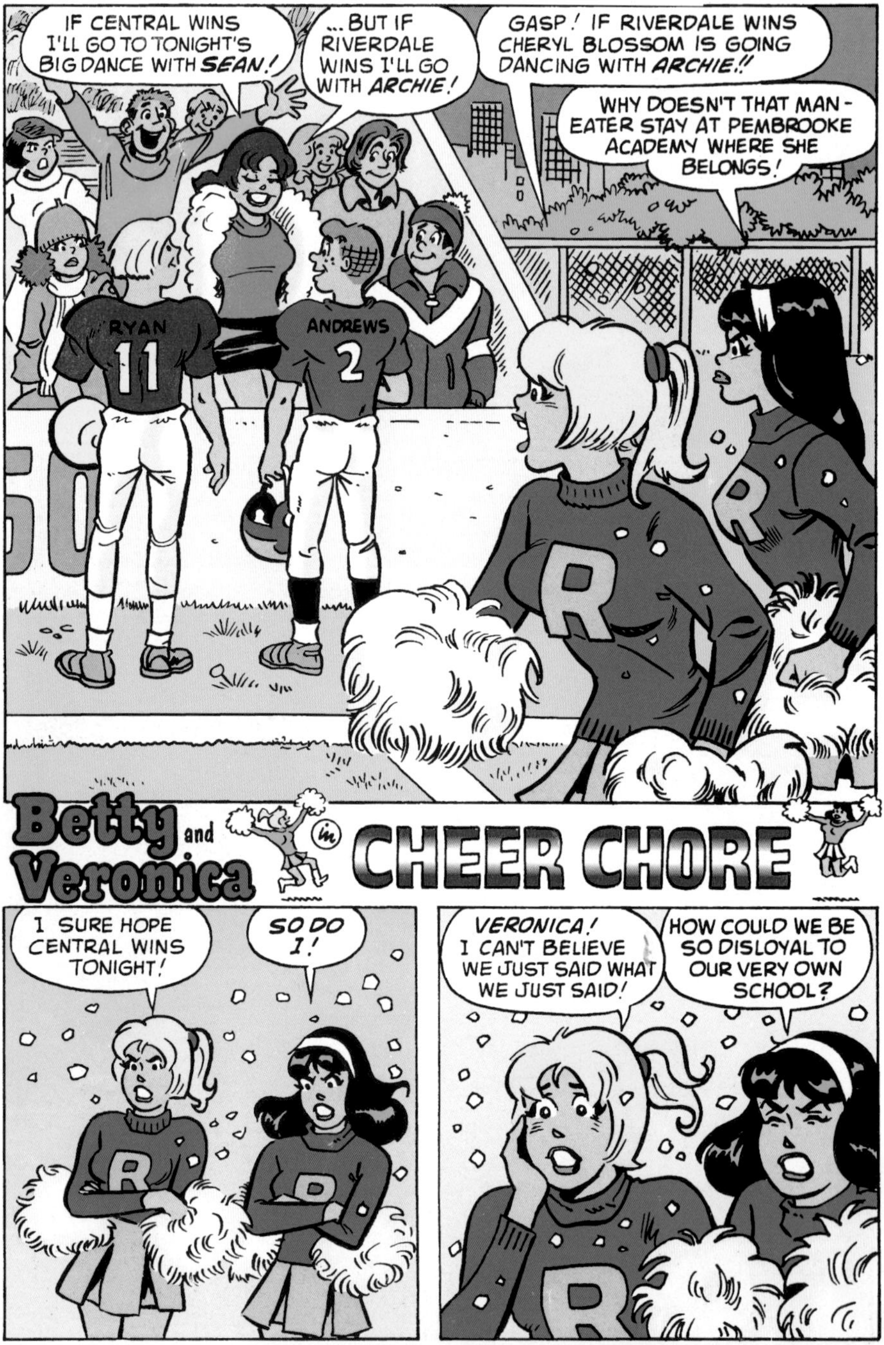
IF CENTRAL WINS I'LL GO TO TONIGHT'S BIG DANCE WITH SEAN!
...BUT IF RIVERDALE WINS I'LL GO WITH ARCHIE!
GASP! IF RIVERDALE WINS CHERYL BLOSSOM IS GOING DANCING WITH ARCHIE!!
WHY DOESN'T THAT MAN-EATER STAY AT PEMBROOKE ACADEMY WHERE SHE BELONGS!
RYAN 11
ANDREWS 2
Betty and Veronica in CHEER CHORE
I SURE HOPE CENTRAL WINS TONIGHT!
SO DO I!
VERONICA! I CAN'T BELIEVE WE JUST SAID WHAT WE JUST SAID!
HOW COULD WE BE SO DISLOYAL TO OUR VERY OWN SCHOOL?

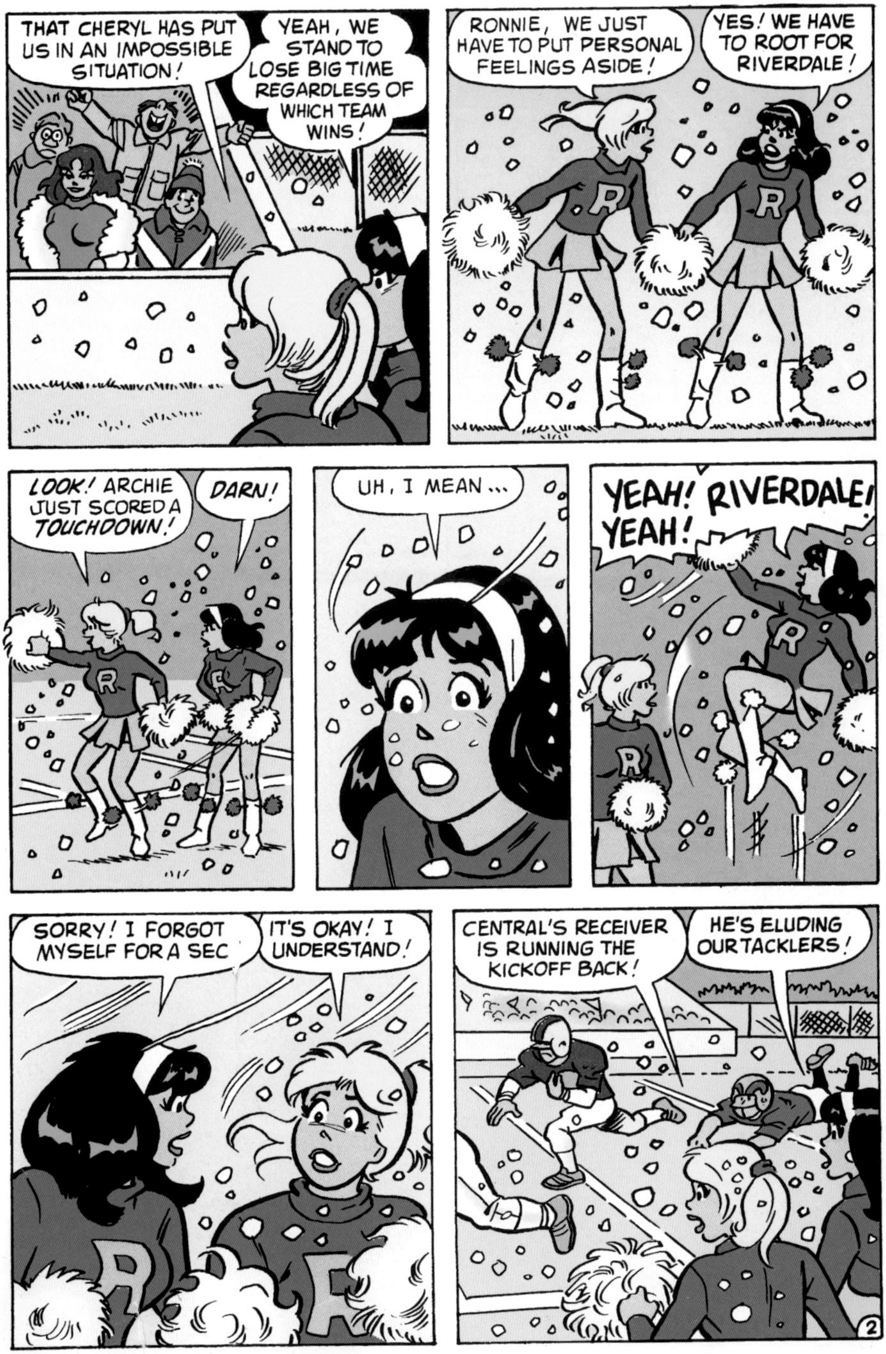
THAT CHERYL HAS PUT US IN AN IMPOSSIBLE SITUATION!
YEAH, WE STAND TO LOSE BIG TIME REGARDLESS OF WHICH TEAM WINS!
RONNIE, WE JUST HAVE TO PUT PERSONAL FEELINGS ASIDE!
YES! WE HAVE TO ROOT FOR RIVERDALE!
LOOK! ARCHIE JUST SCORED A TOUCHDOWN!
DARN!
UH, I MEAN ...
YEAH! YEAH! RIVERDALE!
SORRY! I FORGOT MYSELF FOR A SEC
IT'S OKAY! I UNDERSTAND!
CENTRAL'S RECEIVER IS RUNNING THE KICKOFF BACK!
HE'S ELUDING OUR TACKLERS!
2

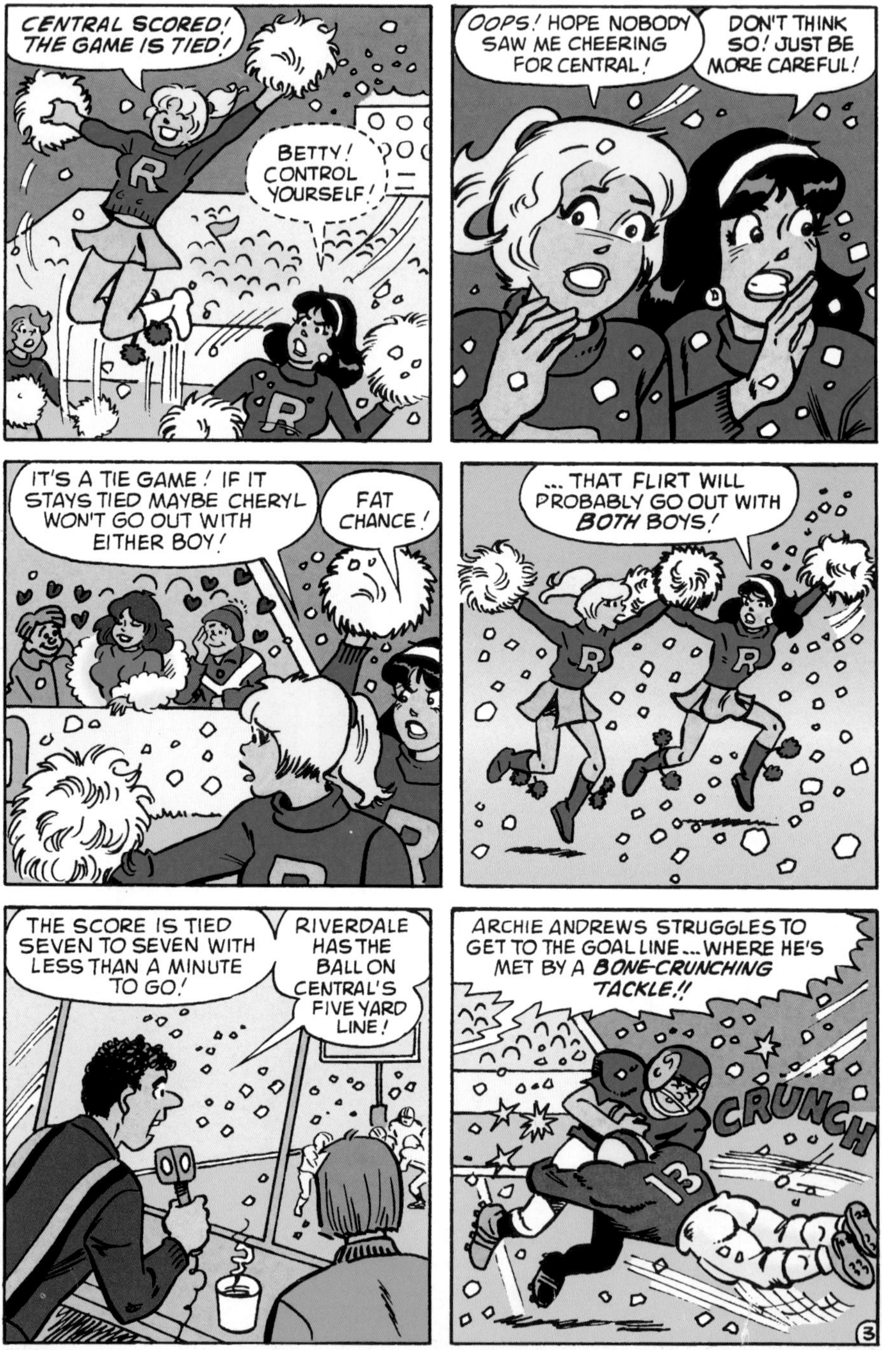
CENTRAL SCORED! THE GAME IS TIED!
BETTY! CONTROL YOURSELF!
OOPS! HOPE NOBODY SAW ME CHEERING FOR CENTRAL!
DON'T THINK SO! JUST BE MORE CAREFUL!
IT'S A TIE GAME! IF IT STAYS TIED MAYBE CHERYL WON'T GO OUT WITH EITHER BOY!
FAT CHANCE!
... THAT FLIRT WILL PROBABLY GO OUT WITH BOTH BOYS!
THE SCORE IS TIED SEVEN TO SEVEN WITH LESS THAN A MINUTE TO GO!
RIVERDALE HAS THE BALL ON CENTRAL'S FIVE YARD LINE!
ARCHIE ANDREWS STRUGGLES TO GET TO THE GOAL LINE ... WHERE HE'S MET BY A BONE-CRUNCHING TACKLE!!
CRUNCH
3

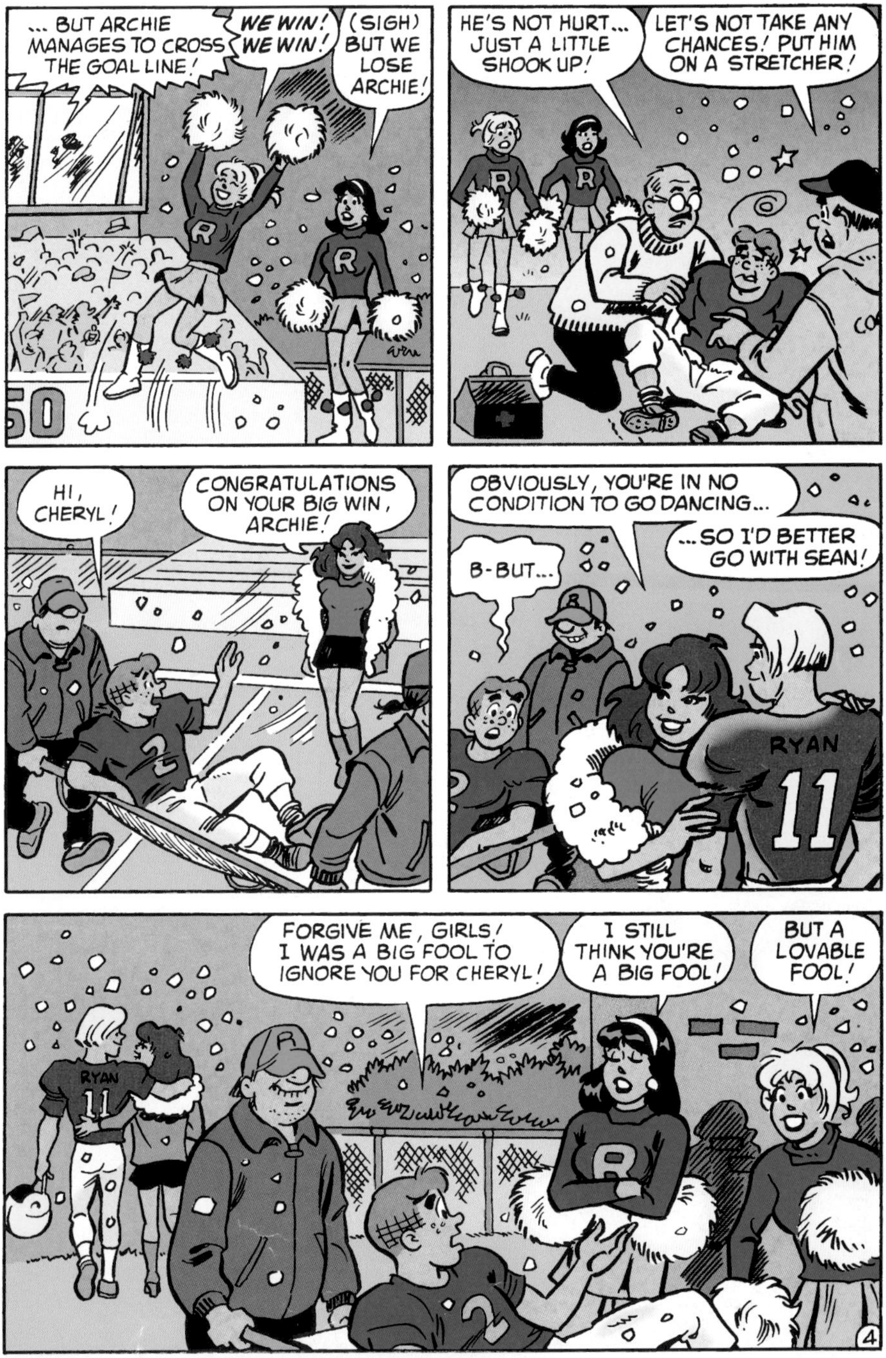
... BUT ARCHIE MANAGES TO CROSS THE GOAL LINE!
WE WIN! WE WIN!
(SIGH) BUT WE LOSE ARCHIE!
HE'S NOT HURT... JUST A LITTLE SHOOK UP!
LET'S NOT TAKE ANY CHANCES! PUT HIM ON A STRETCHER!
HI, CHERYL!
CONGRATULATIONS ON YOUR BIG WIN, ARCHIE!
OBVIOUSLY, YOU'RE IN NO CONDITION TO GO DANCING...
B-BUT...
...SO I'D BETTER GO WITH SEAN!
RYAN
11
FORGIVE ME, GIRLS! I WAS A BIG FOOL TO IGNORE YOU FOR CHERYL!
I STILL THINK YOU'RE A BIG FOOL!
BUT A LOVABLE FOOL!
4

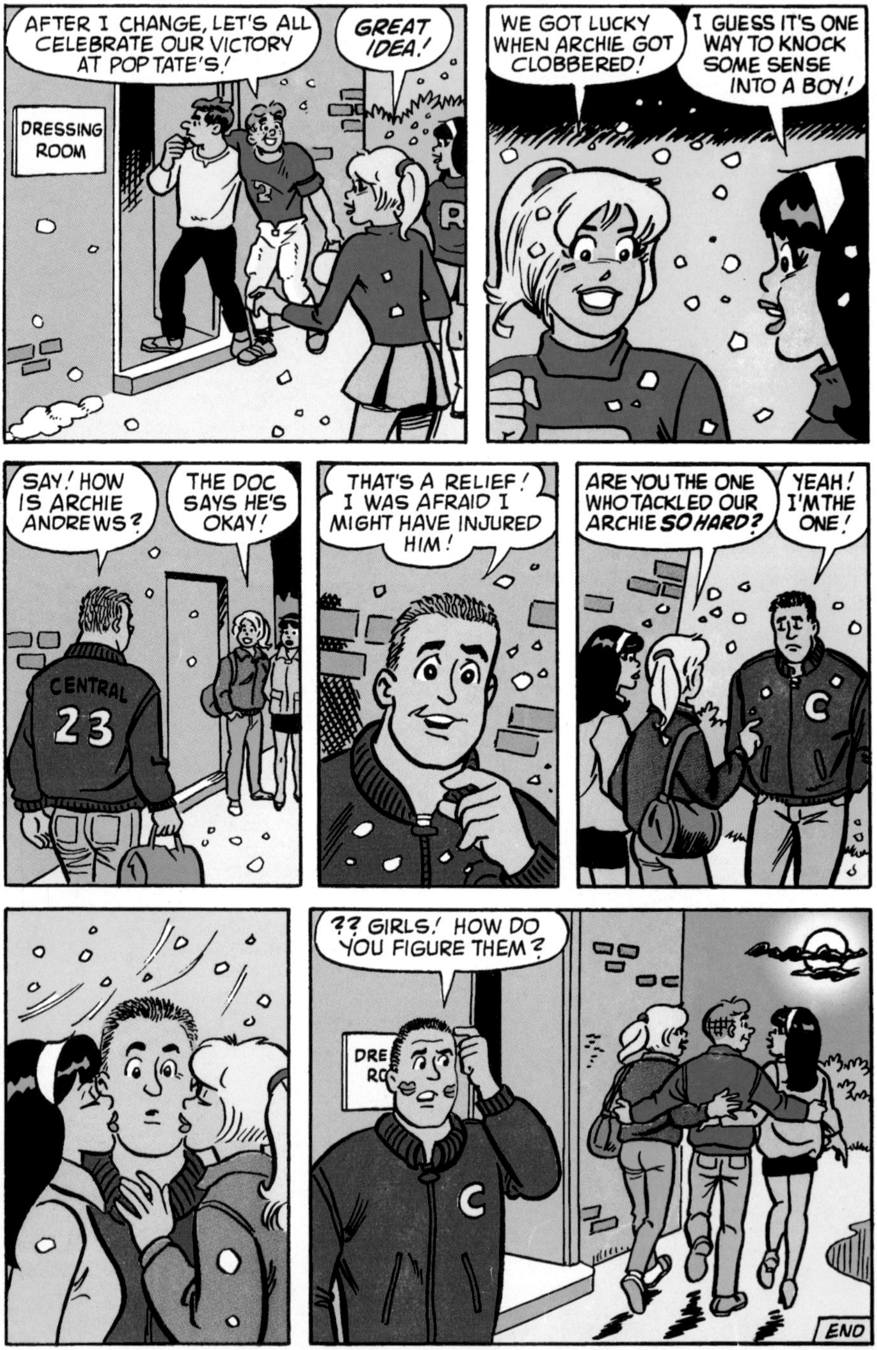
AFTER I CHANGE, LET'S ALL CELEBRATE OUR VICTORY AT POP TATE'S!
GREAT IDEA!
DRESSING ROOM
WE GOT LUCKY WHEN ARCHIE GOT CLOBBERED!
I GUESS IT'S ONE WAY TO KNOCK SOME SENSE INTO A BOY!
SAY! HOW IS ARCHIE ANDREWS?
THE DOC SAYS HE'S OKAY!
CENTRAL 23
THAT'S A RELIEF! I WAS AFRAID I MIGHT HAVE INJURED HIM!
ARE YOU THE ONE WHO TACKLED OUR ARCHIE SO HARD?
YEAH! I'M THE ONE!
?? GIRLS! HOW DO YOU FIGURE THEM?
END

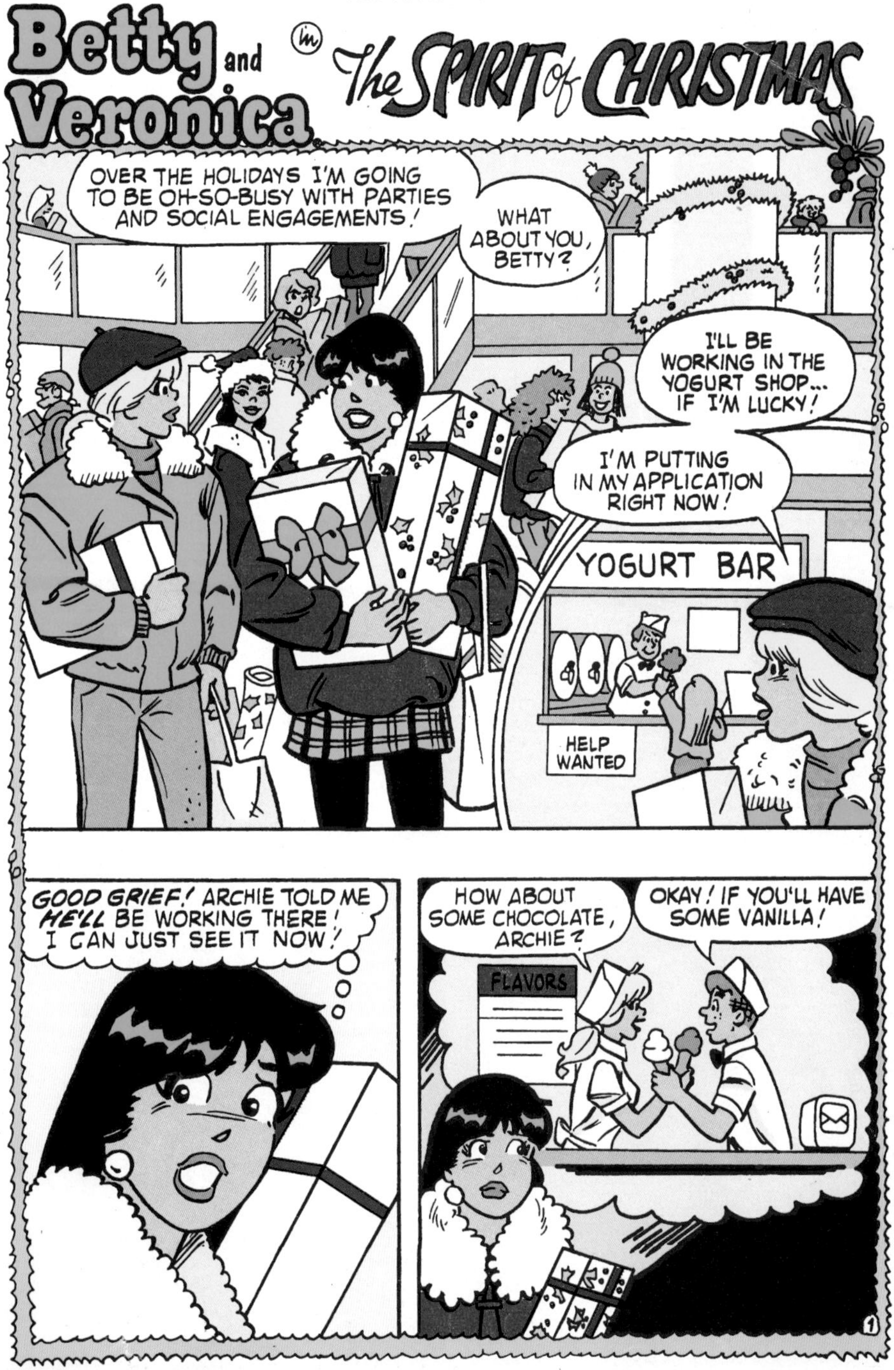
Betty and Veronica in
The Spirit of Christmas
OVER THE HOLIDAYS I'M GOING TO BE OH-SO-BUSY WITH PARTIES AND SOCIAL ENGAGEMENTS!
WHAT ABOUT YOU, BETTY?
I'LL BE WORKING IN THE YOGURT SHOP... IF I'M LUCKY!
I'M PUTTING IN MY APPLICATION RIGHT NOW!
YOGURT BAR
HELP WANTED
GOOD GRIEF! ARCHIE TOLD ME HE'LL BE WORKING THERE! I CAN JUST SEE IT NOW!
HOW ABOUT SOME CHOCOLATE, ARCHIE?
OKAY! IF YOU'LL HAVE SOME VANILLA!
FLAVORS
1

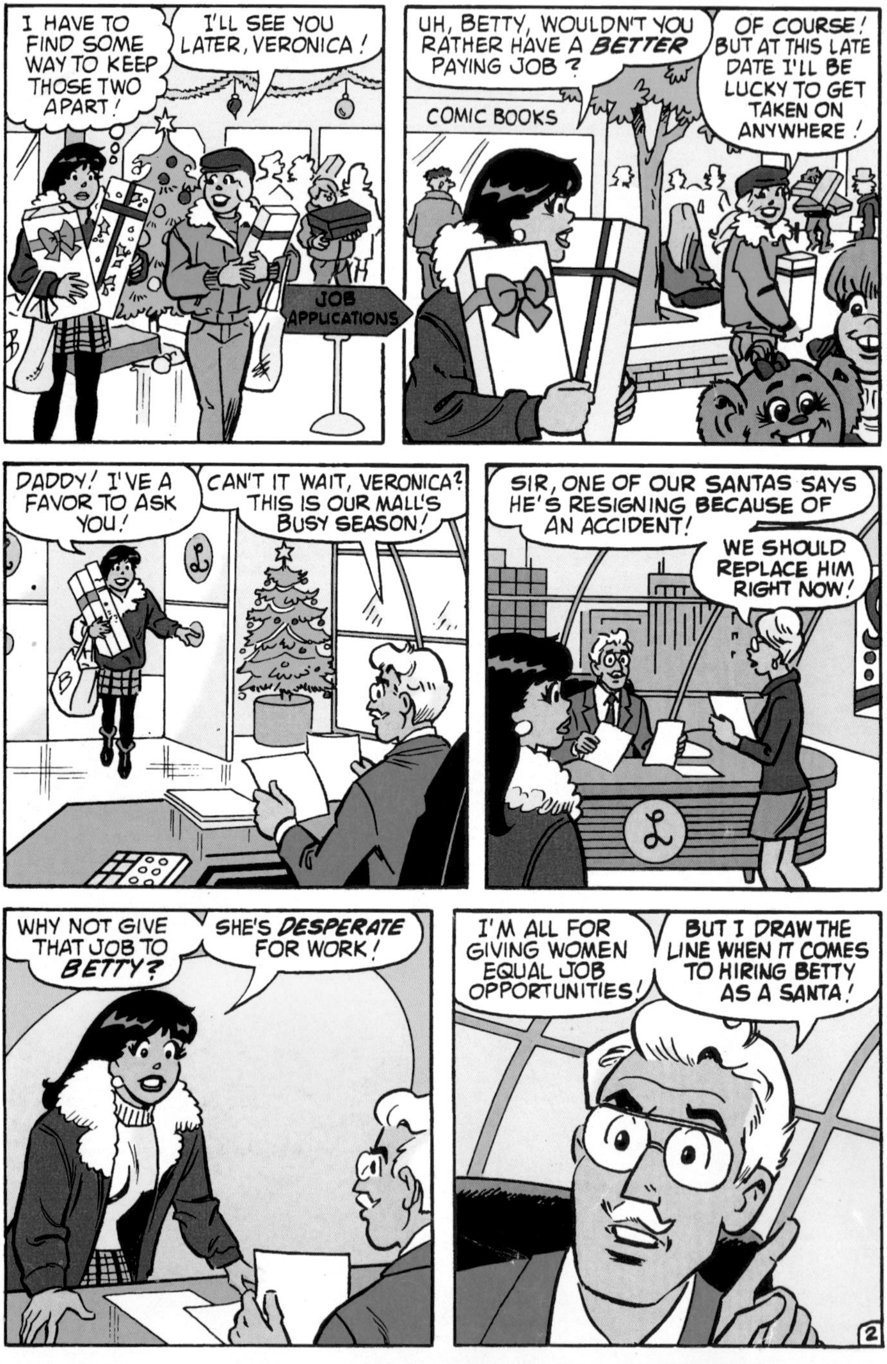
I HAVE TO FIND SOME WAY TO KEEP THOSE TWO APART!
I'LL SEE YOU LATER, VERONICA!
JOB APPLICATIONS
UH, BETTY, WOULDN'T YOU RATHER HAVE A *BETTER* PAYING JOB?
OF COURSE! BUT AT THIS LATE DATE I'LL BE LUCKY TO GET TAKEN ON ANYWHERE!
COMIC BOOKS
DADDY! I'VE A FAVOR TO ASK YOU!
CAN'T IT WAIT, VERONICA? THIS IS OUR MALL'S BUSY SEASON!
SIR, ONE OF OUR SANTAS SAYS HE'S RESIGNING BECAUSE OF AN ACCIDENT!
WE SHOULD REPLACE HIM RIGHT NOW!
WHY NOT GIVE THAT JOB TO *BETTY?*
SHE'S *DESPERATE* FOR WORK!
I'M ALL FOR GIVING WOMEN EQUAL JOB OPPORTUNITIES!
BUT I DRAW THE LINE WHEN IT COMES TO HIRING BETTY AS A SANTA!
2

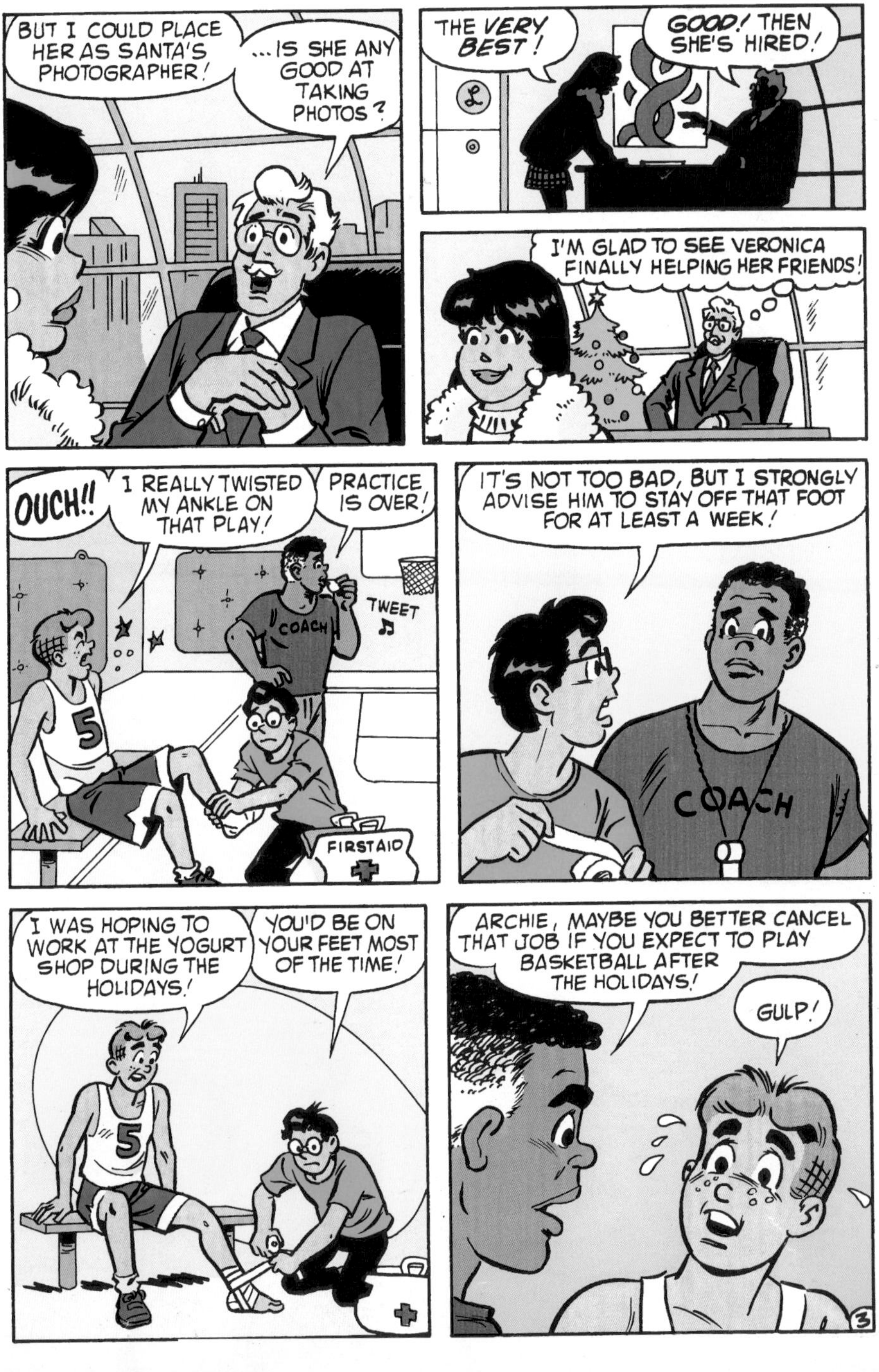
BUT I COULD PLACE HER AS SANTA'S PHOTOGRAPHER!
...IS SHE ANY GOOD AT TAKING PHOTOS?
THE VERY BEST!
GOOD! THEN SHE'S HIRED!
I'M GLAD TO SEE VERONICA FINALLY HELPING HER FRIENDS!
OUCH!!
I REALLY TWISTED MY ANKLE ON THAT PLAY!
PRACTICE IS OVER!
COACH
TWEET
5
FIRSTAID
IT'S NOT TOO BAD, BUT I STRONGLY ADVISE HIM TO STAY OFF THAT FOOT FOR AT LEAST A WEEK!
COACH
I WAS HOPING TO WORK AT THE YOGURT SHOP DURING THE HOLIDAYS!
YOU'D BE ON YOUR FEET MOST OF THE TIME!
5
ARCHIE, MAYBE YOU BETTER CANCEL THAT JOB IF YOU EXPECT TO PLAY BASKETBALL AFTER THE HOLIDAYS!
GULP!
3

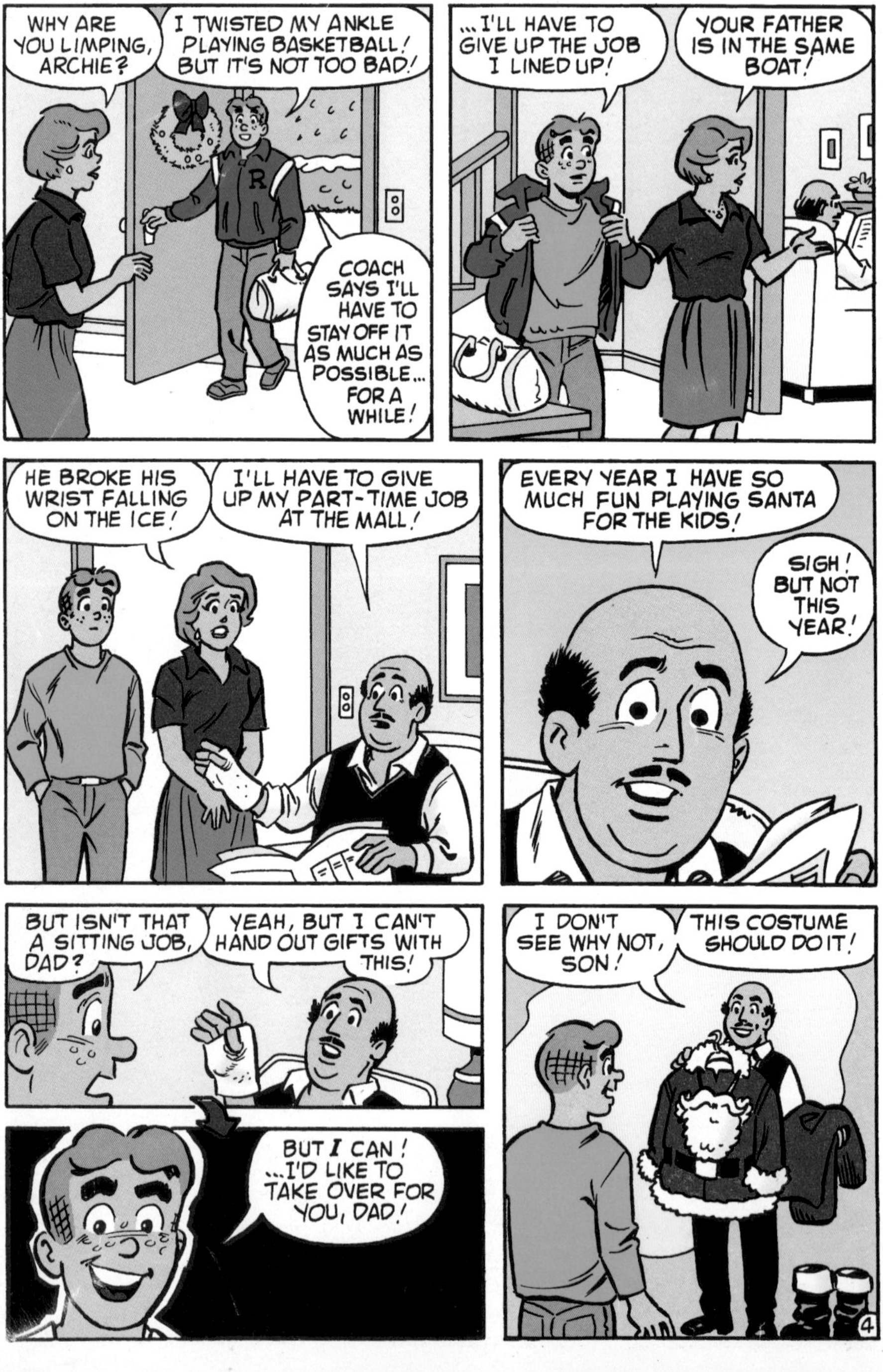
WHY ARE YOU LIMPING, ARCHIE?
I TWISTED MY ANKLE PLAYING BASKETBALL! BUT IT'S NOT TOO BAD!
COACH SAYS I'LL HAVE TO STAY OFF IT AS MUCH AS POSSIBLE... FOR A WHILE!
...I'LL HAVE TO GIVE UP THE JOB I LINED UP!
YOUR FATHER IS IN THE SAME BOAT!
HE BROKE HIS WRIST FALLING ON THE ICE!
I'LL HAVE TO GIVE UP MY PART-TIME JOB AT THE MALL!
EVERY YEAR I HAVE SO MUCH FUN PLAYING SANTA FOR THE KIDS!
SIGH! BUT NOT THIS YEAR!
BUT ISN'T THAT A SITTING JOB, DAD?
YEAH, BUT I CAN'T HAND OUT GIFTS WITH THIS!
BUT I CAN! ...I'D LIKE TO TAKE OVER FOR YOU, DAD!
I DON'T SEE WHY NOT, SON!
THIS COSTUME SHOULD DO IT!
4

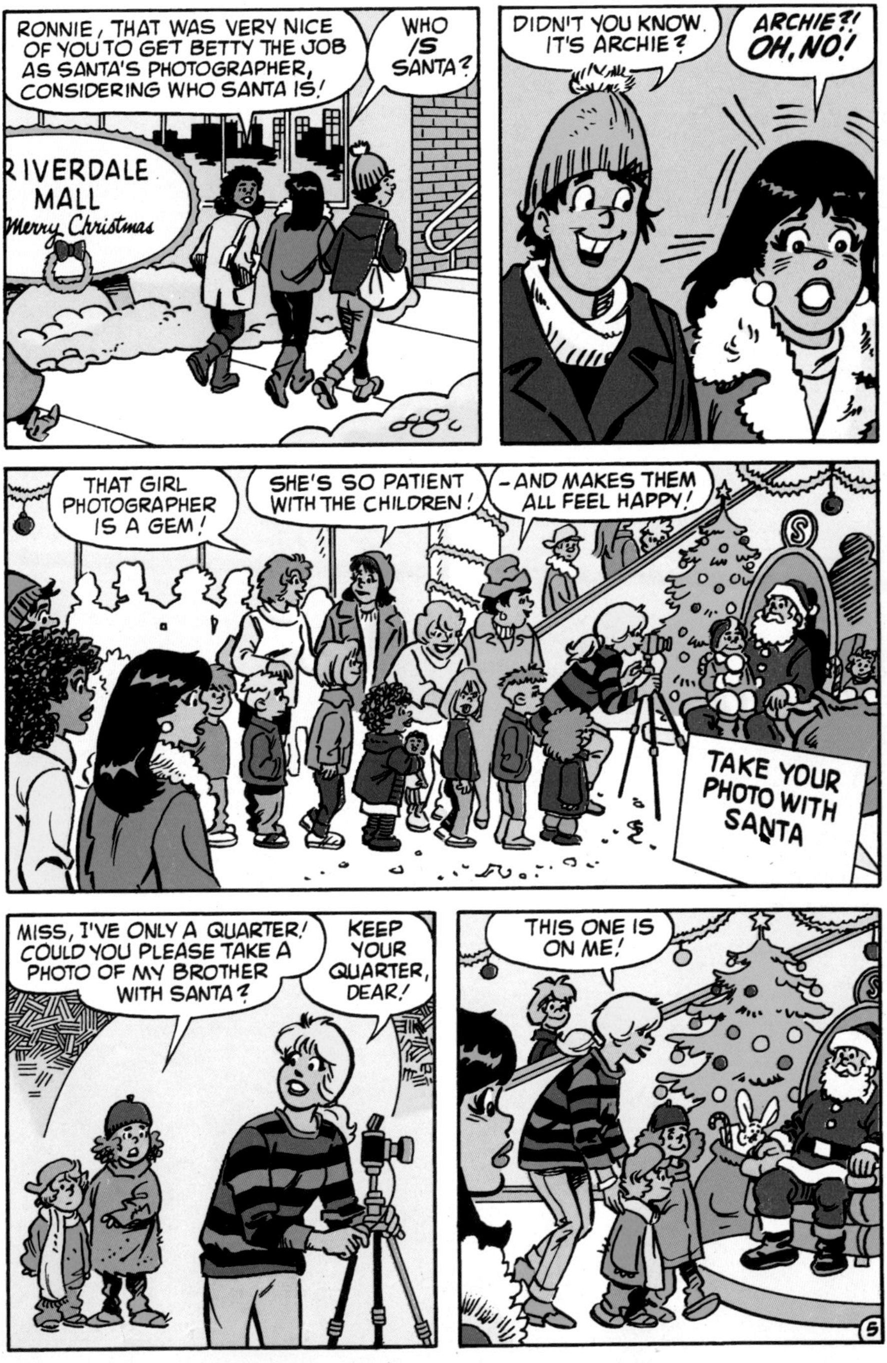
RONNIE, THAT WAS VERY NICE OF YOU TO GET BETTY THE JOB AS SANTA'S PHOTOGRAPHER, CONSIDERING WHO SANTA IS!
WHO IS SANTA?
RIVERDALE MALL
Merry Christmas
DIDN'T YOU KNOW. IT'S ARCHIE?
ARCHIE?! OH, NO!
THAT GIRL PHOTOGRAPHER IS A GEM!
SHE'S SO PATIENT WITH THE CHILDREN!
-AND MAKES THEM ALL FEEL HAPPY!
TAKE YOUR PHOTO WITH SANTA
MISS, I'VE ONLY A QUARTER! COULD YOU PLEASE TAKE A PHOTO OF MY BROTHER WITH SANTA?
KEEP YOUR QUARTER, DEAR!
THIS ONE IS ON ME!
5

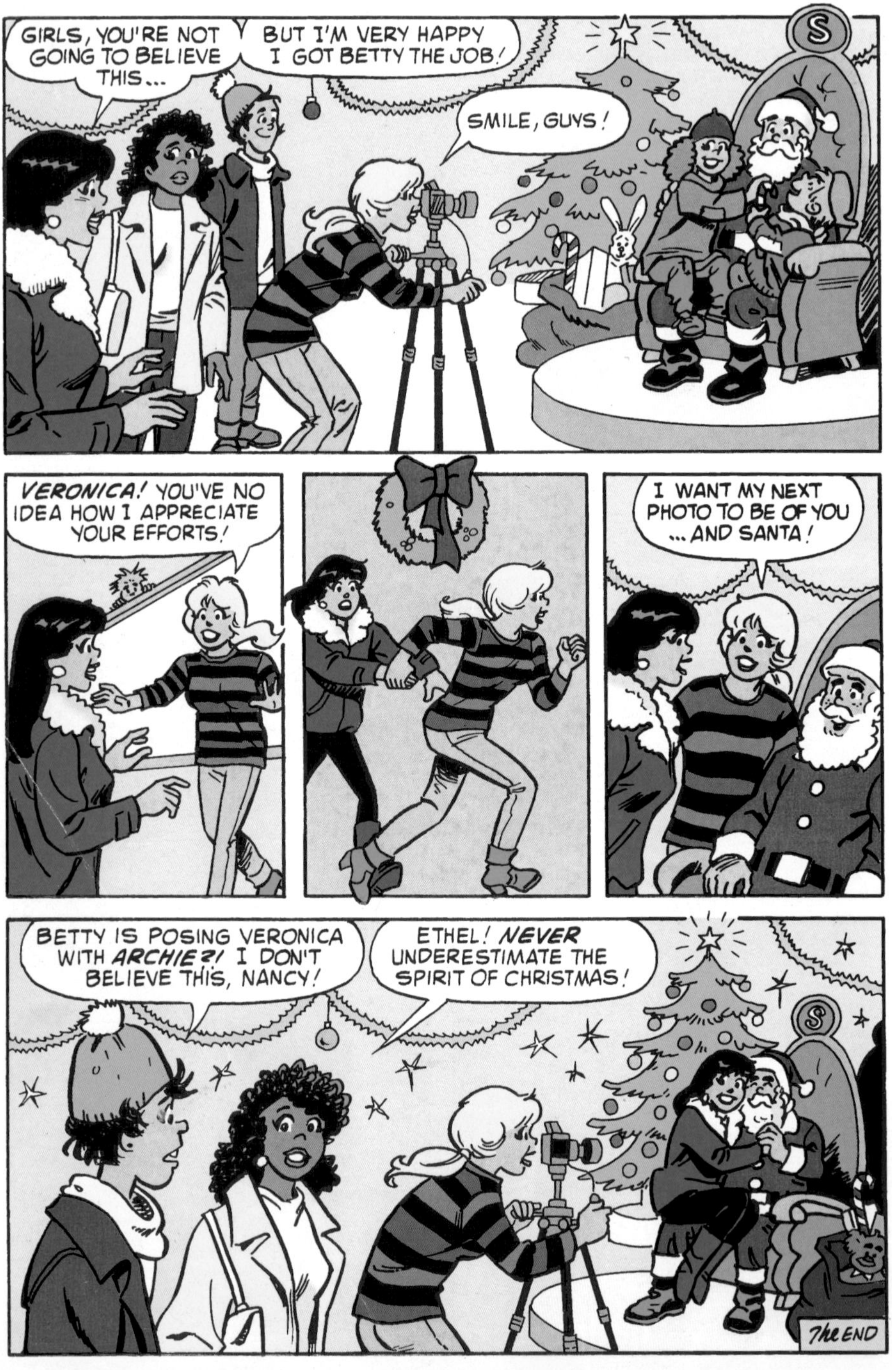
GIRLS, YOU'RE NOT GOING TO BELIEVE THIS...
BUT I'M VERY HAPPY I GOT BETTY THE JOB!
SMILE, GUYS!
VERONICA! YOU'VE NO IDEA HOW I APPRECIATE YOUR EFFORTS!
I WANT MY NEXT PHOTO TO BE OF YOU ...AND SANTA!
BETTY IS POSING VERONICA WITH ARCHIE?! I DON'T BELIEVE THIS, NANCY!
ETHEL! NEVER UNDERESTIMATE THE SPIRIT OF CHRISTMAS!
The END

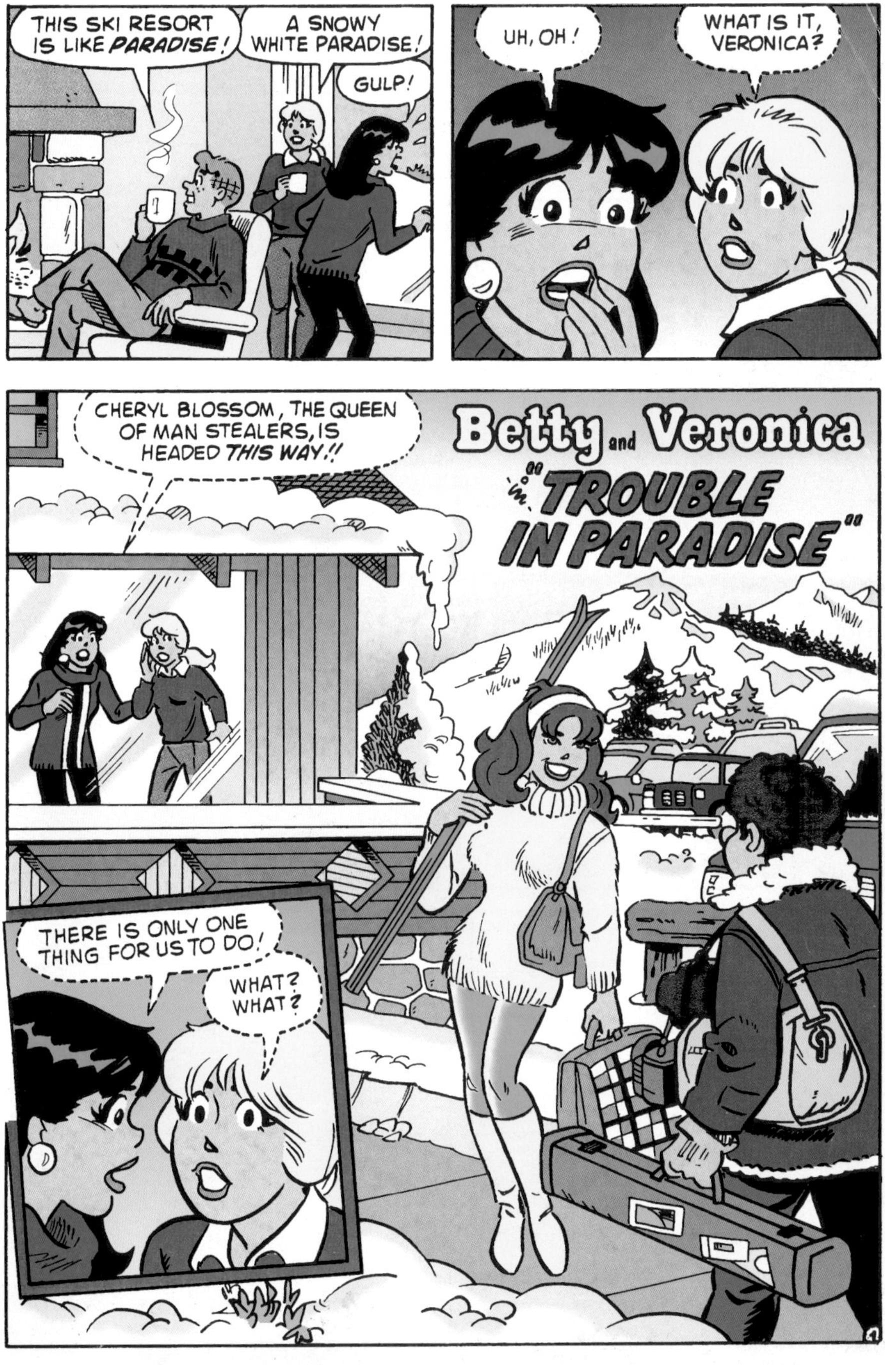
THIS SKI RESORT IS LIKE *PARADISE*!
A SNOWY WHITE PARADISE!
GULP!
UH, OH!
WHAT IS IT, VERONICA?
CHERYL BLOSSOM, THE QUEEN OF MAN STEALERS, IS HEADED *THIS WAY*!!
Betty and Veronica
"TROUBLE IN PARADISE"
THERE IS ONLY ONE THING FOR US TO DO!
WHAT? WHAT?
1

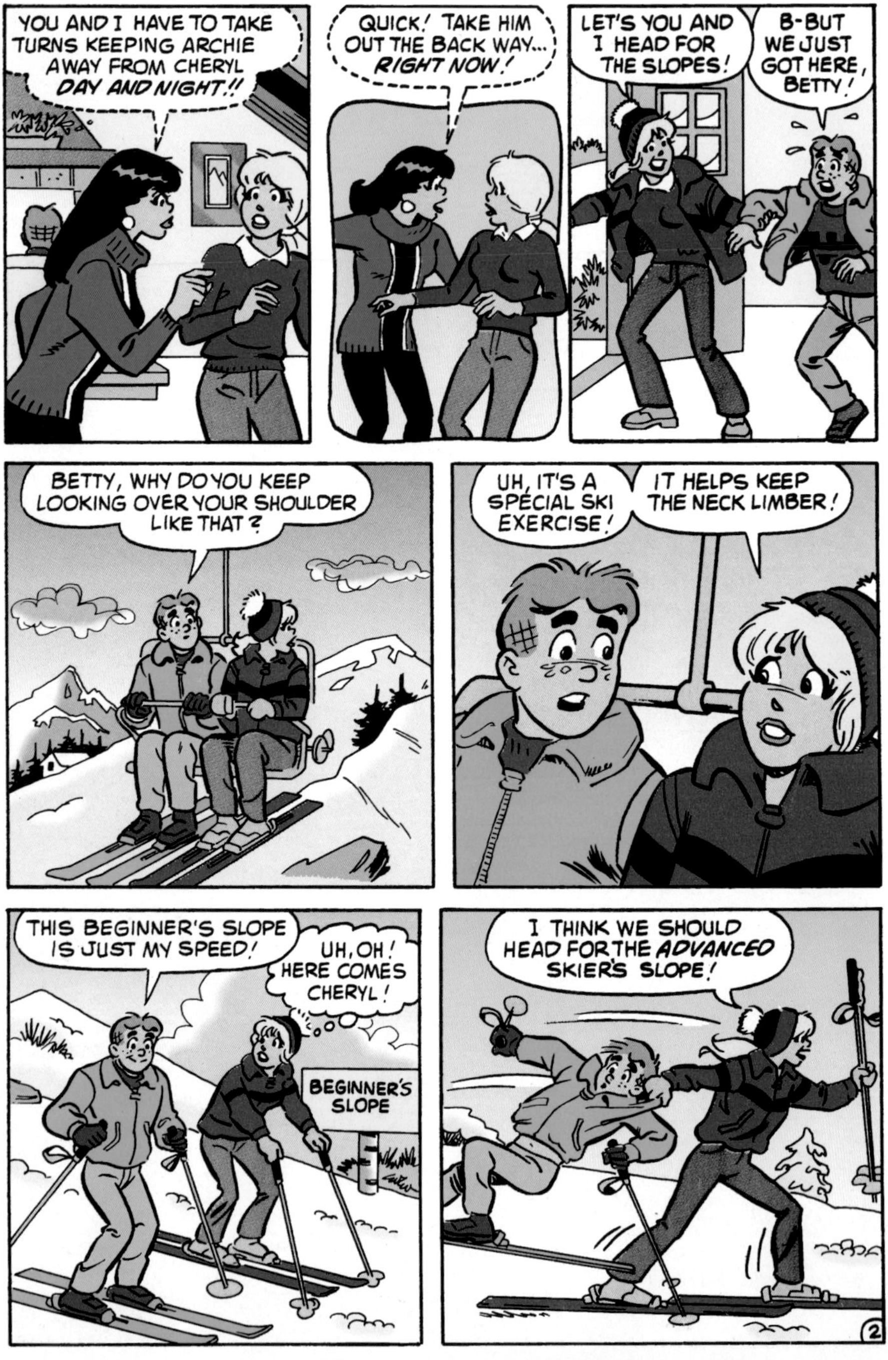
YOU AND I HAVE TO TAKE TURNS KEEPING ARCHIE AWAY FROM CHERYL *DAY AND NIGHT!!*
QUICK! TAKE HIM OUT THE BACK WAY... *RIGHT NOW!*
LET'S YOU AND I HEAD FOR THE SLOPES!
B-BUT WE JUST GOT HERE, BETTY!
BETTY, WHY DO YOU KEEP LOOKING OVER YOUR SHOULDER LIKE THAT?
UH, IT'S A SPECIAL SKI EXERCISE!
IT HELPS KEEP THE NECK LIMBER!
THIS BEGINNER'S SLOPE IS JUST MY SPEED!
UH, OH! HERE COMES CHERYL!
BEGINNER'S SLOPE
I THINK WE SHOULD HEAD FOR THE *ADVANCED* SKIER'S SLOPE!
2

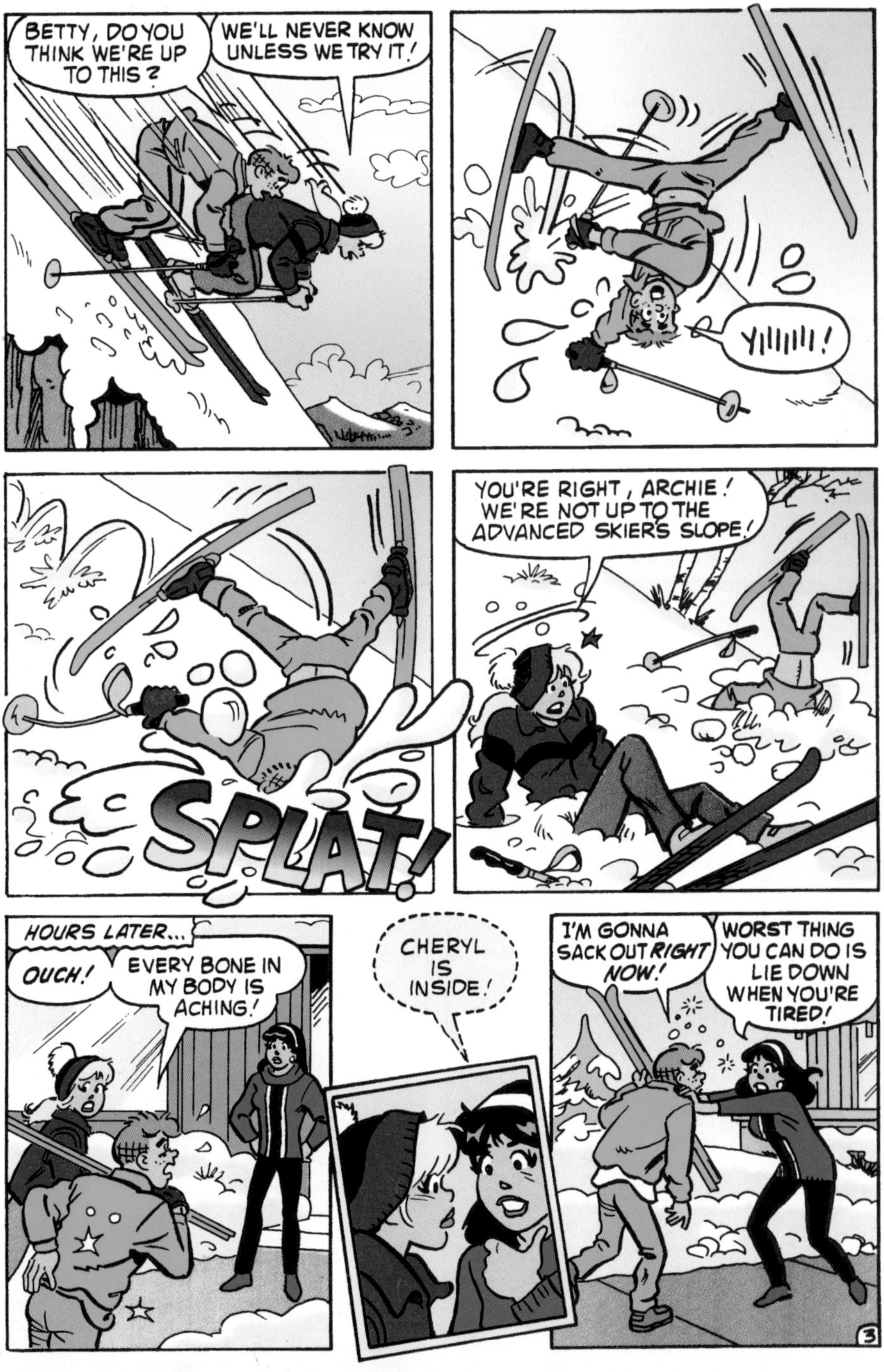
BETTY, DO YOU THINK WE'RE UP TO THIS ?
WE'LL NEVER KNOW UNLESS WE TRY IT!
YIIIIIII!
SPLAT!
YOU'RE RIGHT, ARCHIE! WE'RE NOT UP TO THE ADVANCED SKIER'S SLOPE!
HOURS LATER...
OUCH!
EVERY BONE IN MY BODY IS ACHING!
CHERYL IS INSIDE!
I'M GONNA SACK OUT RIGHT NOW!
WORST THING YOU CAN DO IS LIE DOWN WHEN YOU'RE TIRED!
3

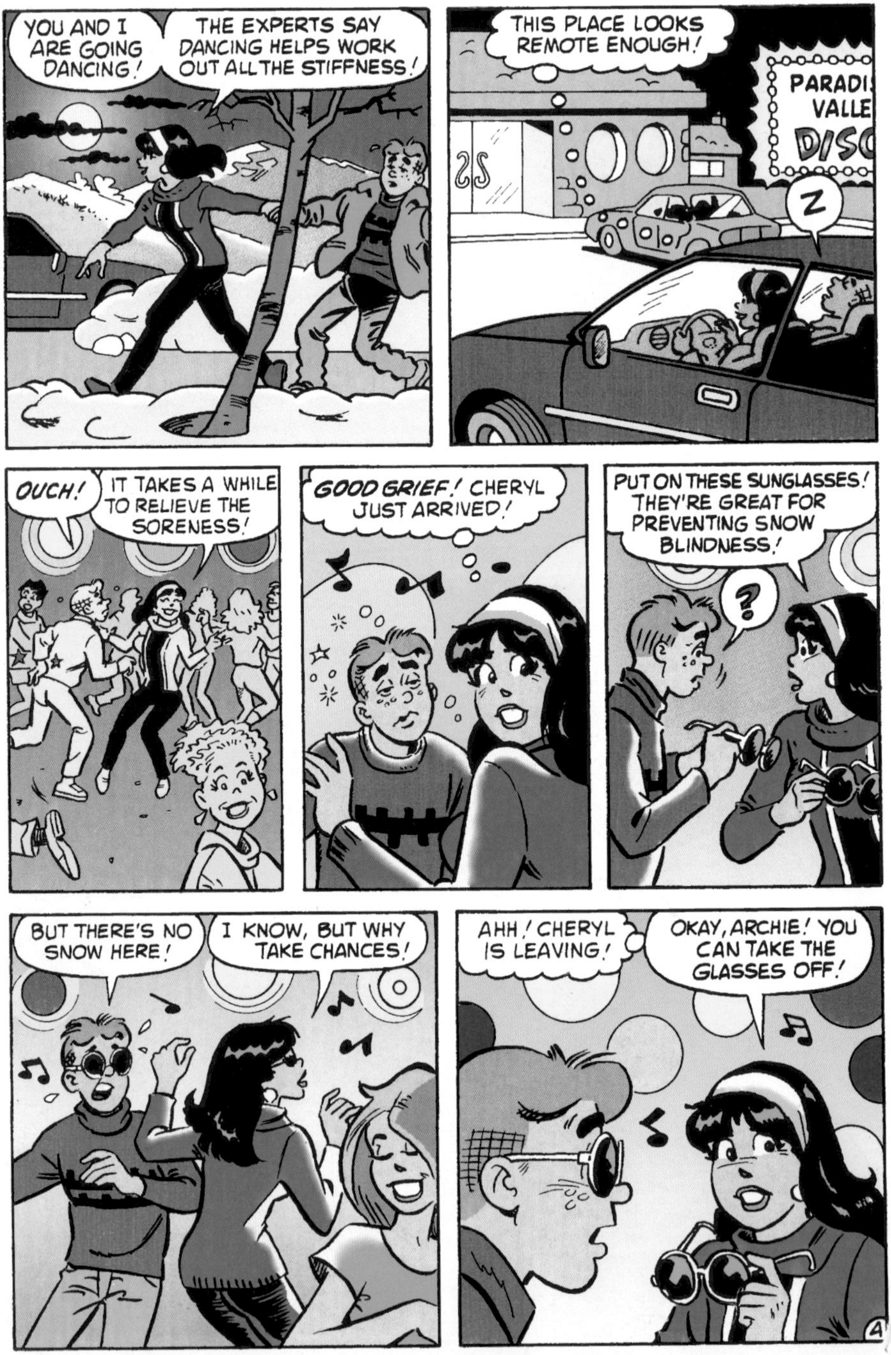
YOU AND I ARE GOING DANCING!
THE EXPERTS SAY DANCING HELPS WORK OUT ALL THE STIFFNESS!
THIS PLACE LOOKS REMOTE ENOUGH!
PARADI VALLE DISC
Z
OUCH!
IT TAKES A WHILE TO RELIEVE THE SORENESS!
GOOD GRIEF! CHERYL JUST ARRIVED!
PUT ON THESE SUNGLASSES! THEY'RE GREAT FOR PREVENTING SNOW BLINDNESS!
?
BUT THERE'S NO SNOW HERE!
I KNOW, BUT WHY TAKE CHANCES!
AHH! CHERYL IS LEAVING!
OKAY, ARCHIE! YOU CAN TAKE THE GLASSES OFF!
4

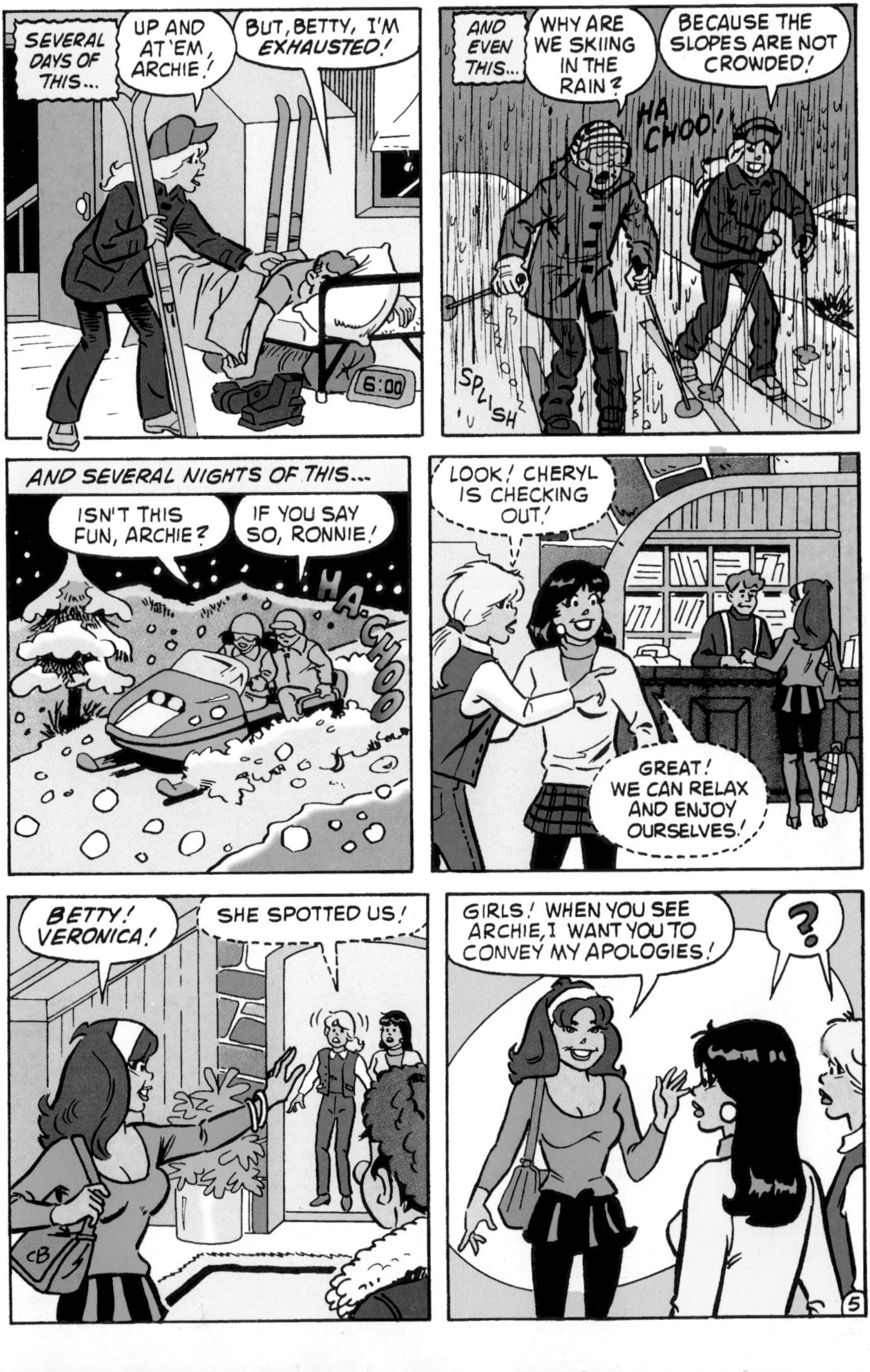
SEVERAL DAYS OF THIS...
UP AND AT 'EM, ARCHIE!
BUT, BETTY, I'M EXHAUSTED!
6:00
AND EVEN THIS...
WHY ARE WE SKIING IN THE RAIN?
BECAUSE THE SLOPES ARE NOT CROWDED!
HA CHOO!
SPLISH
AND SEVERAL NIGHTS OF THIS...
ISN'T THIS FUN, ARCHIE?
IF YOU SAY SO, RONNIE!
HA-CHOO
LOOK! CHERYL IS CHECKING OUT!
GREAT! WE CAN RELAX AND ENJOY OURSELVES!
BETTY! VERONICA!
SHE SPOTTED US!
GIRLS! WHEN YOU SEE ARCHIE, I WANT YOU TO CONVEY MY APOLOGIES!
?
5

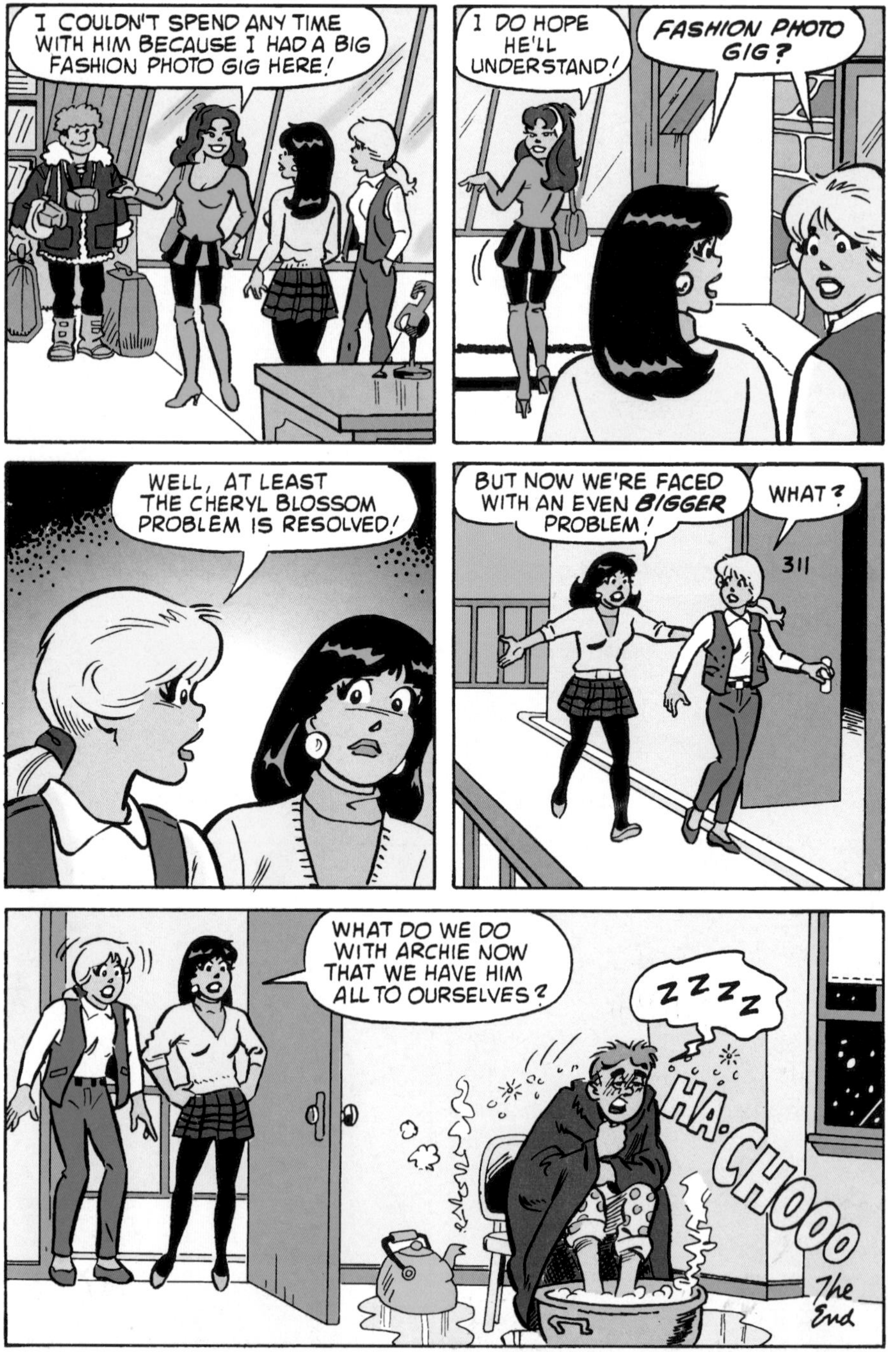

I COULDN'T SPEND ANY TIME WITH HIM BECAUSE I HAD A BIG FASHION PHOTO GIG HERE!
I DO HOPE HE'LL UNDERSTAND!
FASHION PHOTO GIG?
WELL, AT LEAST THE CHERYL BLOSSOM PROBLEM IS RESOLVED!
BUT NOW WE'RE FACED WITH AN EVEN BIGGER PROBLEM!
WHAT?
311
WHAT DO WE DO WITH ARCHIE NOW THAT WE HAVE HIM ALL TO OURSELVES?
ZZZZ
HA-CHOOO
The End

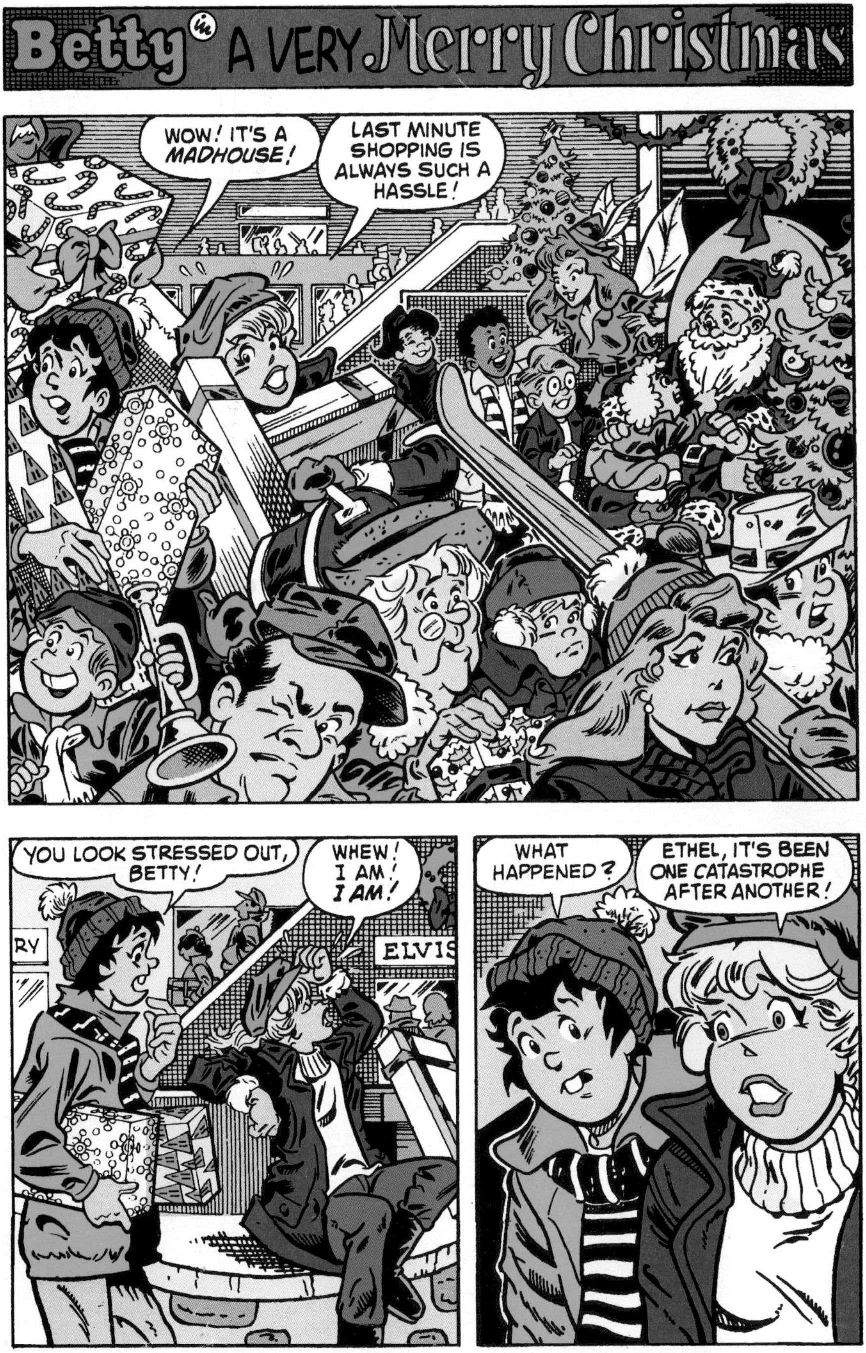
Betty in A VERY Merry Christmas
WOW! IT'S A MADHOUSE!
LAST MINUTE SHOPPING IS ALWAYS SUCH A HASSLE!
YOU LOOK STRESSED OUT, BETTY!
WHEW! I AM! I AM!
RY
ELVIS
WHAT HAPPENED?
ETHEL, IT'S BEEN ONE CATASTROPHE AFTER ANOTHER!

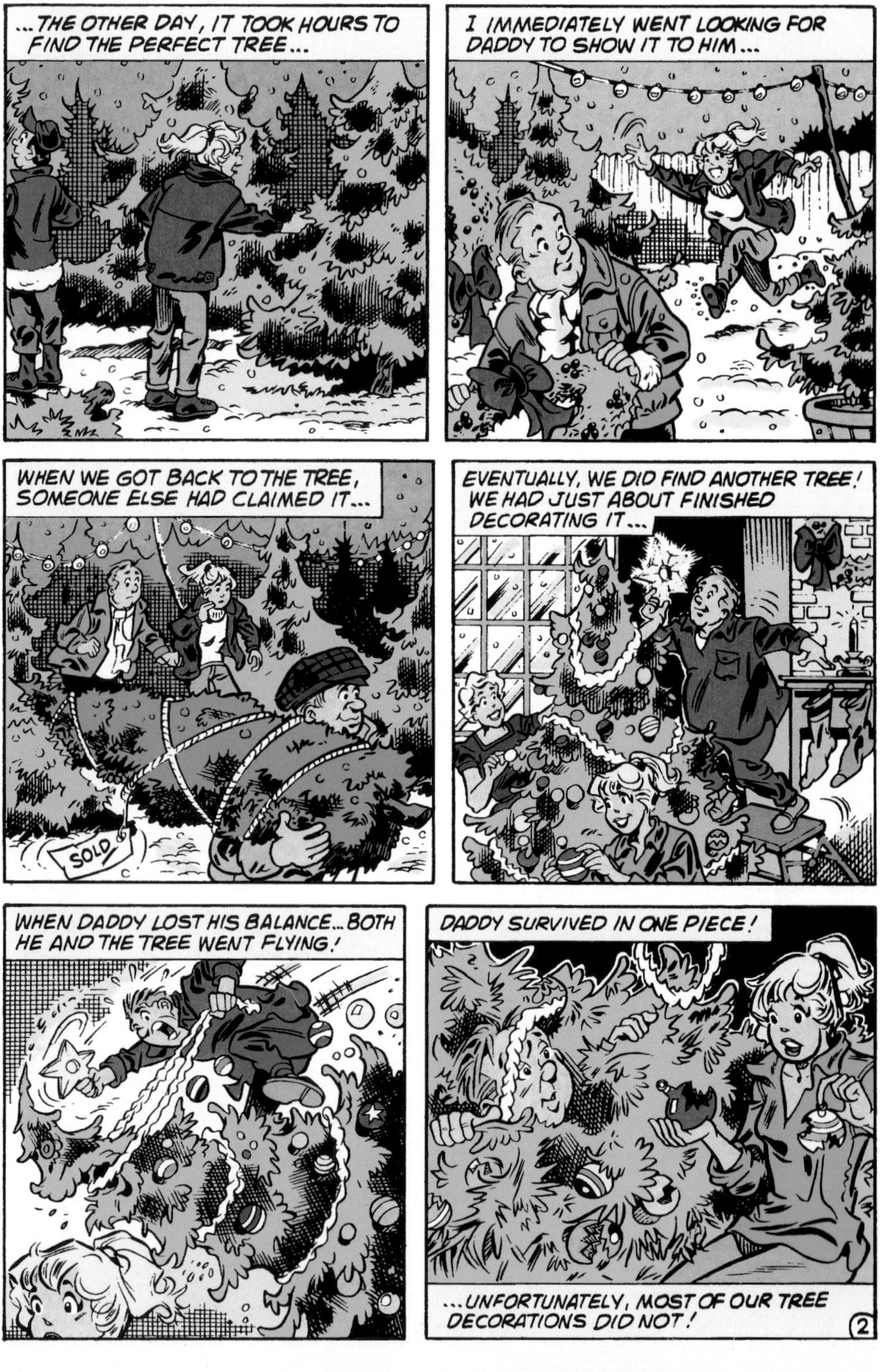
...THE OTHER DAY, IT TOOK HOURS TO FIND THE PERFECT TREE...
I IMMEDIATELY WENT LOOKING FOR DADDY TO SHOW IT TO HIM...
WHEN WE GOT BACK TO THE TREE, SOMEONE ELSE HAD CLAIMED IT...
SOLD
EVENTUALLY, WE DID FIND ANOTHER TREE! WE HAD JUST ABOUT FINISHED DECORATING IT...
WHEN DADDY LOST HIS BALANCE...BOTH HE AND THE TREE WENT FLYING!
DADDY SURVIVED IN ONE PIECE!
...UNFORTUNATELY, MOST OF OUR TREE DECORATIONS DID NOT!
2

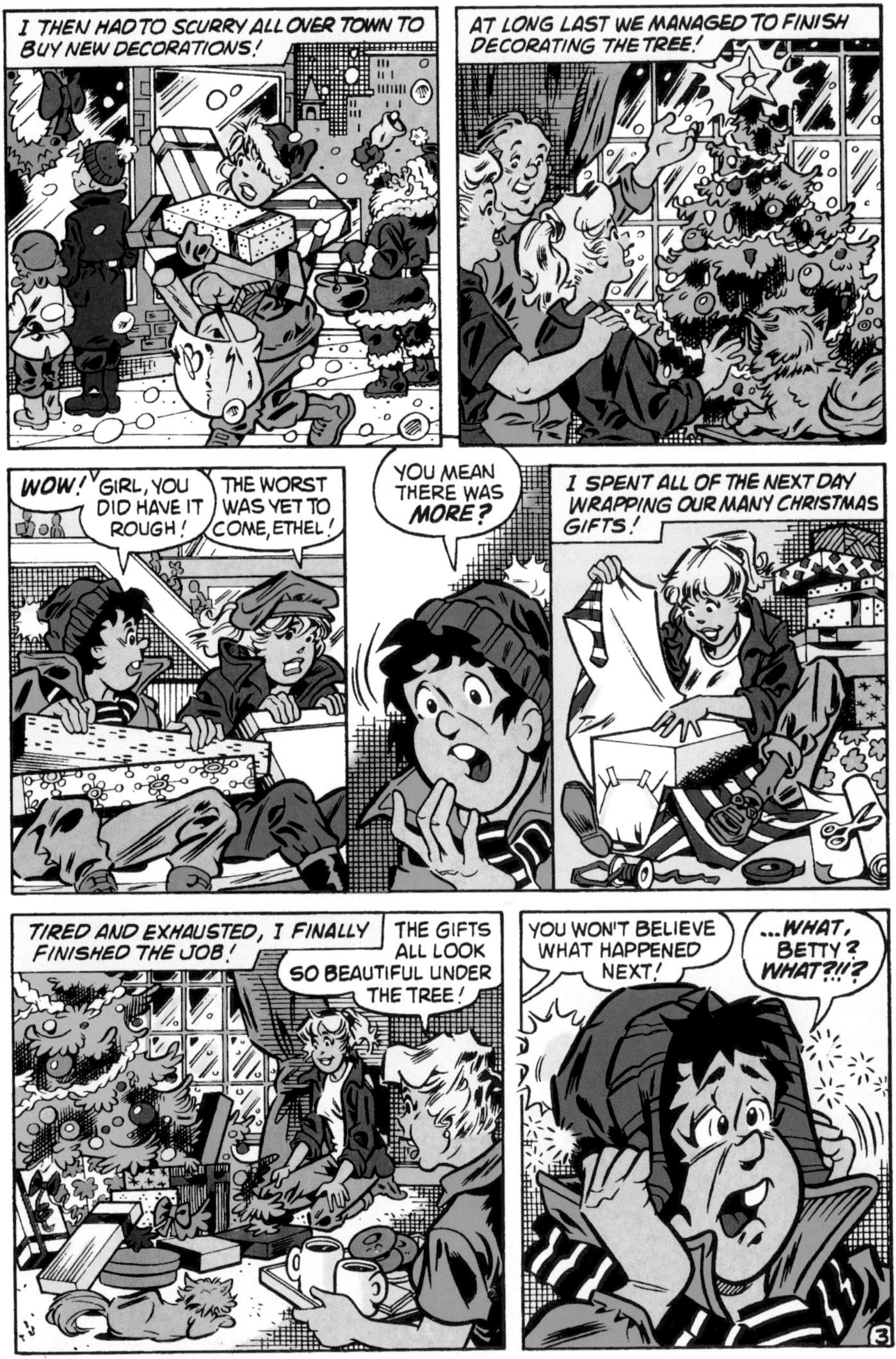
I THEN HAD TO SCURRY ALL OVER TOWN TO BUY NEW DECORATIONS!
AT LONG LAST WE MANAGED TO FINISH DECORATING THE TREE!
WOW!
GIRL, YOU DID HAVE IT ROUGH!
THE WORST WAS YET TO COME, ETHEL!
YOU MEAN THERE WAS MORE?
I SPENT ALL OF THE NEXT DAY WRAPPING OUR MANY CHRISTMAS GIFTS!
TIRED AND EXHAUSTED, I FINALLY FINISHED THE JOB!
THE GIFTS ALL LOOK SO BEAUTIFUL UNDER THE TREE!
YOU WON'T BELIEVE WHAT HAPPENED NEXT!
...WHAT, BETTY? WHAT?!!?
3

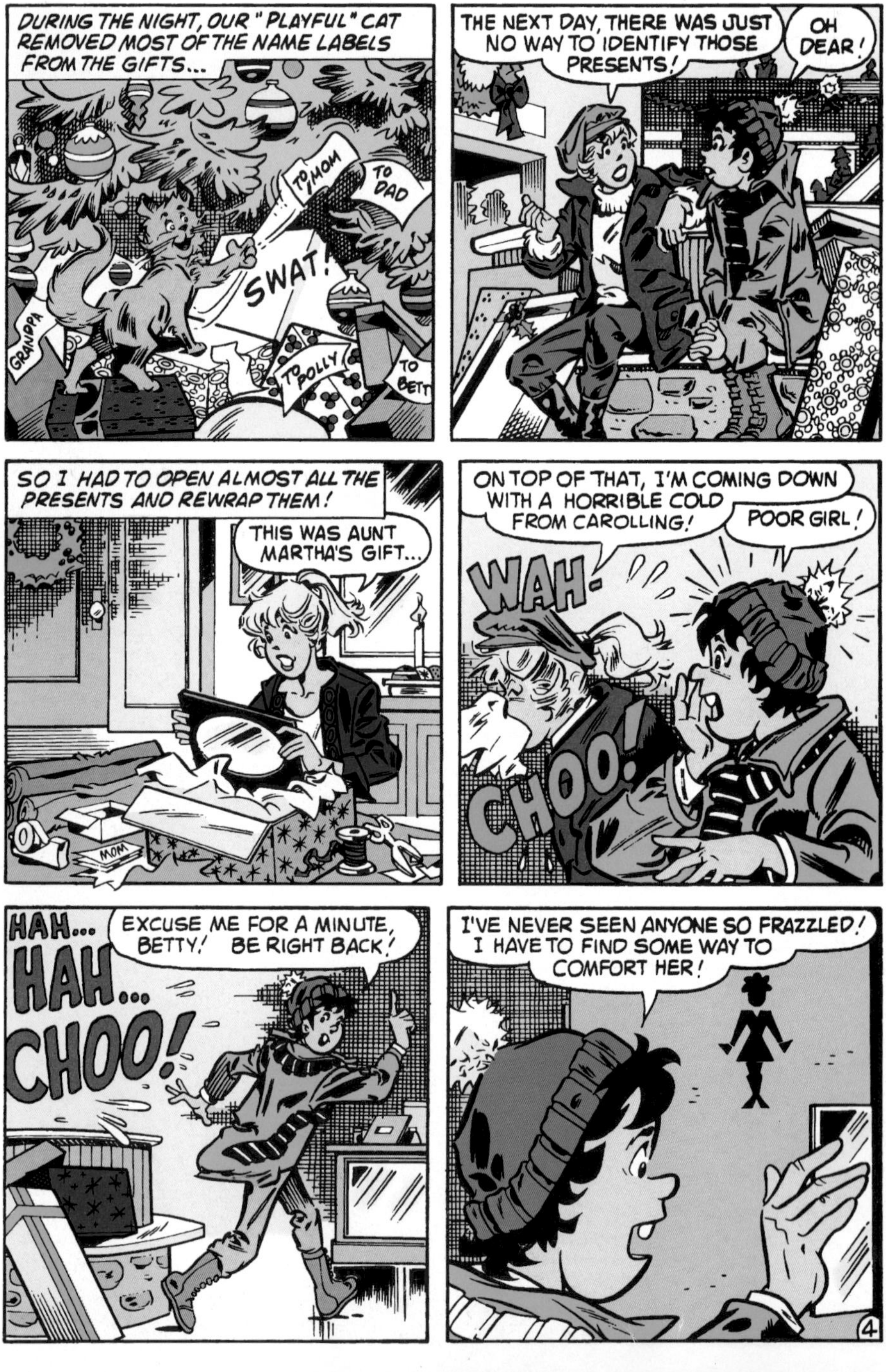
DURING THE NIGHT, OUR "PLAYFUL" CAT REMOVED MOST OF THE NAME LABELS FROM THE GIFTS...
TO MOM
TO DAD
SWAT!
GRANDPA
TO POLLY
TO BETT
THE NEXT DAY, THERE WAS JUST NO WAY TO IDENTIFY THOSE PRESENTS!
OH DEAR!
SO I HAD TO OPEN ALMOST ALL THE PRESENTS AND REWRAP THEM!
THIS WAS AUNT MARTHA'S GIFT...
MOM
ON TOP OF THAT, I'M COMING DOWN WITH A HORRIBLE COLD FROM CAROLLING!
POOR GIRL!
WAH-
CHOO!
HAH...
HAH...
CHOO!
EXCUSE ME FOR A MINUTE, BETTY! BE RIGHT BACK!
I'VE NEVER SEEN ANYONE SO FRAZZLED! I HAVE TO FIND SOME WAY TO COMFORT HER!
4

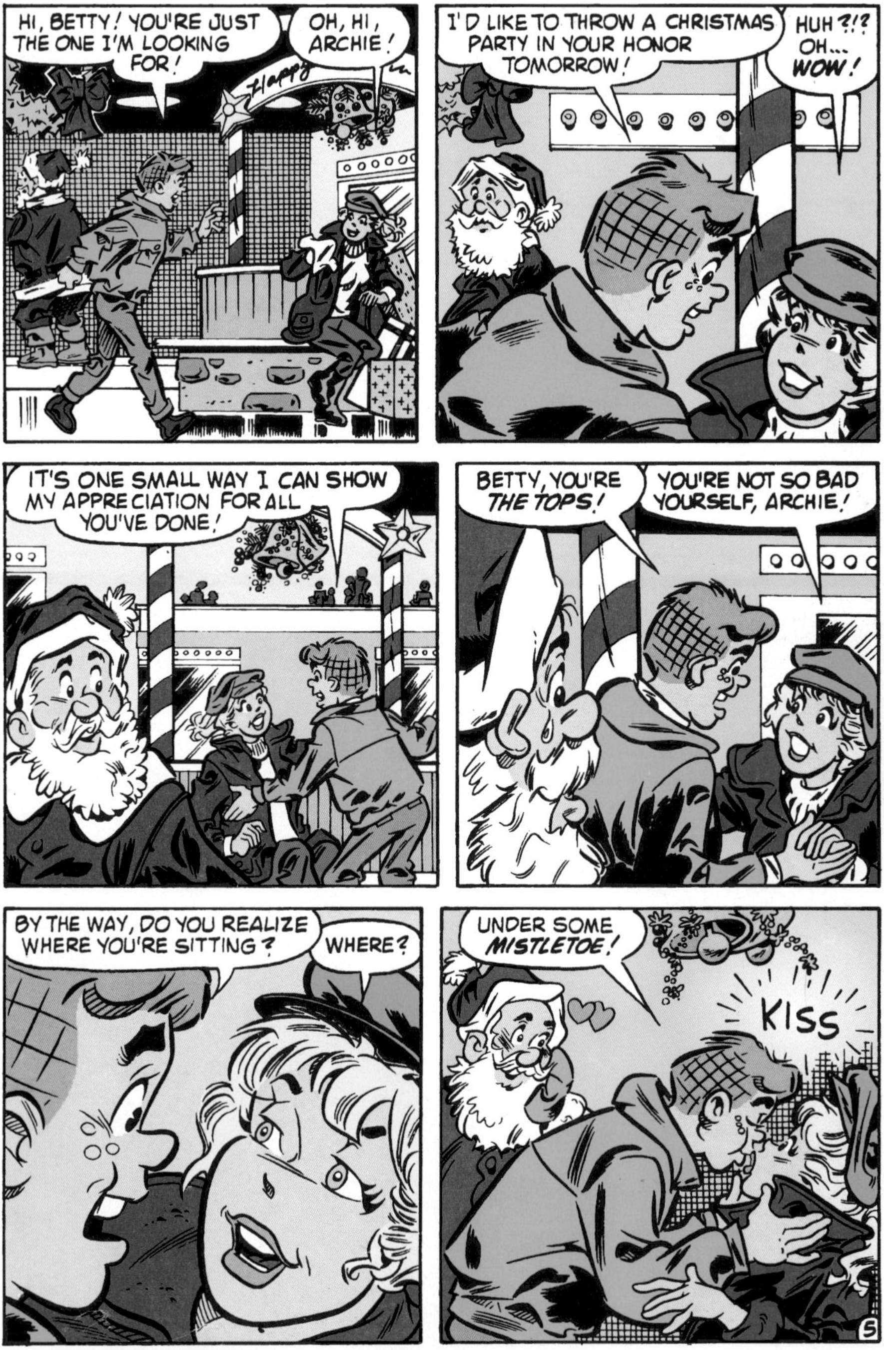
HI, BETTY! YOU'RE JUST THE ONE I'M LOOKING FOR!
OH, HI, ARCHIE!
I'D LIKE TO THROW A CHRISTMAS PARTY IN YOUR HONOR TOMORROW!
HUH ?!? OH... WOW!
IT'S ONE SMALL WAY I CAN SHOW MY APPRECIATION FOR ALL YOU'VE DONE!
BETTY, YOU'RE THE TOPS!
YOU'RE NOT SO BAD YOURSELF, ARCHIE!
BY THE WAY, DO YOU REALIZE WHERE YOU'RE SITTING?
WHERE?
UNDER SOME MISTLETOE!
KISS
5

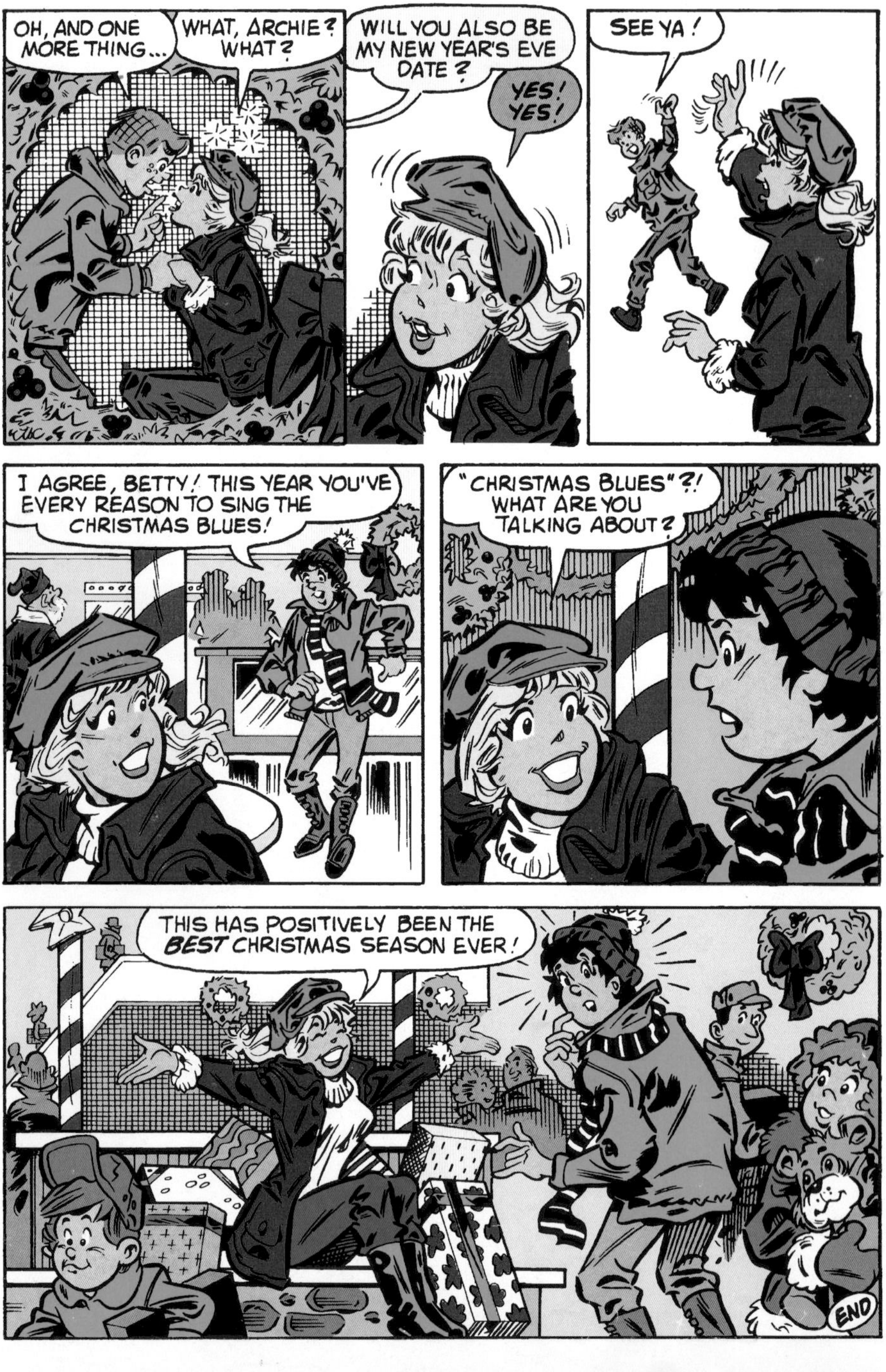
OH, AND ONE MORE THING...
WHAT, ARCHIE? WHAT?
WILL YOU ALSO BE MY NEW YEAR'S EVE DATE?
YES! YES!
SEE YA!
I AGREE, BETTY! THIS YEAR YOU'VE EVERY REASON TO SING THE CHRISTMAS BLUES!
"CHRISTMAS BLUES"?! WHAT ARE YOU TALKING ABOUT?
THIS HAS POSITIVELY BEEN THE *BEST* CHRISTMAS SEASON EVER!
END